PRAISE

Eliza Evans

⋅ ✳ ˙

"Evans infuses the sweetness and warmth of Christmas into her debut novel, perfect for anyone looking to get in the holiday spirit."
                                                                    —*Library Journal*

"*The Christmas Café* is a sweetly cozy, wholesome journey of self-discovery . . . Stocking-stuffed with a sugary plot, a warm and caring hero and heroine, and scrumptious, absolutely drool-worthy festive baking, you'll be yearning for Christmas no matter the season. *The Christmas Café* will bake your spirits bright!"
                        —Lillie Vale, author of *Wrapped with a Beau* and
                                                    The Decoy Girlfriend

"A frothy, feel-good confection of a novel, *The Christmas Café* is a love letter to new beginnings, tiny hometowns, and, of course, the most wonderful time of the year. An unforgettable debut that will make even the most cynical reader believe in Christmas miracles. Plan to devour this delicious tale in one sitting because once you step inside the world of Silver Bells, you'll never want to leave!"
                        —Kristy Woodson Harvey, *New York Times* bestselling
                                            author of *The Summer of Songbirds*

The Christmas Cookie Wars

A NOVEL

ELIZA EVANS

G. P. PUTNAM'S SONS
NEW YORK

PUTNAM
— EST. 1838 —

G. P. PUTNAM'S SONS
Publishers Since 1838
An imprint of Penguin Random House LLC
penguinrandomhouse.com

Library of Congress Cataloging-in-Publication Data
Names: Evans, Eliza, author.
Title: The Christmas cookie wars : a novel / Eliza Evans.
Identifiers: LCCN 2023055110 (print) | LCCN 2023055111 (ebook) |
ISBN 9780593544587 (trade paperback) | ISBN 9780593544594 (epub)
Subjects: LCGFT: Romance fiction. | Christmas fiction. | Novels.
Classification: LCC PS3618.I3452 C47 2024 (print) | LCC PS3618.I3452 (ebook) |
DDC 813/.6—dc23/eng/20231222
LC record available at https://lccn.loc.gov/2023055110
LC ebook record available at https://lccn.loc.gov/2023055111

Printed in the United States of America
1st Printing

Book design by Ashley Tucker

To Amanda
You're an inspiration!

The Christmas Cookie Wars

One

MELODY MONROE WOKE UP FACEDOWN ON THE KITCHEN table, a snowman-shaped sugar cookie stuck to her forehead.

She blinked a few times, bringing the room into focus. Sun streamed in through the window above the copper farmhouse sink, illuminating the crystalline frost that clung to the glass.

Oh no. What time was it?

Heart lurching her out of a sleep-induced haze, she lifted her head and found her twin ten-year-old boys staring at her from across the room, their dark, curly hair still askew from their pillows. Surprisingly, they were already dressed in their typical school-day uniform—sweatshirts and athletic pants.

"Dude . . . what happened to you?" Tate eyed her the same way he did when she rocked out to Def Leppard in the car—with one half of his mouth grimacing in embarrassment while the other side rose in amusement. Someday soon, she feared the embarrassment would totally win out.

"Why'd you sleep on the kitchen table?" Finn asked, bulldozing past her to retrieve a Pop-Tart from the pantry, knocking into the chairs on his way.

Why indeed.

Melody peeled the cookie away from her forehead and tossed it into the nearby trash can before picking sprinkles out of her eyebrows. "You two were supposed to help me decorate the five dozen sugar cookies we signed up to bring in for the bake sale today. *Remember?*"

But there'd been those two birthday parties they'd had to go to on Saturday and then they'd gone sledding with their friends on Sunday, not remembering until last night that they had book reports due today too. "I had to frost all of them myself." A cold splash of reality doused the irritation smoldering beneath her breastbone.

Not so long ago, Finn and Tate would've dropped *everything* to decorate sugar cookies with her. They wouldn't have cared about birthday parties or sledding with friends. Cookie day had always been a big day—a day they wouldn't have missed for anything.

She and Thomas had started the tradition with the boys when they'd been old enough to sit in their high chairs, though back then they'd gotten more frosting on themselves than on the cookies.

The memories descended the way they always did, like an echo—mostly in sounds. She and Thomas laughing, the boys screeching with excitement while they licked the frosting off their spoons. Christmas music had hummed in the background and her husband would circle his arms around her waist while they snapped pictures of the two boys they'd struggled to conceive for five years. *I love you. I love us*, he'd always whisper.

This year would mark their sixth Christmas without Thomas, but she hadn't let any of their Christmas traditions die with him. Each holiday season, she and Finn and Tate still sat around the kitchen table together, slathering buttercream frosting onto the (slightly burnt) cookies they'd rolled and cut out into festive shapes. They always had a contest—because everything was a competition with her boys—to see who could create the most lifelike Santa and the most artistic snowflake. Then, when the sugar rush kicked in, Finn and Tate would chase each other around the house threatening to decorate their faces, while she half-heartedly scolded them.

That was how things had been. Every holiday season. But this year, she felt the icy winds of change blowing in.

"Are we going to school today or what?" Finn sat across from her at the small round table chomping on the strawberry Pop-Tart.

Various sprinkle canisters and bowls of frosting and bits of the cookies she'd ruined in her haste to finish the task still littered the entire surface, but she would have to clean up this mess later.

"Of course you're going to school." Melody couldn't shake the gnawing heartache as easily as she shook the cookie crumbs from her lap when she stood. "I just have to get—" Her gaze landed on the oven clock.

Eight o'clock?

Eight o'clock!

She spun and banged her knee on the table leg, gagging back a word that would put her in the hole with the swear jar yet again. So far, she'd had to pay out more than either of the boys. "Why didn't you boys tell me we were late?" They couldn't be late! She was already skating on thin ice with Mr. Braxton. The principal had personally called her about the boys' tardies last week, and she'd assured him they would be on time every day through the end of the year.

Tate shrugged and calmly sat down next to his brother. "I thought you knew what time it was."

"I didn't know!" She flailed around the cramped kitchen, stumbling to get the rest of the cookies packed up in the box she'd set out on the counter last night before apparently passing out facedown in a pile of frosting.

"Get your backpacks ready," she called on her way up the steep, narrow stairs. When she and Thomas had bought this old Victorian, the pitched roof and the wraparound front porch and the turrets had charmed her into believing it was a dream come true, but she'd lost count of how many times she'd tripped going up the ancient staircase.

Inside her room, she quickly shed yesterday's sweats and pulled on a pair of somewhat wrinkled jeans and an asymmetrical tunic sweater she'd designed for her boutique. There'd be no helping her hair now, though, so she left her messy bun intact and practically skied back down the steps, gripping the railing so she didn't crash.

Finn and Tate had gotten their backpacks on but were currently playing Frisbee with one of the cookies.

Melody intercepted the confection midair and slam-dunked it into the trash can. "Get in the car, you two." Swiping the box of cookies off the counter, she managed to snatch her purse off the hook by the door and followed them into the garage, nearly tripping over Finn's bike, which lay right in her path to the driver's side.

"Sorry, Mom." He aimed his repentant smile at her, batting his thick dark eyelashes for good measure, and wisely moved the bike before a word could escape her lips, the little angel.

"Buckle up," Melody advised before easing the car out of

their garage. A new layer of snow blanketed the driveway, so she'd better take it slow.

Don't look at the clock . . .

But it was too late. They were officially thirteen minutes behind schedule. The bell had already rung and the rest of the kids would be sitting in class when Finn and Tate ambled in. Again.

"Are we gonna have to go to Mr. Braxton's office?" Tate uttered a heavy sigh. "We were already in there four times last week."

"Yes, I'm aware." Melody paused at the stop sign and waited for their neighbor, Mr. Munson, to cross the street. Even with her blood pressure spiking, she buzzed down the window and called, "Good morning!" because the poor man had lost his wife two months ago.

"Nice to see ya, Melody." He waved. "And you too, boys. Drive safe. It's real slick out this morning."

"Will do. Have a good day." She buzzed the window back up and blasted the heat.

"I still don't see why we had to go to the principal's office for trying to set the ants from Mrs. Altman's ant farm free," Finn mumbled. "They shouldn't be stuck in one dirt tunnel. They should be able to live their lives outside of captivity."

That was the thing about her boys. They didn't *mean* to get into trouble. It was like she'd told Mr. Braxton on more than one occasion: They were spirited. And curious. And busy. But they were also respectful kids and they listened to authority. For the most part anyway.

"The ants belong to your science teacher, though, so you can't set them free without permission." She shot a stern glance into the rearview mirror. "And can we make a pact?

How about we refrain from any more visits to the principal's office for the rest of the year?" After today, that was. That would be the best Christmas gift she'd ever gotten.

Lately, she'd spent entirely too much time with Mr. Braxton. Seriously. She hadn't received this many lectures since *she'd* been ten years old. She and the principal were roughly the same age—so she'd heard—but every time she sat in that overstuffed chair across from his desk, she regressed.

"It's not our fault Mr. Braxton is so strict," Tate complained. "He's no fun at all. I don't think he even knows how to smile."

He tended to be long-winded too. During a lot of their "talks" she smiled and nodded but then found herself analyzing his taste in books from the crowded shelf behind him. He appeared to like mysteries and suspense novels, so maybe they could give him the benefit of the doubt. "There could be more to Mr. Braxton than we can see."

"I doubt it," Tate mumbled.

"Well, let's keep an open mind." She'd do her best, even while she endured another one of the principal's sermons on the importance of punctuality today. "And I'd like you to do your best to stay out of trouble. You wouldn't want to be on Santa's naughty list this year, would you?" Speaking of . . . "You two still haven't written your letters to the North Pole yet." She watched for their reaction in the rearview mirror and, sure enough, the boys exchanged a pitying look.

Melody braced herself. She'd known this was coming, after all. Tate and Finn had spent most of last December asking questions about Santa, which she'd expertly deflected. In an effort to keep them believing, she'd also gone to great lengths to make their elf Barney extra convincing. She'd even snuck into their rooms after they'd fallen asleep to take selfies with Barney and them on her phone.

But this year they'd mainly ignored poor Barney. A weight pressed against her heart, crushing her hope. Were they really giving up on Santa? They were only in fifth grade. They had their whole lives to learn that magic wasn't real.

"If Santa knows everything, we shouldn't have to write him a letter to tell him what we want," Tate said wisely. "Besides, I was doing some calculations about how long it would really take to drive a flying sleigh around the entire earth and, even if he went the speed of light, he'd still never be able to stop at everyone's house. The whole thing goes against physics."

Physics schmysics. "Santa is magic." The words wobbled out. "He doesn't need physics." That was the truth. Christmas should be full of magic, even if it only truly existed in the traditions they'd always shared. Every year, late Christmas Eve night, Thomas had gone outside to make reindeer prints and Santa's boot prints in the snow. He ate the goodies the boys left out—cookies for the big man himself and carrots for the reindeer, leaving the remnants, and he'd even written them each a note in wacky handwriting.

"Right. Santa is magic," Finn recited loyally. "He only needs us to believe. Don't worry, Mom. I'll write a letter when I get home from school. All I really want this year are those lit Beatbox headphones."

"Oh, is that all?" The headphones that happened to cost three hundred dollars? Boy, she missed the days of Hot Wheels and yo-yos and candy canes in their stockings.

"Yeah, all I want are the headphones too," Tate said. "Silver for me."

They might as well be made of real silver. "We'll have to

see." She'd need to come up with some magic of her own to be able to afford those headphones plus a few other small gifts they could open.

Holding back a sigh, she slowed the car on a particularly icy patch of asphalt on Main Street. "It looks like the city finally got the decorations up." The familiar sight of the *Welcome to Christmas in Cookeville* banner settled her. "I can't wait for Cookie Daze." Her tone turned so wistful and sappy, she wouldn't be surprised if the boys started gagging in the back seat.

She couldn't help it. No matter what else changed, their town would always be the Cookie Capital of the Rocky Mountains. The claim to fame had started back in the early 1900s when Edmund Heinrich, a German baker, opened a cookie factory for the miners. Word spread and people started to travel from all across the country to taste his cookies.

In the early seventies, the town had even been listed in the *Guinness Book of World Records* when more than half the residents got together to make the biggest chocolate chip cookie ever recorded. That was how the Cookie Daze festival had been born, along with a host of other holiday-themed events that she and the boys attended every year. Even though the factory was long gone, the elementary school's cookie committee had closely guarded the traditions, partnering with local businesses to raise money for extra programs and supplies at the school.

"Cookie Daze is awesome." Tate undid his seat belt before she'd even finished parking in the school lot.

"Yeah, Cookie Daze'll be a ton of fun!" Finn scrambled to get out of the car first, and the twins raced to the sidewalk.

Well, at least they still had something to look forward to.

She'd take it. Melody climbed out of the car, collected the cookies from the back seat, and followed Finn and Tate into the school, trying to keep a low profile in case they happened to see—

"Good morning." Mr. Braxton appeared in the hallway outside the office, stern frown already in place. Today, he appeared even more buttoned-up than usual in a crisp gray shirt covered by a charcoal sweater vest and black slacks that had not even one tiny wrinkle. The dark-rimmed glasses were new. Maybe he'd recently started needing readers too.

The principal made a show of looking at his watch. "Running late again?"

"Sorry. But it wasn't our fault this time." Tate shrugged off the blame. "My mom passed out at the kitchen table last night."

"Tate!" A high-pitched laugh squeaked out. "I didn't *pass out*," she clarified. "I fell *asleep*. I mean, I don't even drink much. Maybe an occasional glass of wine but certainly not enough to pass out." Her weird laugh was not helping her case here. "I learned my lesson after one party in college . . . Anyway, while I was decorating the cookies for the bake sale"—she held up the box so he could see she'd been hard at work doing her parental duty—"I must've gotten sleepy. We were a little short on time this weekend, what with birthday parties and sledding, so . . ." She let an awkward silence fill in the blanks.

"She was real tired," Finn told the principal gravely. "She didn't even wake up until we came downstairs this morning and she had a giant cookie stuck to her forehe—"

"Why don't you two get to class?" Melody nudged Finn and Tate away before they further incriminated her. "We don't want to be any later than you already are. Have a good day," she called as they shot down the hall.

When she looked back at Mr. Braxton, the frown had deepened, creasing his mouth with obvious concern. "Why don't we step into my office for a minute, Ms. Monroe?"

"Melody." She'd told him to call her Melody on multiple occasions. That was what Mr. Drake had called her. He'd been the principal for fifteen years, until Mr. Braxton had taken over after his retirement. Man, she missed him. He'd been cheerful and friendly and understanding. Mr. Drake hadn't lectured her.

"After you." The principal gestured for her to complete the walk of shame through the entire office.

Melody tried to smooth her hair as she waved at Nancy—Mr. Braxton's faithful assistant—and stepped through his door. The office looked exactly how a principal's office should look—especially one who wore sweater vests and bow ties. Neat and orderly. No paper mess on the desk like hers at the boutique. No old coffee cups or take-out containers in sight. She sat in one of the chairs that faced his polished desk. What was that scent? Cinnamon? Cloves?

Mr. Braxton sat across from her and methodically removed his glasses, folding them up and then slipping them into the pocket of his shirt underneath his sweater vest. "Are you doing okay, Ms. Monroe?" Those dark eyes assessed her with the same laser focus that probably coerced kids into confessing to their crimes.

There she went, tumbling backward through the years to find her unsure ten-year-old self again. "I'm good." She reinforced the declaration with a winning smile. "Better than good, actually. I'm great!"

"You have something in your eyebrow." He pointed to the left side of his face, guiding her to the spot.

"Oh." She used her pointer finger to scrub the crusted blob of frosting away. "Oopsie. Guess I missed that part when I showered." Actually, how long had it been since she'd showered? Three or four days? She'd have to add that to her to-do list.

Mr. Braxton continued to assess her. "This is already the boys' fourth tardy this month, and I'm concerned." He used the gentle but firm tone she'd heard him use on Finn and Tate more than once. "As you're aware, punctuality can really affect classroom learning . . ."

His voice droned on, but her gaze drifted to the color-coded bookcase behind him. Wait. Was that a Nicholas Sparks novel? Yes! *The Notebook.* She never would've pegged him as a romantic.

"Ms. Monroe?" The principal tilted his head into her line of vision. "I hope we're on the same page."

Maybe they could be if they were discussing a Nicholas Sparks novel. She couldn't wait to tell her sister he had a romance novel on his shelf! Kels wouldn't believe it. "I agree with everything you said." Punctuality was very important. It simply wasn't her reality right now. She kept smiling. "There's so much going on in December, as you know." And now, on top of the typical busyness, she was being forced to face the fact that her boys were growing up, letting go of what had always made this season so magical and meaningful. He likely wouldn't understand that. Rumor had it Mr. Braxton had a daughter who lived in Denver with her mom, but no one seemed to know much about her.

"Don't worry. Everything's fine, Mr. Braxton!" Her enthusiasm overcompensated. "We won't be late anymore. I promise." At least not for the rest of the year. Surely she could get the twins here on time for the rest of the semester. "The cookies turned out to be a lot more work than I'd anticipated, that's all." Because she'd thought three of them would be decorating. *Together.*

"Well, it's unfortunate you put all of that work in." Mr. Braxton opened his laptop. "Didn't you get the email I sent out on Friday?"

Email? When was the last time she'd checked her personal email? "Uh, no." It had probably been a week. Not that she'd admit it to him.

"There won't be a bake sale this year." He turned his computer to show her the latest school newsletter, which she hadn't read for at least the last month. "The school's cookie committee disbanded, and all cookie-related fundraising events for the rest of the year have been canceled."

Melody scanned the announcement, her stomach twisting and tightening. No Cookie Contest? No Cookie and Cocktail Crawl? *No Cookie Daze?* "I don't understand. It's not the holidays in Cookeville without Cookie Daze." Despite her best efforts to contain it, panic squeaked through. They couldn't cancel everything!

Mr. Braxton recentered his computer, his eyes focused on the screen. "We can't make it happen this year. Charlene Templeton disbanded the entire committee over a disagreement about her leadership style."

"Right before the holidays?" Melody lurched to her feet. "But those events make the school a ton of money. They fund the entire STEM club!" The one thing her boys loved about school. Not to mention, those events were part of their cherished traditions. They'd been going ever since Finn and Tate had been born.

"Believe me, I know how bad this is for the school." Mr. Braxton stood too. "I hate to see this happen on my watch. But I've asked around to see if we can find someone else to take over, and no one's willing. Probably because of all the drama. No one wants to cross Charlene."

Of course not. Charlene Templeton was one of those moms who ruled the school. She sat on every committee, planned every event, volunteered for every party. Her son, Blake, had been in the boys' class for years, and his mom had never given Melody the time of day. But who cared about Charlene? Christmas was on the line! "I'll take it on." She'd gladly cross the woman if it meant she got to attend Cookie Daze with Finn and Tate this year. Besides, how hard could running the cookie committee be?

"*You?*"

Melody couldn't decide if his veiled expression hinted at wariness or amusement. The man was so hard to read. "Sure. Why not?" He could probably list about a hundred reasons why she wasn't qualified to lead the school's most important fundraising efforts, but she didn't give him a chance. "I run a very successful boutique in town." Maybe she wasn't always on time or on top of every detail, but she could step up and bring people together for a good cause when she needed to.

Jonathan eyed the cookies in the box that still sat on his desk. "But you don't really bake." He paused, looked away. "Wait. That didn't come out right. What I meant was—"

"I can bake." A defensive heat clouded her face. "These might not be my best effort . . ." And they might've been made from refrigerated store-bought dough. ". . . but I know how to follow a recipe." And how much baking would she really have to do anyway? "Besides, isn't the cookie committee more about building community than anything else?" Practically the whole town turned out for Cookie Daze.

"I guess." Skepticism narrowed his eyes. He clearly didn't think she was capable! "Do you really want to take this on, though? It's a lot of work and you said yourself December is a busy month for you, both at work and at home. I mean, there are a ton of meetings, and the events are very time-consuming."

Was he seriously mansplaining how busy her December was? Now Melody narrowed her eyes at him. "Kelsey can step up at the boutique more." Her younger sister could run that place by herself if she had to. "I know I can do this. Even if you don't think I can."

"That's not what I meant." His mouth pinched in frustration. "Sorry. I wasn't trying to imply you're not capable."

Then what was he trying to say? Melody continued to glare at him while he shifted uncomfortably in his chair.

"We'd be happy to have you lead the committee," he finally muttered. "If you really want to."

She didn't even try to analyze the mysterious look on his face. "I'm in." She was doing this.

Whether Jonathan Braxton liked it or not.

Two

"*YOU'RE* GOING TO BE THE COOKIE COMMITTEE PRESI-dent?" Kelsey belted out her signature raspy laugh. She sounded like Stevie Nicks.

"What's so funny?" Melody taped off the box she'd packed up with four tunics she'd designed. When she'd opened Timbre Couture the year after Thomas's death, she'd never dreamed her modest little boutique would take off because of online sales. In five years, she'd taken over an additional adjacent storefront on Main Street just to house inventory and run the shipping operation. This side of their space was a perpetual mess—folding tables covered with piles of the clothing, stacks of collapsed cardboard boxes, their printing and labeling equipment. But without her mini warehouse, they'd barely be scraping by financially, given they were a fashion boutique in a small mountain town that relied on seasonal tourism.

"I've tasted your cookies, that's all." Her sister slapped a printed label on the box and then reapplied her lip gloss. They looked a lot alike, with soft brown highlighted hair (there was only one decent color stylist in town) and they were the same height, but the similarities weren't obvious because Melody didn't put as much effort in. Out of the two of them, Kelsey took more care with her appearance these days.

While Melody hadn't had time to go home and change after her stint in the principal's office, her sister showed up to work in the hand-embroidered cardigan Melody had designed as part of their exclusive Cookeville Collection, along with the black velvet skinny pants Melody had loved creating but could never quite pull off wearing herself. She rarely appeared as put together as Kels, but her sister also still had her husband, Doug, to help her out during the morning routine. Not to mention, their six-year-old daughter, Genevieve, was already going on twenty. Kels didn't have to remind Genevieve to shower or comb her hair or change her socks like she was constantly doing with the twins.

"I can't believe Charlene stepped down," her sister said. "I mean, didn't she go to the Culinary Institute of America or something? She owns a catering company, for crying out loud."

"So?" Melody rifled through the stock of magenta slouchy-fit sweaters to find a medium and then carefully wrapped it in their branded silver tissue paper, sealing the package with a sticker. Presentation was everything, after all. "Charlene also has an ego problem, which is why she tried to disband the committee and sabotage Christmas."

The woman had probably designed the whole debacle to force Jonathan to get on his knees and beg for her to come back. "I can totally handle the cookie committee." It might even be a good way to reconnect with Finn and Tate. She could get them involved—they'd said themselves how much they loved Cookie Daze. This could actually be the perfect scenario.

She taped the seam of yet another box and set it on the growing stack. "And anyway, I'll have all the help I need to make this holiday season a huge success. Starting with you."

"Ha! I can't bake either." Kels plastered the label on their last box of the day's orders and then traipsed underneath the archway that led back into the main store.

"Baking is irrelevant." Melody followed her sister to the cash registers near the entrance. She'd kept the design for the storefront chic and simple, leaving the walls as the original exposed brick and adding floating shelves between tiered clothing racks. The colors of the accent chairs and checkout counters were soft and calming—seafoam green and a subtle coral. Of course, she and Kels had gone all out in the holiday decorating department. They'd placed white trees in every corner of the space, adorning them with ornaments in all shades of blue. Blingy snowflakes dangled from the open ceiling, and pink garlands outlined every leaded-glass window.

"We're both creative. I have big ideas and you're good at bringing them to life." Kels had been her sidekick since she'd been born. Melody simply couldn't run the cookie committee without her. "Besides, you still owe me for dog-sitting Turk while you were in Maui." Two of her rugs hadn't survived her sister's Great Dane.

"Fine." Kelsey sighed, drama queen that she was. "What do we have to do?"

Melody paused from unlocking the computer. That was a good question. She wasn't sure exactly how the cookie committee went about their business. She'd attempted to contact Charlene for a knowledge transfer but hadn't heard anything yet. "We need to recruit new members," she decided. Maybe some of the old ones would come back too. "And then we'll need to have a meeting. The annual cookie swap is supposed to happen next weekend." That would kick off the chain reaction of holiday events that would consume her life until Christmas.

"Just let me know when and where to show up." Kels drifted to the center of the boutique and started to straighten a shelf of sweaters.

Another good question. Melody logged in to the system in preparation for opening. "I guess I'd better ask Mr. Braxton when and where the committee usually met." Maybe she should've gotten a few additional details before storming out of his office in a huff.

"Why would you ask Jonathan about the meetings?" Her sister moved to a rack of scarves, carefully refolding them one by one. That was why they made such a good team. Kels was meticulous while Melody was . . . well . . . flexible.

"As the principal, he's on the committee. He just can't run it."

"Really?" Kels whirled and smirked at her, bouncing her eyebrows. "Why didn't you say so in the first place? If Mr. Braxton will be at the meetings, I'm definitely in."

"Oh, come on." Melody threw a feather pen at her. "You'll join for him but not for your own sister?" She shouldn't be surprised. When Jonathan took over as principal at Cookeville Elementary, the school suddenly had more volunteers than they knew what to do with. It was pathetic the way women threw themselves at him. And now Kels was all gaga too! "I have to say, I'm disappointed in you."

"Jonathan Braxton is hot stuff, honey, like a homegrown Idris Elba, in case you hadn't noticed." Kels crept a few steps closer. Her prying gaze intensified. "*Have* you noticed? You've been spending a lot of time with him lately."

Ha! Melody opened a drawer to restock their stack of tissue paper for checkout. "It's difficult to notice how hot someone is when they're constantly lecturing you." The only thing she'd really noticed about Mr. Braxton was his diverse reading tastes, but now didn't seem like a good time to inform Kels about the Nicholas Sparks novel. That would likely only add to Mr. Braxton's appeal in her sister's book. "He's downright stodgy. And then there's the issue of his geriatric wardrobe. He must've inherited a whole crate of sweater vests and bow ties from his great-grandfather or something."

"You could help him out in that department." Her sister squealed and hurried to the men's section near the back of the store. "Picture him in this." She ripped a royal blue cashmere sweater off the rack, waving it in the air.

Uttering a tortured groan, Melody went back to staring at the computer screen. She got so tired of her family trying to match her up with every eligible bachelor they knew. Did it ever occur to them that she didn't mind being single? "I don't want to picture Mr. Braxton in anything, thank you very much."

Kels let out a cackle. "That works too."

"I mean, I don't want to picture him at all!" Leave it to Kels to make her blush. This was the boys' principal they were talking about! "Mr. Braxton can't stand me. He thinks I'm irresponsible and flighty." Which were some of her best qualities, in her opinion. "Basically, we have nothing in common."

"Seems to me that man could use a little more spontaneity in his life." Her sister traipsed back to the checkout counter, leaning in across from her while she batted her eyelash extensions. "And you might be the perfect person to help him with that."

"I can assure you, I'm not." Melody turned away to dust off

the glass jewelry case. "Hello! I have no room in my life for any kind of relationship. Especially with my kids' principal." She couldn't even imagine what kind of scandal that would cause around here. "I'm happy with things the way they are." Maybe her life wasn't easy, but it was simple.

"The problem is, things don't stay the same forever." Kels delivered the words in a gentle murmur. "You said yourself the boys have gotten a lot busier lately. They're growing up, Melly. The older they get, the more room you're going to have in your life."

She didn't want more room. Single parenting had been the hardest thing she'd ever done, but she wanted her life consumed with Finn and Tate. She wanted them to fill her time and her thoughts and her heart so much that there was no room for anyone else. They'd already lost a parent and, no matter how old they were, they deserved to have her be completely available for them with no distractions or complications. All she wanted to do was keep the magic alive for them, keep their *father* alive for them, during one more holiday season. "I should go on my committee-recruiting mission." Before the tears came. She loved this time of year, but boy did it make her heart ache sometimes. "Can you hold down the fort for a while?"

"Yep. I've got it." Her sister's tone held one part sympathy and two parts defeat, but she let Melody slip out the door without another word.

Out on the street, she could breathe again. The cold air unlocked her chest and chilled the sting out of her eyes. She and Kels had had similar conversations over the last couple of years, and she understood where her sister was coming from.

Each member in her family had tried bringing up the

dating thing from every angle. *Thomas would want you to be happy. It's okay to move on. You need to focus on yourself too.* Those were all true statements. She didn't disagree with them. But they didn't understand—it wasn't guilt that kept her from moving on. It was a lack of desire. Sure, she'd noticed a man here and there. She'd admired some, even. But no one except for Thomas had ever stirred her heart. So she'd filled her soul with love for other things—for her boys and her family and her business.

And for romance novels from the used bookstore, if she was being honest.

Maybe those things were enough for her. Even if they weren't enough to satisfy her family.

Refocusing on her mission, Melody ambled down the sidewalk, passing the T-Shirts & Trinkets shop and the Tough Cookies Winery, both of which were still closed at ten o'clock in the morning. In fact, most places on the main drag in Cookeville didn't open until noon during the winter—everyone typically liked to let the snowplows get out to clear the roads before they ventured to work. She inhaled the crisp air, tinged with woodsmoke, and reveled in the quiet. Winter in the mountains might be cold and bitter, but all that snow sure did create a wonderland, especially this morning. Sunlight poured down from the royal-blue sky, highlighting glitter in the layer of powder.

The town beautification committee took their job seriously during the holidays. Decorations lined the streets and storefronts and stayed up until January 15. Most of the trappings centered on the town's cookie-themed past with colorful fiberglass confections standing between wrought-iron lampposts and garlands of cookie lights strung up between buildings. Funny, hand-painted signs hung in many of the shop windows. *A balanced diet is a cookie in each hand. Christmas: when eating cookies for breakfast is totally acceptable. Joy to the cookies, the oven has dinged! Official Christmas Cookie Tester. Christmas Cookie Guru.*

Now that she had an official position on the cookie committee, she'd have to find a kitschy sign for her storefront too.

Continuing on, Melody maneuvered around the gingerbread cookie house built between two trees and pulled open the door to Chester's Coffee Café—the only other business that was brave enough to open in the morning.

Nearly every table had already been occupied, one in particular by some of her favorite people.

"Hey, Mom and Dad." She removed her gloves and stuffed them into the pockets of her peacoat.

"Melly!" Her dad tossed down the playing cards he was holding to lurch to his feet and dragged over another chair so she could join them at the table, along with Aunt Bernice, Uncle Clive, and their friend Joan. Her parents and their besties met at the coffee shop three mornings a week to play poker with pennies before her mom went to her part-time job as music teacher at Finn and Tate's school. Right now, it appeared her mother was winning.

"Surprised to see you this morning," her mom mused, brows pinched together as she focused on her cards. As usual, her curly hair was pulled back into a loose braid the way Melody always remembered—though now the lovely auburn had salty streaks of gray. She could only hope she aged as well as her mother. "Kelsey said the online shop has been extra busy this month."

"So busy." But you didn't hear her complaining about that

extra business. Though it still wouldn't be enough for her to bust the budget with headphones for the boys.

"I bought each of my granddaughters that sparkly sweater you designed for Christmas." Joan peered up at her above the tops of her bifocals, which were perched on the end of her nose. With her perfectly coiffed white hair and painted red lips, she looked like she should be the cover model for an AARP publication. "They're going to love them, honey. Beautiful."

"And I bought those darling sweater dresses for my daughters and the grandgirls." Aunt Bernice was never one to be upstaged when it came to supporting Melody and Kelsey's endeavor. "Plus a few scarves and those silk pajamas. So elegant!" Her mother's twin sister beamed victoriously.

"Oh, you two," Uncle Clive muttered, adjusting his Coke-bottle glasses. "Everything's gotta be a competition, doesn't it?"

"We all know I spend the most money at Melody and Kelsey's store." Her mom rearranged the cards in her hand. "So let's quit the squabbling and get back to our game before I have to get to work."

Melody clamped her lips to stave off a laugh. If her mother hadn't had that huge pile of pennies in front of her, she would've been the one trying to distract the group. "Thank you *all* for shopping Timbre for Christmas. We wouldn't survive without you." These Golden Girls had literally picked her up and carried her after Thomas had died. "Which is one reason I'm here. I need some help."

Joan set down her cards, offering her full attention. "Sure, Mel. Anything for you."

"As long as it doesn't involve capturing more bats from your attic," Aunt Bernice caveated.

"No, it doesn't have anything to do with bats." Thank the

good lord. Three years ago, she'd heard these strange noises coming from her ceiling in the middle of the night and had called her parents in a panic—and they'd then called Uncle Clive and Aunt Bernice, who'd rushed right over. When they'd opened the attic door, the bats had flown out, dive-bombing them, and they were all running around screaming until her father had saved the day by opening a window and shooing them out with a broom. "This favor has to do with cookies."

"Cookies?" Her father dropped his playing cards on the table again. "I'm listening."

"Well, it actually has to do with the cookie committee. I'm taking it over." Melody made a ta-da gesture.

The entire table blinked at her.

"But you can't bake." Her mother finally set down her cards too.

Why did everyone keep saying that? "I *can* bake. I just don't do it very often." Sheesh. She didn't have time to bake. She had a lot going on. "Running the committee doesn't have much to do with baking anyway. There's all the event planning and the fundraising for the school. Charlene tried to disband the committee right before Christmas, which would have meant there'd be no Cookie Daze this year."

Joan gasped. "No Cookie Daze?"

"Well, that's just plain ridiculous." Aunt Bernice snatched the carafe from the center of the table and poured herself another mug full of coffee. "That Charlene. She's always causing trouble around here."

"The woman loves attention," her mother agreed. "I'm not surprised she created drama before the biggest event of the season."

Melody didn't have time for drama. "I can't imagine a

holiday in Cookeville without Cookie Daze, so I told Mr. Braxton I would run the committee this year."

"Mr. Braxton," Joan murmured dreamily. "He's on the committee too, right? As a staff representative?" She patted Melody's hand. "You can count me in, sweetie."

"He's a little young for you, don't you think?" Aunt Bernice muttered. "I'm in too, Melly. I can do it all—bake, organize, fund-raise. As you'll remember, I was the president of the Junior League for many, many years."

"Over three decades ago," Melody's mother pointed out.

"Two and a half," Bernice countered.

She'd better interrupt before the argument delved into the history of the Junior League. "So you three will help me out?"

"You bet." Joan leaned close to her. "Mr. Braxton may be too young for me, but he's certainly not too young for you."

No, but he made her *feel* too young. Like a flighty, irresponsible teenager who constantly had to look over her shoulder to make sure she hadn't done something wrong. "He's Finn and Tate's principal. And Mom's boss. Seeing as how the boys don't have a great track record at school, we all have a complicated relationship with Mr. Braxton."

"Hooey." Her mother picked up her cards again. "My grandsons are angels, and I dare anyone to say differently. I'm definitely joining that committee. And I'll tell you something: I love Jonathan to death but if he gets too snooty for his own good, I'll put him in his place. Don't you worry."

"I don't want you to get fired." That would mean her mom would spend her afternoons at the boutique, which might be a little much. She wasn't exactly shy about sharing her honest opinions about how customers looked in the clothes they tried on. "So let me handle Mr. Braxton, okay?" She didn't need to give Finn and Tate's principal one more reason to dislike her.

After her mother gave a noncommittal grunt, Melody stood up and scanned the coffee shop. Having these three ladies would help, but they would need more worker bees if they were going to save the STEM program. She scanned the rest of the café for potential volunteers. Aha! Around the counter sat Adele, Prisha, and Eden—three of the other STEM club moms.

Melody bid her family goodbye and traipsed to their spot. "Hey, ladies."

"Hey, Mel." Prisha pushed out the chair next to her. "Want to join us?"

"Only for a few." Kels shouldn't have to run the store alone all morning. "I'm glad I ran into you three. I'm sure you've heard by now that the cookie committee disbanded."

The three of them traded knowing looks.

"We've heard, all right," Eden said. "Such a bummer. I'll bet they nix the STEM club by the end of the year."

"Not if we all step in." Her heart started pounding at the possibilities. They could do this. They could save their kids' club and the entire holiday season! "I told Mr. Braxton I'd lead the committee. Right now we desperately need more members. And I'd love to count on your support."

Adele's expression was the first to fall. "Oh. Um. Wow. That's great, Mel. Really." She picked up her mug and held it in both hands. "But I can't join the committee. We have too much going on this month. Sorry."

What was with her dodgy gaze?

"Us too," Prisha added quickly. "You know how chaotic the holiday season is." She waved a hand through the air. "Busy, busy, busy!"

Her voice hit too high a note. "Eden?" Melody glared at the other woman.

Sure enough, she squirmed too. "Look, Mel . . . we can't. Okay? I'd hate to see the STEM program go as much as you, but none of us want to get in the middle of this."

"The middle of what?" she managed to ask even with her jaw locked up. She had a feeling she already knew what was coming.

Prisha looked around them. "Charlene disbanded the committee because Deb complained she wouldn't listen to anyone else's ideas," she whispered.

Melody almost laughed. "Well, she *doesn't* listen to anyone else's ideas."

Adele swiveled her head too, glancing around them like she was afraid they were surrounded by spies. "All I know is that three people sided with Deb and now no one at school will talk to them. They're being completely ostracized. We can't risk it. I mean, our kiddos have auditions for the spring musical coming up, and you know who's directing the play."

Her shoulders slouched against the chair back. "Let me guess. Charlene?"

"Levi will be devastated if he doesn't get a part," Eden half whispered.

"So will Saanvi." Prisha's downcast expression apologized. "I'm so sorry, but she's been working too hard for this. She wants the lead this year."

"So we'll go to Mr. Braxton and tell him she's intimidating everyone who crosses her." This was ridiculous. There had to be some accountability here.

"He can't fire a volunteer," Adele argued. "And you won't find enough people who are willing to complain out loud. She has too many connections."

"Fine." They could chicken out but she wasn't going to back down. "Even if you won't be on the committee, you'll come to the cookie swap next week, right?" They needed as many people as possible to show up and pay the suggested donation in order to get this train back on the tracks.

There went that guilty look bouncing between the three of them again.

"The thing is, we already have plans." A grimace warped Eden's mouth.

Melody crossed her arms and waited. *This should be good . . .*

"Charlene is hosting a special pre-tryout practice for the play that afternoon," Prisha blurted.

That seemed about right. Charlene knew exactly how many kids participated in the spring musical. She'd likely planned a competing event on the off chance someone was clueless enough to take over the cookie committee. "I can't believe this."

"If the kids miss it, they won't get a part, or at least a good one." Adele's tone begged Melody to understand. "You know how Charlene works."

"Charlene works that way because she gets away with it." They were *letting* her get away with it. "That's the way Charlene will always work unless someone stands up to her."

And Melody was not afraid. It was time someone put an end to the queen's reign.

Three

THE MASSES HAD BEEN RIGHT. MELODY REALLY *COULDN'T* bake.

Waving away the curl of smoke, she slid the cookie sheet out of the oven, wincing at her attempt to make the Christmas pinwheels recipe she'd found in a stack of her mother's *Better Homes & Gardens* in an article titled "The Ten Easiest Christmas Cookie Recipes." Easy? Ha! The red and green and white dough was supposed to be swirled together in clean lines, but somehow the colors had bled when she'd rolled it out, so she'd had to press and fold and squeeze the strips of dough into submission. Sometime during the baking process, the cookies had expanded and melted, blurring the lines to make them look more like blobs than wheels.

"Whoa." Tate cruised past the oven, both his mouth and his forehead furrowed. He looked so much like Thomas sometimes. "What happened to those?"

"Nothing." She snatched one up and took a bite to prove they were salvageable. The recipe had claimed they melted in your mouth, but this cookie crumbled in her mouth, dry and a little too salty. "I don't understand. I followed the recipe exactly." It had to be the altitude—baking at seven thousand feet above sea level posed unique challenges that she obviously wasn't qualified to address.

"It was a good try, Mom." Finn patted her shoulder in solidarity. "I'll bet they'll be the most delicious cookies at the swap."

While Tate *looked* more like Thomas, Finn had inherited his father's buoyant optimism. But she tended to be a realist. "There is no way these will be the most delicious cookies at the swap." Especially since Mr. Braxton had a long-standing reputation as the best baker at Cookeville Elementary. Legend had it that his grandma was some kind of baking champion and had passed all her knowledge down to him. No one was going to take one of her blob wheels when Mr. Braxton's cookies were available.

Both boys stole a cookie off the pan and crammed the whole thing into their mouths, chewing thoughtfully.

"Mmm," Finn murmured, his smile too big and toothy to be believable.

"I think maybe you went a little overboard on the salt," Tate informed her in his matter-of-fact way.

"I did what the recipe said." But it didn't matter how bad they were. She didn't have time to make anything else before the swap. She started to transfer the blob wheels into the containers she'd set out earlier. "Are you two about ready to head to the school?" They couldn't be late when she was the one in charge, as much as she'd like to procrastinate. She had no idea how many people were coming—or if anyone would show up at all. Since Charlene had officially canceled the event on the school's social media site, Melody had spent a whole day reposting the details, doing her best to get everyone excited. So far, they only had twelve interested and seven going, which would be a lot less than last year's record attendance.

"Do we have to go?" Tate's shoulders slumped. "It's a *Saturday*. We don't want to go to school on the *weekend*."

"There are going to be a million cookies there, and you can eat as many as you want," she reminded them. They'd never complained about going to the cookie swap before. "Come on. Go get your coats on."

Just when she thought Tate's shoulders couldn't possibly slump anymore. He'd also added a scowl into the mix, but he knew better than to argue with her.

She sealed the lid on the cookies, the burn of embarrassment already simmering. Maybe she wouldn't have to put them out. Maybe she could walk around instead of standing at her spot behind a table and then no one would know where the blob wheels came from . . .

"I've gotta change real quick." Finn disappeared and she heard him bounding up the steps.

Change? He was wearing his typical uniform of athletic pants and a long-sleeve T-shirt—the same thing he wore to school every day. "Well, hurry up," she called after him. "Here, honey." She handed Tate the container of cookies and squeezed past him into the mudroom to get her coat on.

"Okay. I'm ready." Two minutes later, Finn rushed past her and she had to stop and do a double take. "Is that *gel* in your hair?" And was he wearing the button-up shirt and khaki pants she'd gotten him for the fall choir concert?

"Oh. Yeah." Her son tapped the new stiff wave of hair over his forehead. "I call shotgun!" He bolted out the garage door, beating both her and Tate in one lunge.

Was he seriously dressed up? For a cookie swap? She had to be dreaming. For years she'd begged and negotiated and bribed the boys to dress up—only for special occasions, mind you—but those were battles she'd mostly lost. Melody stepped past Tate, holding the door open for him, and then climbed into the driver's seat next to Finn, openly staring. "You look really nice."

"I know." Her son straightened his collar, wearing the same smile that always got him an extra scoop of ice cream at the old-fashioned parlor three doors down from the boutique.

Melody started up the car and headed for the school. "So, what's the occasion?" She did her best to strike a casual, disinterested tone. She couldn't make too big a deal over this or he'd never wear another button-up shirt again, but seriously. She'd been waiting for this day. For the day that one of them actually cared about their appearance. Maybe she could take him shopping!

"He has a crush," Tate said blandly from the back seat.

"Shut up," Finn snapped.

A crush? Melody stepped hard on the brake and cranked her head to stare at Finn. The one who qualified as her baby since he was six minutes younger than his brother. "Who do you have a crush on?"

"No one," he mumbled, turning his head to stare out the window. "Tate doesn't know what he's talking about."

Evidently, Tate *did* know what he was talking about because Finn's face had turned as red as Santa's suit.

Before she could say another word, her younger twin reached forward to turn up the radio.

But she couldn't even hum along with "Walking in a Winter Wonderland." Finn had a crush? An actual crush? Just last year he'd practically been gagging when he'd told her about how his friend Stella had tried to kiss him on the playground. He'd run away, of course, and he'd steered clear of her the rest of last year. But this year he liked someone enough to dress up for them?

Melody drove for a while, again doing her best to maintain a neutral expression until she parked in the lot near the school's gymnasium doors. Tate was out of the car before she'd even cut the engine, giving her the perfect opening. "You can talk to me, buddy," she told Finn. "About anything." While she couldn't quite believe they were at this stage, she was supposed to be the one helping him navigate crushes and figure out what he wanted to wear to impress someone special. That was her job.

"It's nothing, Mom." Her son huffed. "No big deal." He climbed out of the car and followed his brother in through the gymnasium doors, leaving her to carry in the container of Christmas blob wheels all by her lonesome.

Melody slung her purse over her shoulder and leaned halfway into the car through the back door to get the container. There'd been a day when her kids had told her everything—especially Finn. He would come home and spend a half hour giving her a play-by-play of his day. Yet now here they were. He was starting to keep things from her already—

"Ms. Monroe?"

A cringe worked its way up her neck. Mr. Braxton. Hiding the cookies under an arm, she whirled. "Hi. And it's Melody."

The principal walked briskly across the sidewalk to meet her, his forehead furrowed.

"Didn't you get my email?"

Why was he always asking her that? "No. I didn't see any

email." Didn't the man know by now that email was not the best way to communicate with her—or with probably half the school? There were spam filters and junk emails to wade through and pointless forwards from relatives. Who had time for all of that? "I haven't exactly been on my computer lately." She'd been too busy developing a new Christmas cookie—the blob wheel. Melody made sure her arm covered the top of the container so Jonathan couldn't get a look at the monstrosities inside. After everyone witnessed her walking in with a contribution, she would have to find a place to hide them the first chance she got.

"I emailed you to tell you that we can't use the gym today." For always wearing such a stern expression, Mr. Braxton had a nice voice. Velvety smooth and lulling. Too bad he mostly used it for telling her what she didn't want to hear.

"What do you mean we can't use the gym?" The cookie swap had always been in the gym. "Why not?"

"Mom!" Finn appeared at the door. "They're doing the play practice in here. Where're we supposed to set up the tables for the cookie swap?"

"Are you serious?" Melody seethed. No wonder Charlene hadn't returned the three messages she'd left on her voicemail. She was trying to sabotage them.

"That's what I told you in the email." Mr. Braxton spoke with a stern patience. "It seems Charlene booked the space for the play right after she canceled the swap and before I could get into the system to reschedule. So I asked you to come up with another plan."

"Right." Melody took a good long glance at her watch. They had exactly half an hour before they were supposed to welcome people—assuming anyone came—to one of the best events of the season and they had no space.

"There's still time to call if off." Mr. Braxton pulled a phone out of his pocket. "I'll send a text through the communication chain and—"

"No." That was what Charlene wanted them to do. "We'll figure something out." This was her first event as the head of the cookie committee, and she wasn't about to let it fail. They simply had to improvise. "What about classrooms?" She didn't wait for a response before hurrying up the sidewalk toward the double glass doors. "We can put four tables in every classroom, and then people can wander through the building swapping the cookies. It might be nice to be spread out." Having a huge crowd in the gym always created a sense of mass chaos anyway. This way people could meander.

"That wasn't the plan." Mr. Braxton had caught up to her. "We've *always* had the event in the gym and—"

"Finn, Tate!" Melody called to the boys. "You need to take two of the folding tables to each classroom and find a place to set them up." It would be like a progressive dessert experience through the building. Parents would get to tour all of the classrooms. How fun would that be?

The boys saluted her and disappeared down the hall.

"We aren't prepared to host this event in the classrooms." The principal fell in stride with her. "I didn't warn the teachers and—"

Oh, for the love! Melody stopped and faced him. "Jonathan. Er, I mean Mr. Braxton . . . do you really want to cancel *now*? This is one of the biggest events in the school's holiday fundraising season. That would be saying no to money that could help us make sure you don't have to make any difficult decisions about extracurriculars."

He hesitated, his gaze darting around her while his jaw flexed. The pause gave her a second to study his face. To really *see* him. God, Kels was right. That strong structured jaw and those fiery intense eyes and full, symmetrical lips. Her eyes went wide. *Stop staring at his lips!* She had to focus.

"I guess you're right." He delivered the words through a re-signed sigh. Obviously she didn't have his vote of confidence.

"We can do this. I know we can." She might not be as organized as he was or as good at executing a set plan—or even having a plan to begin with—but she could improvise with the best of them. Flying by the seat of her pants was where she shone. "Trust me. Please. We can still pull this off and start the season right."

Judging from the worry lines in his forehead, he didn't agree, but a definitive nod sealed the pact. "Fine. We'll set up the tables in the classrooms."

"Thank you." She set the container of blob wheels on top of the coat rack outside the office, her mind already spinning ahead. "You help the boys get the tables set up, and I'll go find the linens and decorations so we can make this every bit as festive as it's been in the past." She'd dig through the storage closet in the teachers' lounge after a quick stop in the gym.

Jonathan muttered something when they parted ways, but she couldn't make out the words. It didn't matter. He'd likely already formed an opinion of her over the years, but she could still prove him wrong. In fact, today was the perfect opportunity to prove him wrong. She would fix everything and then he would see that she could be a valuable asset to the school community.

After shedding her coat and purse in the office, Melody booked it down the hall and ran into Adele outside the gym. "Hey, Mel." She looked around nervously, likely because she didn't want Charlene to see them talking.

"Hi there." Melody caught a peek through the window on the door. There had to be fifty kids in there and at least that many parents, which could work in their favor. "So glad you're here. I can't wait for you to walk around the swap and see what delectable offerings there are today." Ha! Little did Charlene know, she'd given them a built-in customer base by taking over the gym.

Adele winced. "Um, actually, Charlene said parents have to stay during the auditions. To supervise their kids. We're not supposed to leave the gym."

Was she joking? Either way, Melody laughed. She couldn't help it. "This is an elementary school. Not a prison. I'm pretty sure you could leave the gym for ten minutes to collect some cookies for a good cause."

"Like I said, I can't get into the middle of any drama with Charlene right now." She sidestepped Melody and opened the door. "Sorry."

"So am I," she muttered, following Adele inside. Most of the chairs that had been set up facing the stage were occupied by parents and their kids. Charlene stood in front of the stage behind a lectern chatting with Prisha while kids milled around them.

Backbone firm, Melody marched down the aisle between the rows.

Charlene looked up as she approached, amusement curling her shellacked lips. She wasn't surprised to see her. "Oh, hi, Melody. I didn't expect to see you here. Are Tate and Finn interested in trying out for the play?"

"Not even a little." She made sure her tone told the woman to cut the BS. "I'm here because I'm running the cookie swap— the event that you canceled at the last minute. Remember?"

Prisha looked back and forth between them, wide-eyed, and then slowly backed away.

"That's right." Charlene's smile had a snide bent. "I think I did hear something about you *trying* to run the cookie committee. How's it going?"

Oh no. She was not going to let this woman bait her into a fight. Not while everyone was watching them. She had to be the bigger person here. "It's going great. In fact, I stopped in to invite everyone here to walk around the swap while they wait for their kids. We have a variety of bakers who—"

"Sorry, Melody." Charlene had started to speak louder. "I need all the parents to stay for the duration of the rehearsal. There's no way I can supervise this many kids myself. It's against policy."

Against whose policy? Melody looked around. No one would meet her eye. None of these people would dare go walk the halls for fear of their kid getting blacklisted from the play.

"Now if you'll excuse us, we have a schedule to keep." Charlene waved her away. "All right, Sam. You're up next. Stage left, please."

Music started up—giving Melody her cue to leave. She did so with her head high.

By the time she'd made it to the teachers' lounge to look through the stash of event decorations, she was practically breathing fire. All she wanted to do was save the STEM program and preserve the town's holiday traditions, and Charlene was declaring an all-out war. The problem with a war, though, was that both sides lost too much. So Melody couldn't get drawn in. She had to rise above and stay focused on her goals instead of on simply beating Charlene.

Old tables crammed the lounge, and the kitchenette along

one wall looked like a throwback to the early nineties with honey oak cabinets and a mauve vinyl countertop. The smell of tuna fish made her nostrils flare. You'd think the district could do more for the people who were shaping all those young minds.

She couldn't solve all the world's problems in one day, however, so she started to open the doors of the closets lining the far walls. Ah. There was one labeled *Cookie Committee*. Melody pulled open the door and immediately froze. What in the world? No. This couldn't be right. The Christmas decorations had been destroyed—the tablecloths, the sparkling poinsettias, the centerpieces, the papier-mâché votive holders the third graders had made in art class. They were all a mess! Nothing was salvageable.

"The boys informed me that they have the tables under control." Mr. Braxton appeared in her peripheral vision. "Do you need help with the decorations?"

"There are no decorations." She stared at the shreds of fabric and plastic, dread building behind her ribs. It looked like someone had taken scissors and shredded everything.

"What do you mean?" He joined her at the closet. "It looks like some mice might've gotten in here."

Right, mice. In this particular closet.

"Didn't you do inventory in the closets this week? That was a checklist item in the president's introduction email. You were supposed to check the closet to make sure everything was ready."

There was an official checklist for this job? And to think she'd been waiting for Charlene to call her back and give her some instructions. Melody held out her hand. "Unlock your phone and give it to me right now."

Mr. Braxton shrank away from her. "What? Why?"

"I'm going to give you my cell number and then you can text me everything I need to read instead of emailing me." She held out her hands and wiggled her fingers until he reluctantly acquiesced.

"Trust me. This will be much more efficient." She typed in her name—adding a smiling emoji for good vibes—and then punched in her number. "There." She handed it back to him. "No more emails." Every time she opened her computer there were fifty new orders for the boutique and that always became her first priority. She didn't have time to wade through a hundred other emails.

Jonathan still held his phone out and away from him like he didn't know what to do with it now that it contained her number. "I can't send personal texts to every parent in this school."

"You won't be sending personal texts." He likely didn't even know what a personal text was—a friendly *Hi there!* or *How's your day going?* In all of her interactions with him, Mr. Braxton had been professional and . . . well, borderline robotic. "Besides, I'm not *only* a parent. I'm the president of the cookie committee now. And I'm implementing a new bylaw." Or whatever the heck they called it. "No more emails for the president of the cookie committee. Only texts." She grinned at him because she couldn't resist. "Do I need to sign an official decree or something?"

"That won't be necessary."

Wait. Was Mr. Braxton smiling?

"So, Cookie Club President, what's the plan for decorations?" The shadow of a smile he'd been sporting evolved into a smirk.

That was a new look for him.

"We're running out of time," he prompted. "Everyone will start arriving in twenty minutes."

Hopefully some people would arrive, other than the new committee members who'd agreed to bake for the swap. "Okay." She exhaled slowly, letting go of the earlier tension. They were already on crisis number two of the day and it wasn't even noon, but she could handle this. "No problem." This was the moment that single-momming twin boys had prepared her for. She traipsed out of the lounge, waving the principal along down the hall and into the library.

"We're going to use these." She gestured to the holiday display adorning the wall. "We'll borrow the paper chains and streamers." Carefully, she detached a red-and-green section from the wall. "And you can collect all of the miniature trees from the bookshelves for centerpieces. Oh! We can also stop by the art room and cut paper to fit the tables and then kids can color on them!" Securing the paper chain around her neck like a scarf, she hurried to one of the book carts in the corner. "Let's put everything on this so we only have to make one trip."

For once, Jonathan didn't argue. He moved alongside her, collecting the decorations and carefully setting them on the cart while she disconnected the rest of the streamers and paper chains. Then they quickly stopped in to the art room and worked together to cut long sheets of white paper.

After that, they developed quite the distribution system, with her focusing on placing the trees and Jonathan taping the garlands to the tables.

"Mr. Ponder won't be happy if he finds out we moved his library trees." Jonathan glanced around them as if he half expected the librarian to jump out from behind a door.

"He won't even know," Melody assured him. "We'll clean up and put everything back the way it was when we found it."

"Hey, Mom!" Tate ran out from the fifth-grade classroom across the hall. "We're done with the tables. Can we go watch the play auditions?"

"Maybe later." Charlene likely wouldn't let them in the door if Melody wasn't there to supervise them. She handed Jonathan one of the paper chains. "I'll need your help to get people checked in," she called to the boys, who were now playing tag in the hall.

"You and I can check people in." Jonathan hung the last paper chain on the table in the kindergarten classroom. "It would be good for the president and the principal to greet everyone when they arrive anyway. We can hand out our cookies first."

Cookies! *Ugh.* The blob wheels were still sitting on the coat rack. "Right. Sure." They could hand out their cookies together. Unless hers mysteriously disappeared ASAP. "Um. I'll get ready to greet people, if you take this cart back to the library." Then no one would witness her getting rid of the evidence that the blob wheels belonged to her.

"Sure. Sounds good."

Jonathan walked away, but before she could get to the cookies her mother glided in through the doors. "Hey, sweetie girl."

"Mom. Thanks for coming." She hugged her around the platter she held. "Are those your spritz cookies?" She had fond childhood memories of her mom cursing the day she'd bought that cookie press every year. "They look great." Much better than the blob wheels. Her gaze fixated on the container that sat on the other side of the hallway.

"Hey, Nonna!" Finn beelined toward them and nearly tackled his grandma with a fierce hug.

"Finny, look at you. You're so sharp!" She straightened his collar with her free hand. "What's the occasion?"

"Nothing." Her son detached himself and bolted down the hall again, calling "Gotta go!" over his shoulder.

"Did you make him dress up?" her mom asked sternly. Heaven forbid Melody force her grand-angels to do something they didn't want to do.

"No, before we left the house, he said he had to change and then he came downstairs dressed like that all on his own. Tate said it's because he has a crush on someone."

"He does," Mr. Braxton said behind her.

Fabulous. He'd already returned from taking the cart back to the library. How was she ever going to hide the cookies?

"Finn has a crush on Ms. Sanderson."

Melody gaped at him. "As in the cafeteria lady?"

Her mother chuckled. "Isn't that adorable?"

How had she missed this? "Ms. Sanderson is well over fifty years old." Or maybe even sixty. It was hard to tell because she dyed her hair blond.

Jonathan's second smile of the day appeared, and this one changed his face, crinkling the corners of his eyes and mouth. "She's funny and friendly and she makes one heck of a chocolate fudge brownie. What's not to like?"

"I'd marry her," her mother agreed. "If I weren't already taken by the man of my dreams, of course."

Sure, Ms. Sanderson was amazing. Melody loved her as much as anyone else. But why had no one informed her that her son had been flirting with the cafeteria lady? Usually she counted on her mother to keep her in the loop about their goings-on at school.

"Did *you* know about this?" she demanded.

"I didn't have a clue."

"Great." At some point she'd have to figure out how to talk to Finn about age-appropriate dating. But right now she had to act like a president. Or at least fake it till she made it. A few cookie swappers were already walking through the doors. That was a good sign, right? Charlene couldn't confine everyone to the gym all day. "Mom, why don't you go set up in one of the second-grade classrooms?"

"Got it. But I need to make my sizable contribution first." She pulled a folded check out of the pocket of her flannel shirt and shoved it into the cash box Jonathan had put on the table to collect the donations. Which was a good catch. Melody hadn't even thought about where they would put the money.

With more people streaming in, Melody stepped behind the table alongside Jonathan, greeting the familiar faces from around town and directing them to their stations while collecting donations in the process. Finn and Tate pitched in too—escorting people to their tables and helping to carry boxes of cookies. When there was a lull, Jonathan disappeared and Melody took the opportunity to catch her breath. Okay. Even with Charlene's obvious sabotage, this event would be a complete success. Things had started out rocky, but they'd saved the—

"Do you know whose cookies these are?" Jonathan approached the table carrying the container of blob wheels. "I found them on top of the coat rack."

Heat exploded in her cheeks. She'd totally forgotten to hide those damn cookies. "Oh. Uh. Huh. Nope. I don't recognize those." The lie tumbled out before she could stop it. "Must've been someone who walked in and forgot they left them there. I can go ask around." She stole the container out of his hands. "I need to check on everyone anyway—do my job as president."

"Sounds good. I'll hold down the fort here." He took up his post behind the table. "It looks like one of our kindergartners or first graders helped make them, if that guides you in the right direction."

"Yeah. Totally." She wasn't sure if she was smiling or grimacing. A kindergartner? They weren't *that* bad. "I'll be right back." She took off down the hall and then veered to the cafeteria since the lights were out. A huge trash can sat by the door. She hesitated. The boys would likely end up eating them if she brought them home—they'd eat pretty much anything with sugar. Then at least the cookies wouldn't go to waste. Glancing around, Melody hid the container behind the trash can and then returned to the table. She could go back for them after everyone left.

"Did you find out who they belonged to?" Mr. Braxton asked.

"Yep. Sure did." She assessed the next group coming through the door. "Look at that. At least people are showing up." Not in masses or anything, but they wouldn't be standing here alone for the next two hours.

"I was a little worried." He paused, then squeezed his eyes shut for a beat. "Not because of you being in charge or anything. That's not why I was worried. I just didn't—oops, I forgot to put out my cookies." Mr. Braxton stiffly lifted the box that had been sitting on the chair next to them and removed the lid, revealing run-of-the-mill chocolate thumbprints.

They didn't look like anything special to her.

He cleared his throat. "What I meant to say before was, Charlene didn't love the fact that the committee was going to continue on with the events under new leadership."

"I'm aware. But maybe new leadership is exactly what the cookie committee needs."

"It might be." Something new glinted in his eyes, but before she could decode the change, another group of people came in.

They settled into the routine again, signing in swappers, accepting donations, explaining how the event worked.

Her sister arrived twenty minutes late, with no cookies. No surprise there. Kels hated spending time in the kitchen.

"What a fun idea to do the swap in classrooms." Kels aimed her smile at Jonathan.

"Thank you." Melody decided to take all of the credit. He'd wanted to cancel, after all. "We thought it would be good to change it up this year. Didn't we?" She lightly elbowed Jonathan in the ribs.

He grunted.

"Personally, I think putting the cookies in the classrooms is too cumbersome."

Charlene.

At some point, she'd snuck up behind Kels.

"I always like to get a look at all of the cookies side by side so I can pick the best." She wedged herself in front of the table next to Kelsey. "Speaking of cookies . . . *Mr. Braxton*, these look *divine*."

Melody eyed the cookies in the box between them. There was nothing special about them! And yet any woman who'd walked past them ogled both Mr. Braxton and his offering.

"Oh my." Charlene chewed slowly, her eyes closing with a look of rapture. "Mmm mmm mmm."

Maybe Melody should leave the two of them alone. She shared a look with her sister, their thoughts flying back and forth. After years of practice, she and Kels could read each other.

Right now, her sister really wanted to say something like *Get a room, Charlene*. And she was fighting off a laugh.

"Is that *toffee* I taste?" Charlene ran her tongue over her bottom lip.

"It is, actually." Could the principal really be clueless? "My grandma always put toffee into her thumbprints."

"You baked with your grandmother?" Charlene fawned. "That's *so* sweet."

Oh please. Everyone knew he'd baked with his grandmother. Especially Charlene. She knew everything about everyone.

If Finn and Tate had been around they definitely would've been making gagging noises by now. Melody was too mature to do that, but she looked at Kels again and they snickered together. "I thought no one was supposed to leave the gym during the rehearsal." Melody made her tone as sweet as toffee.

"The kids needed a few minutes to study the next song. They won't miss me. I thought I should come and see how everything was going out here." She caught Melody in a calculating gaze, then looked around. "Where are your cookies, Melody? I'm *dying* to try the new president's offering."

Uh-oh. "You know, I think I misplaced them somewhere." She threw up her hands. "Oh well. I'll be too busy walking around to stand behind a table the whole afternoon anyway. I have to make sure to greet everyone and recruit more new committee members." She stepped away, but Tate rushed up to her, holding something above his head.

"Hey, Mom. I found our cookies behind the trash can."

Melody's heart lurched to her throat. She darted a glance around but there was no way to stop this impending disaster—no place to hide, no magical portal offering her an escape.

Her darling son deposited the container of blob wheels onto the table right next to Jonathan's thumbprints. "Can you believe that? Do you think someone tried to throw them away?"

The principal's brows pinched together but he didn't say anything. No one said anything. Not Kels. Not Charlene. They all only stared at her.

Melody's cheeks burned so hot the smile melted off her face.

Tate looked truly offended on her behalf. "I mean, I know they didn't turn out that good, but you did your best, and then someone tries to put them in the garbage? It's a good thing they missed or I'd find 'em and put *them* in the garbage."

"Thanks, Tate!" She prodded her son away, the rash of humiliation now inching up her neck. "Why don't you go do some more taste testing, hmm?" She couldn't bring herself to look at the blobs, or at anyone else's face.

Finally, Charlene interrupted the deafening silence. "I'd better get back to the gym." The words had a singsongy ring to them. She probably couldn't wait to go back and report to everyone there how truly awful their new cookie committee president was.

"Wow, Mel," Kels finally said after the woman had gone. "Those look . . . *interesting*. Very creative."

Her hands stiffened as she removed the lid. There was no going back now. These were her cookies and she had to sell them, darn it. She wouldn't *let* Charlene make a fool out of her. "Do you want to try one?"

"Uh . . . you know how I am with food dyes. They really mess me up. But I *will* take one of these." She stole a thumbprint from the box and bit into it right away. "My God! These

THE CHRISTMAS COOKIE WARS 🥠 49

are incredible!" She held it in Melody's direction. "Have you tried this cookie? I mean, you pick it up thinking it's going to be just another chocolate thumbprint and then you put it in your mouth and . . . *wow*. That toffee in the middle truly melts."

Melody shot her another tried-and-true sisterly glare. Traitor!

"I'm glad you like it. This is an old family recipe." Jonathan beamed. She'd never seen such a light in the man's eyes. He picked up the box and held it out to Melody. "Maybe you'd like to try one?"

"No, thanks." Averting her eyes from the gooey chocolatey goodness, she held a firm stance.

She'd never wanted a cookie so badly in her life, but she wasn't about to become a Jonathan Braxton groupie.

Four

"HOW'S IT GOING, HON?" KELS SNAGGED MELODY'S EL-bow and dragged her into the bathroom at the end of the second-grade hallway.

"It's going *great*. I've never had so much fun in my whole life." Sarcasm had always been her love language. Two hours had passed since Tate had outed her cookies, and her insides were still smoldering. "Jonathan totally knows I lied about the blob wheels." Which was why she'd avoided him as much as she possibly could while standing next to him at a table. "And Charlene has me pegged for a complete failure."

"Yeah, Tate created quite the awkward moment." Her sister winced on her behalf. "But at least Jonathan didn't react."

"Not yet." Though she was fully anticipating a lecture about lying later. She leaned close to the mirror and assessed her face. Faint red splotches still streaked her cheeks. "The worst news is that we're three hundred dollars behind in fundraising compared to last year's cookie swap. So it would appear I *am* a total failure." What had she been thinking taking this on? Not only did she suck at baking, she clearly did not have enough star power in this community to pull everyone together. Not when she was competing with Charlene.

"Come on. The day's not over yet." Kels's wide grin attempted to rally her.

"No one has come in for the last half hour." So she might as well wave the white flag now. "I don't think I can face Mr. Braxton."

"Well, I can." Her sister sighed dreamily. "I need to snag myself another one of those chocolate thumbprints before they're gone. I can't resist them." Kels elbowed her. "Jonathan is very hard to resist."

Pshaw. For some women, maybe. Melody gasped. "Wait a minute . . ." The thumbprints. Mr. Braxton's undeniable popularity with the moms . . . and some dads. "That's it!" She spun to face her sister. "We'll have Mr. Braxton load the cookies on a cart—along with the donation box—and he can take the cookie swap on the road!" Charlene had said parents couldn't leave their kids in the gym unattended, but she'd never said anything about not bringing the cookies to the people.

"That's pretty brilliant, Mel." Kels hugged her. "See? You *are* the right person for this job."

"Maybe I am and maybe I'm not, but I refuse to give up. Come on." She grabbed her sister's hand, and they raced down the hall.

"You have to take your cookies into the gym," Melody called to Mr. Braxton before they'd even reached the table. "Get the cart! We're taking the cookie swap on the road!"

He stared at her with his typical bewildered frown.

"Let's move, move, move." She clapped to get him going. "We only have a half hour before people start leaving the rehearsal and we have three hundred dollars to make up."

Understanding dawned on his face slowly, followed by a grin. "A mobile cookie swap sneak attack. That's perfect."

"Exactly. No one can resist you." Wait. She hadn't meant to say that. "I mean a lot of people can't. Some people. Not this person." She pointed to herself.

"Here's the cart!" Kels rolled it out of the office at the perfect time to shut her up. What was the matter with her?

Thankfully, Mr. Braxton didn't seem to have noticed. He was busy positioning his sixth, seventh, and eighth boxes of cookies on the cart.

Melody added the donation box without saying another darn word. Who knew what would come out of her mouth if she opened it?

Jonathan started to push the cart down the hall. "You're coming with me, right?" he called over his shoulder.

"Of course she is!" Kels pushed her forward, setting Melody's legs in motion.

Truthfully, Mr. Braxton didn't need her help soliciting donations. Most people likely wouldn't even notice her standing next to him. But she *didn't* want to miss the look on Charlene's face when Jonathan walked in with his thumbprints either. That in mind, she got the door for him.

Inside the gym, everyone stood around chatting.

"Jonathan." Charlene hurried over, not bothering to acknowledge Melody. "What a surprise. We were just getting ready to finish up here."

"Perfect timing, then." He flashed a charming, somewhat self-deprecating smile. "I still had too many cookies left, and we thought you all would be hungry after working so hard to supervise the rehearsal. Anyone care to offer a donation to take some of these home?"

Charlene's smile curdled, and Melody had to gag back a laugh as a line formed with kids begging their parents for a cookie.

Melody stood in the background while moms flirted with the principal, stuffing cash into the donation box like they would into a naughty firefighter's pants.

Twenty bucks here, ten there, along with some fives and ones and comments like "These look so *scrumptious!*" and "You'll have to give us the recipe!"

"Sorry. I'm not at liberty to share it." Jonathan continued to serve up a side of charm along with the cookies.

"You really can't?" one woman asked. Melody didn't recognize her. "I'd be *happy* to take you out to dinner as a thank-you."

Melody gasped but turned it into a cough before she drew attention. Exactly how many times had he been asked out today?

"Sorry." Now *that* expression she recognized—polite indifference. "My grandma made me promise to keep her baking secrets in the family. Besides, it's bad form to go on a date with a parent." He said the last part with a perfect blend of regret and sincerity.

"Oh, all right," the mom whined. "If you change your mind, you have my email."

Melody rolled her eyes. Email. The woman probably loved email. She and Jonathan were perfect for each other.

By the time the line dwindled, she was sure they'd made up the difference in donations. "Hey, Charlene, there's a few cookies left," she called over to where the woman was hastily boxing up a microphone. "Wouldn't want you to be left out."

"Maybe I'll take some if you go get your cookies too."

Melody could read Charlene's smirk all the way across the room. "Why ever didn't you bring them in?"

A couple moms standing around her snickered, and Melody felt herself shrink a few inches.

"Sorry, everyone. It looks like I'm officially out of cookies." Mr. Braxton wheeled the cart to the door, and she ran ahead to open it for him before any tears fell. Clearly Charlene had told them all about the blob wheels.

"That was a solid plan, Ms. Monroe," he said when they'd cleared the doors.

Her voice was too fragile to correct him on her name, so she only mumbled, "Thanks."

"Hey, Mom!" Finn bounded to her, out of breath and holding a football. She stole it before Mr. Braxton busted them for playing in the hall.

"Why don't you two start taking down the tables in the classrooms?" The faster they cleaned up, the faster she could get out of here. She'd endured enough humiliation for one day. "Find Nonna to help you. And make sure you put the miniature Christmas trees back exactly the way they were in the library."

"Okay!" Her sneaky younger twin stole the ball back out of her hands, and they both took off down the hall with Tate threatening to tackle Finn.

"How'd it go in there?" Kelsey was waiting for them at the table outside the office.

"It was a total success." The principal started to pull cash out of the box, counting it under his breath.

"My sister is brilliant, isn't she?" Kels slung an arm around her.

"That's two thousand and thirteen bucks." Mr. Braxton held the fistful of money over his head. "We beat last year's total."

That took some of the sting out of Charlene's earlier dig.

"All right. I gotta run." Kels gathered up her purse from the table. "We're going Christmas tree hunting."

"Aren't you bringing any cookies home?"

"My box of cookies is already in the car." Kels grinned. "I snagged a few more of Jonathan's thumbprints and hid them before they were gone."

"Why am I not surprised?"

"Bye, hon. I'll see you at the boutique later." Her sister gave her a half hug and then bolted out the door, leaving her standing alone with Mr. Braxton.

"You did it."

The disbelief beaming from his gaze gave Melody her edge back. "What can I say? I shine when people underestimate me." Like he had. "Mission accomplished. We can all go home now." As soon as they cleaned up. She snatched the container of blob wheels to move it so he could clear the tablecloth, but Mr. Braxton stepped up toe to toe with her.

"Can I try one?" He nodded toward the cookies in her hand.

"You don't have to do that." Melody automatically stepped back. She hated it when people felt sorry for her. She'd dealt with far too much pity after losing her husband so young. Besides, she didn't *want* him to try them, to know how truly awful they tasted.

"I know I don't have to." He took a step closer to her like they were part of some choreographed dance. "I'd really like to try one of your cookies, Ms. Monroe."

"*Melody*," she grumbled. What was his endgame here? Did he want to humiliate her too? Whatever. She had to get rid of the cookies anyway. "Suit yourself. But I can't be responsible for what happens to you." She peeled off the lid.

He laughed, low and gravelly. The sound stirred something in her.

"I'm not worried." He selected an extra blobby red-and-green cookie and took a bite, chewing thoughtfully. "It's not so bad," he finally said.

"Right. I'm sure it's delicious." She happened to know they were too dry and salty from her ill-fated taste test at home.

"This isn't the worst cookie I tasted today. I promise." He took his time methodically finishing the cookie and then dusted the crumbs off his hands. "You need to let the butter sit out at room temperature next time. The eggs too. That'll help the texture. And the colors wouldn't have bled so much if you'd chilled the dough longer."

Melody simply blinked at him. Was he being . . . nice? It seemed like it, although his facial expression stayed neutral.

"I didn't mean to lie," she blurted. "About my cookies. They didn't turn out quite right and I was . . . a little embarrassed, that's all."

"You don't have to explain saving face to me." Jonathan's mouth finally softened into something resembling a smile. "I lie sometimes too." He stacked the cash box on his empty cookie containers and disappeared into the office for a second, leaving her to wonder.

"Mostly to my daughter, Ainsley, when she asks me if I know a band she's really into," he said when he came back into the hallway, without the box. "I don't want to seem obsolete, so I tell her I know whatever band she's talking about and then I have to spend a week listening to make the lie true."

The confession disarmed her. Ainsley. What a pretty name. "I get that." The older Finn and Tate got, the less she seemed to have in common with them. "I didn't want people to know

THE CHRISTMAS COOKIE WARS 🍪 57

I'm an incompetent baker, so I hid my own cookies behind the trash can." As long as they were trading confessions, she might as well come clean. "I didn't want to hand them out because I knew no one would want them."

"I won't tell anyone, if you don't tell anyone I'm a fake when it comes to music." He folded up their card table. "Ainsley would die if she knew that I really listen to reggae."

"*Reggae?*" She had to take a second to process this information. Buttoned-up, sweater-vested Mr. Braxton listened to reggae? She sharpened her gaze on him. Maybe he was messing with her. "Really?"

"I know." His head swiveled side to side like he wanted to make sure no one was eavesdropping on them. "Now I know one of your secrets and you know one of mine."

Yes, and she had a sudden desire to learn more. "How old is Ainsley?"

"She's fifteen." He leaned the folded table up against the opposite wall. "After the divorce, we let her decide where she wanted to be, and she chose Denver with her mom. I told her I would be okay with whatever she chose, but I lied about that too."

Melody couldn't look away. She'd truly never seen this side of him. "I'm not sure that's lying as much as it's sacrificing what you want for your kid. That's one of the harder parts of the job."

"For sure." His sigh said it all. "I don't get to see her as much as I want, but we talk all the time. And, even though she's busy, she always spends the whole winter holiday with me, so I can't complain."

"That's swee—"

"Hey, Mom!" Her boys came charging down the hall until

they caught sight of their principal and then they quickly put on the brakes.

"All the tables are put away," Finn reported, eyeing Mr. Braxton with caution.

"No one ate your cookies?" Tate took the container out of her hands and appeared to count.

"Nope." She eyed Mr. Braxton. "Except for one. I guess people aren't interested in blob wheels. Their loss."

"I'll have one." Her son dug into the container and shoved the whole cookie into his mouth.

"It's delicious, Mom," he said, still chewing. "I'll bet you're gonna win the Cookie Contest next week."

Yeah, she was thinking about finding a way to recuse herself from the next cookie committee event. "I'm not sure I'll enter—"

"You boys know I've won the Cookie Contest three years running," the principal broke in.

That was true. "Yep. So what's the point in entering anyway?" She was almost relieved. Let Jonathan win it again. If today was any indication, she should definitely *not* enter. It was one thing to have her cookies passed over. At the contest, the attendees publicly voted on all of the cookies, ranking them from first place to last.

"You're not going to win this year." Tate marched to his principal and then quickly added, "Sir. Because we're gonna help my mom bake the best cookies anyone in this town has ever tasted. And then *we're* gonna win. Isn't that right, Mom?" He moved to stand by her.

"Oh. Well . . ." They were going to help her bake cookies like they used to? Visions danced in her head—the boys measuring out ingredients, mixing, and rolling and singing along

to Christmas music in their cozy kitchen. A few uninter-
rupted hours with them. She'd pretty much do anything—
even humiliate herself again. "I mean, I guess we could try..."

"You're absolutely sure you want to enter?" There was
something almost playful about Jonathan's question. "Nothing can beat my grandma's recipes, you know."

"My mom can." Finn lunged to her other side, his hand on
her shoulder, chin lifted up the way it did when he wanted to
look taller.

Her heart melted. In probably two years they would be
bigger than her, but for now, they were still looking up at her,
both of them. Expectantly. How could she back down in front
of them? "I can't beat his grandma's cookies. But we can. Together." She winked at her boys and then shot Jonathan a
glare to let him know the challenge had been accepted.

"Come on, Mom." Finn hurried to the office and found her
coat and purse. "We should get going so we can decide what
cookie we're going to make."

She hesitated. The boys hadn't been this interested in
spending time with her since she'd bribed them by taking them
to a water park last summer... but she had to see to her responsibilities here, so Mr. Braxton wouldn't think she was any flak-
ier than he already did. "We have to do a walk-through first—"

"Don't worry about it." The principal still had that glint of
a challenge in his eyes. Or was she misreading him? "I'll make
sure everything's back in its place before I go home. You only
have a week to come up with a cookie that will beat mine.
Trust me. You're going to need all the time you can get."

Was he seriously trash talking right now? Her competitive
streak might have been lying dormant since high school volleyball, but it fired right back up. "You seem pretty confident

for someone who's only comfortable using recipes from the 1950s."

Jonathan's eyes widened with surprise before a smirk narrowed them again. "My recipes are tried-and-true. Time tested—"

"And outdated," she interrupted. "No offense, but I have a creative edge—"

"Yeah, my mom is a *fashion designer,*" Finn added. "She's going to design the coolest cookie ever and then we're going to win the contest."

Mr. Braxton slowly lowered his gaze to the container of blob wheels in her hands. "I'm not worried."

A fiery indignation boiled over. The nerve! She'd thought they'd had a moment earlier—that they'd almost crossed a line into friendship. But she'd obviously been mistaken. He'd probably been messing with her, telling her to leave out the butter and eggs so they were room temperature. "If you're that confident, maybe we should make this more interesting."

"Yes!" Tate jumped into the fray. "A bet! Let's make a bet!"

Oops. Maybe she was getting carried away . . .

"I'm game." Jonathan paused. "We've been in need of a volunteer to help out in the cafeteria during lunch the last day of school."

The cafeteria? Right before Christmas, when the kids were all hopped up on sugar and restless for a break? That was her worst nightmare. The smell of that place alone was enough to drive her to drink. Not to mention the chaos and the noise and the spills . . .

"Unless you're too afraid." He seemed to know exactly how to bait her.

"I'm not afraid." She sized up his typical uniform—dark-colored sweater vest and slacks with a boring crisp button-up shirt. "Fine. If you win, I'll take cafeteria duty. But if I win, you have to let me style you for a week. In clothes I've designed."

Jonathan glanced down at his ensemble. "What's wrong with my clothes?"

"His recipes aren't the only thing from the fifties," Tate muttered.

"What was that?" Mr. Braxton leaned closer to her son.

"Nothing!" Melody shoved the cookie container into Finn's hands and then slung an arm around each boy, dragging them toward the exit. "We should get going. Hope you're ready for your new wardrobe if I win."

For the first time his expression registered concern. "Only for a week," he called, following behind them. "And nothing too wild."

She'd take that caveat as a compliment. "You have to agree to give me full creative license—wild or not—or we don't have a deal."

"Fine." Mr. Braxton moved in front of them with a stubborn lift to his chin and stuck out his hand. "We'd better shake on it."

"Right." A sudden breathlessness hit her the second his hand swallowed hers. Warmth radiated all the way up her arm.

"I look forward to beating you."

"Not gonna happen," Finn assured him. "Just you wait. We're gonna make something epic."

"You're not gonna know what hit you," Tate added.

"All right, you two." She prodded them out into the cold, and they all got into the car. "We need to do some serious brainstorming." They had no idea what Jonathan had up his sleeve, so they would have to think big.

"How about we make some gingerbread people?" Tate clicked in his seat belt. "We could decorate them like ninjas."

"Maybe." Christmas ninja cookies? Somehow she didn't think that would be enough to give them an edge.

Melody started the car and drove out of the parking lot, heading for the boutique. "Not sure if gingerbread people would have enough pizzazz." Considering the batch she'd made last Christmas had a texture like cardboard. She wasn't sure she wanted to attempt that again. "We need to think outside the typical Christmas box."

They might not be able to beat Jonathan on taste, but she was a fashion designer, dang it. She could take him down with presentation. "We have to come up with something so amazing that everyone'll notice." And somehow they had to make it taste good too.

"I've got it!" Finn leaned between the seats. "We can put two cookies in one!"

"Yes . . . like a chocolate and a mint," Tate said. "People love that."

"Or chocolate and peanut butter." Finn had never liked mint.

"That's a good idea. But we'd probably need to stick to traditional holiday flavors." She turned onto Main Street and slowed her speed. A sign hung in the coffee shop's window: *Today's specials—Eggnog Crème Brûlée Latte and Cinnamon Latte.*

"Crème brûlée and eggnog," she mused.

"I love eggnog," Finn reminded her.

"We all love eggnog." And she happened to know that those specials at the coffee shop were favorites of the majority of people in town. "We can make some eggnog cookies and cinnamon cookies." A visual formed—huge cookies adorned with rich, creamy frosting. They could caramelize the sugar on top and dust them with gold edible glitter.

They would make them so beautiful and so unique that no one would be able to pass them up. "We've got this, boys. We're going to win the Cookie Contest."

Hopefully Mr. Braxton liked Sea Island cotton.

Five

"WHAT D'YOU THINK, MOM?" FINN HELD UP THE PAPER he'd been working on while sitting on a stool at the checkout counter.

Markers and papers were strewn across the surface, some having rolled off onto the reclaimed-wood floors. Her younger twin definitely took after her, while neat and orderly Tate was like a miniature Thomas.

"It's perfect." Every Sunday, both boys accompanied her to the boutique, and she paid them minimum wage to do odd jobs like dusting and price tagging and restocking the shelves. This morning, however, Finn had been obsessing over the cookie plan. Meanwhile, Tate was over in the men's section, refolding the sweaters because they weren't up to his symmetrical specifications.

Melody walked to the counter and inspected the drawing more closely. "Wow. You even put in the green and gold detail." He'd sketched swirls into the layers of frosting, though she had no idea how they would translate that level of detail into cookies. In fact, she had no idea how they would translate the eggnog and cinnamon flavors into the cookies.

Her son nodded, chewing thoughtfully on the edge of the marker cap. "I think the colors will be perfect."

"I agree." He'd captured the gold sparkles beautifully— exactly what she'd been picturing. However, since yesterday when she'd shaken hands with Jonathan, gambler's remorse had started to set in. She'd never gambled in her life, and these stakes were high.

It wasn't the cafeteria duty that had her losing sleep. It was the way her boys kept looking at her when they talked about the big Cookie Contest. How their eyes lit up with such hope. Those looks had driven her to spend most of last night surfing the Internet on her phone while she tried to look up recipes and formulate a plan for how to actually put the ingredients together into something that tasted decent.

And she hadn't gotten very far.

The door scraped open, setting off the chimes.

"Morning, loves!" Her mother paraded in, followed by Aunt Bernice, Joan, Kels, and three other members of the newly formed cookie committee.

"Welcome, everyone!" Melody rushed to greet them. With such limited time before their next big event, she'd called an emergency meeting at the boutique. That way, she and Kels could listen for any customers to come in and they wouldn't have to close the store. "You can all head right back to the break room." She smiled especially wide at Nancy, Mr. Braxton's assistant, and Deb and Tracey, two moms of kindergartners, apparently the only other moms at the school who didn't fear Charlene's reign of terror.

"I'll go to the break room after I get kisses from my grandest boys!" Her mom smothered Finn and Tate.

"Me too." Aunt Bernice opened her arms, and the boys walked into the obligatory hug knowing there was no escaping it. But she rewarded them each with a sucker from her pocket.

"Help everyone get situated back there," Melody said to Kels. "I'll wait for Mr. Braxton."

Her sister winked, then herded the group to the back of the store.

"I can't believe Mr. Braxton is coming *here*," Finn muttered. "I'd better hide my drawing so he doesn't spy on us."

"Yeah, he can't find out about the cookie we're making." Tate eyed the door. "I can't wait to see the look on his face when we win. It'll be the—"

The door whooshed open with the wind and the principal strode in, looking mighty out of place against the whimsical décor.

Finn immediately threw his upper body down over the paper, hiding his creation.

"Good morning, Finn. Tate." Mr. Braxton hung out by the door, stomping the snow off his boots onto the mat.

"Good morning, Mr. Braxton," the boys recited dully.

Melody raised her eyebrows at them. Reason number five hundred she should've never made that bet. Now she'd made their principal their nemesis.

"We have classified information over here." Her older twin moved to stand between Mr. Braxton and Finn. "You're not allowed to see our cookie plan. Sir."

"I promise I didn't come to spy." He shed his coat and hung it on the rack by the door. "But, since I'm here, maybe I could take a look at that drawing and give you some pointers." His sly grin made it clear he was teasing them, but the joke sailed over the boys' heads.

"No way!" Finn quickly folded up the masterpiece and stuffed it into his pocket. "We don't *need* your help."

"Yeah. We've got this in the bag." Tate swiveled his head to gaze at her. There went that hope again, beaming straight at her, making her stomach hurt.

"We sure do." Her smile was showing too many teeth. She could feel it.

"Suit yourselves." Jonathan stepped farther into the space, glancing around like he was lost.

Oh right. He'd never been into the store before. She didn't sell any sweater vests here. "We can head to the break room." Melody beckoned him away from the boys. "Everyone else is waiting back there."

"Great." Mr. Braxton walked alongside her, slowing his pace to study the clothing racks they passed.

He seemed . . . distracted. Or confused?

"Did you want to do some shopping?" Melody meant it as a joke but, to her utter surprise, Mr. Braxton stopped. "Maybe. After the meeting? And I might need your help. Would that be okay?"

She blinked at him a few extra times. Was he being serious? "Sure. Um, it's fine with me."

"Great." He strode into the break room.

When Melody caught up, everyone had already been seated and most of them had steaming mugs of coffee in front of them too. She shot her sister a grateful smile and took her place at the head of the long table. "Thank you all for coming. I know it's a bit unorthodox to meet here instead of at the school."

"It is much easier to meet in the conference room or library." Mr. Braxton pulled a small leather-bound notebook out of his pocket. "But this will do for today."

Well, good. She was glad she had his approval. Melody gave her head a slight shake. "Anyway, I thought we should touch base quickly about the Cookie Contest since it's only days away." A burst of panic squeezed her throat. She *had* to get that recipe perfected ASAP! "As of now, we have five competitors." Her and Jonathan, of course. She'd also talked Chester, the coffee shop owner, into entering by bribing him with the silk pashmina he'd had his eye on for a while now. Thankfully, her mother and Bernice had roped in two friends from the next town over. It seemed no one in their community was overly excited to go up against Mr. Braxton. "I've been in touch with each contestant, letting them know they need to bring along three dozen cookies for judg—"

"If I may, I had a thought," Mr. Braxton interrupted. "What if this year, instead of everyone bringing their cookies from home, we actually made them during the competition. In real time?"

Melody's mouth went dry. That was a terrible idea. How could she put this nicely? "That sounds like a lot of work, and we don't have much time to pull off such a large-scale change." Why did he want to change things up? Now? Days before the competition? Did he think she was going to cheat and *buy* cookies? Okay, the thought might have crossed her mind, but she'd never actually do that! "I don't think a live competition would work." For her.

"Why not?" He leaned back in his chair, looking more casual and comfortable than she'd ever seen him. "The school has a huge kitchen—plenty of oven space. And with only five of us there'll be plenty of room to set up prep stations in the gym." He seemed to aim the argument at her. "I think a live competition would really draw people in. We could charge more for entry that way."

"I love it." Joan gazed dreamily at Jonathan across the table.

Melody wished she were close enough to give the woman a gentle kick under the table.

"We need all the attendees we can get," Nancy agreed. "Everyone loves a good competition."

"It sounds fun!" Deb added. "A live competition like *The Great British Baking Show*!"

Not exactly like that because Melody couldn't bake. She looked from one person's smile to the next. She couldn't do this. She got stressed enough baking in the privacy of her own kitchen! How would she ever be able to measure and mix and roll and decorate with a hundred people watching her? She tried to send her sister a telepathic message. *Come up with a reason this won't work!*

But Kels was smiling and nodding along too. "I think that'll put the perfect spin on an old tradition."

"It's settled, then." Her mother drove the final nail into the coffin. "Oh, what fun. Can I be the host? With a microphone and everything?"

"I don't see why not." Jonathan looked to her. Because she was supposed to be the president here, yet he was the one making all the decisions, coming in here with all these great ideas that he should've run by her first.

It was too late now. She couldn't pull a Charlene. "Sure, Mom. You can be the host."

"Great." Mr. Braxton jotted some notes. "We can set up the stations in the front of the gym and add tables and chairs for the spectators."

Wasn't he full of extra good ideas today? Melody tried to loosen her jaw so she didn't glower at him.

"Oh, I bet Chester would bring his mobile coffee and hot cocoa station and sell drinks to the audience," Bernice said. "I'll ask him during poker tomorrow morning."

"Sounds like a great plan." It appeared this group didn't need her at all. Maybe she could resign and withdraw from the cookie competition.

"I'll talk to Ms. Sanderson about using the kitchen." Mr. Braxton added another note in his leather-bound book. "And I'll have the building engineer set up the tables for us." His gaze fell on Melody. "You'll contact all of the contestants and let them know about the change?"

"I guess I will." Since he seemed to be the one assigning roles. "Now that that's settled . . ." She'd better take back the reins before Mr. Braxton got any other brilliant ideas that would make her life harder. "Does anyone have any questions about the plans for the Cookie and Cocktail Crawl or Cookie Daze?" She'd sent them a lengthy email—yes, email!—two days ago about her ideas for making some changes to those events. Mr. Braxton must be so impressed.

"I thought everything looked great." He had his gaze glued to his phone now. "There are some good ideas here."

Murmurs of agreement went around the table.

"I haven't read the email yet," Kels admitted.

A sister after her own heart. "That's okay. We can talk about the other events at our meeting next week. I wanted to keep this one brief anyway." She needed all the time she could get to formulate a plan for their cookie. Especially now. "Let's adjourn until then."

"Sounds good to me." Mr. Braxton stuffed his notebook back into his pocket. "See you all on Saturday."

The words held an ominous ring in Melody's ears. She took her time collecting mugs, carting them to the sink.

Deb and Tracey ambled out the door first, talking excitedly about watching a live competition. Nancy and Mr. Braxton exited next, leaving Melody standing in the break room with her family members.

"Have you figured out your cookie for the contest yet?" Aunt Bernice brought her another mug.

"I mean, Finny's drawing is beautiful, but do you have a recipe?" Her mother stared at her as though seeing an impending disaster. "Have you ever tried to make eggnog crème brûlée cinnamon cookies?"

"Not yet. We're still working on that part." God, they were so screwed. "Maybe one of you should enter the contest too. Or better yet, all three of you." That would take some of the attention off her—

"Are you kidding?" Bernice scoffed. "No one's going to beat Jonathan anyway." She didn't even have the decency to look apologetic. "Not only do his cookies always *taste* the best, he's also got the whole sexy librarian look going for him."

Her sister nodded but then her sheepish expression backpedaled. "Not that you're not sexy too, Melly. You're just not *Jonathan Braxton* sexy."

"I couldn't care less about being sexy." She was lucky to get a shower and swipe on some mascara once in a while. Melody dumped the last dregs out of the coffeepot and rinsed it in the sink. "This contest is supposed to be about baking. Not about how we look during said baking." She already knew what her persona would be in front of the crowd—harried, stressed, mediocre baker.

"What was it Jonathan made last year?" Mom tilted her head toward Kelsey's, as she often did when they had to share thinking powers.

"Something with a jelly filling, wasn't it?" Bernice asked.

"No, no. That was the year before." Her mother tapped at

her forehead. "Ah yes! He made those delicious butter cookies dipped in chocolate."

Kelsey moaned. "They were *divine*."

That seemed to be everyone's favorite adjective to describe Mr. Braxton's cookies. Talking to these three was not helping her confidence.

"It doesn't matter what Mr. Braxton made last year." Finn marched into the break room. "We're still going to beat him. We *have* to beat him. Mom made a bet."

"A bet?" Mom, Aunt Bernice, and Kels said it at the exact same time, their full attention on Melody.

"You made a *bet* with *Mr. Braxton*?" If Melody had been regretting that decision earlier, now she truly hated it, especially seeing the blatant disbelief on her mother's face. What had she been thinking?

"Yep," Tate said proudly, following his brother to the table, where they both plopped down. "If we win the contest Mom's gonna make him wear nicer clothes for a week, and if he wins she has to volunteer in the cafeteria the last day of school."

"But that's not gonna happen," Finn assured them. "She won't have to work in the cafeteria because our cookies will win."

Her mother was still too busy gaping at Melody to hear him. "You're going to *dress* Mr. Braxton?"

Her sister laughed. "Amazing!"

"I'm not going to actually dress him," she clarified. "I'm going to be his fashion consultant. Only for a week. I'm sure he's fully capable of getting dressed himself." Melody peeked out into the store to make sure no one was listening to them talk about Mr. Braxton's sexy factor. He was still there— talking to Nancy by the registers. "The bet is no big deal," she said quietly. Heck, maybe he wouldn't even hold her to it. They'd only been joking.

"No big deal?" Her sister snorted. "Have you ever volunteered in the cafeteria?"

"Nope." She'd pretty much done every other volunteer job in that school, but she'd always avoided the lunchroom.

"She won't have to." Frustration broke through Finn's words. "We have a plan. Remember?" He pulled the drawing out of his pocket and held it up.

Melody couldn't even look at the picture. The boys might've already forgotten how her blob wheels had turned out, but she sure hadn't.

"It's a very pretty drawing." Aunt Bernice patted Finn's nest of curls. "But people at the Cookie Contest will judge on taste, I can promise you that."

"And your cookies didn't exactly go over well at the swap." She could always count on her mother to keep her humble.

"This will be different." They had to win. She would pull all-nighters for the entire week if she had to. She would make fifty batches until they had the perfect cookie. No matter what, she would not let her boys down. They were counting on her. "All right. I've got to get back to work." Melody shooed her aunt, sister, and mom out of the break room, but she stopped the second she caught sight of Jonathan wandering through the juniors section.

"I have to run and pick up Gen." Kels's eyes were wide. "I'm assuming you can handle the customer?" She nodded toward the principal.

"Yeah. Sure." Melody had completely forgotten he'd already requested her help. "I'll take care of him." What? "It." She cleared her throat. "I'll take care of it."

Smiling, her sister rushed out of the boutique.

"Are you shopping?" Leave it to her mother to embarrass someone who already looked like a deer caught in the headlights.

"Kind of?" Mr. Braxton rubbed his forehead. "I need something for my daughter. For Christmas." He turned to Melody, looking slightly puppylike and vulnerable. "I kind of don't have any ideas. I thought maybe you could help me pick something out."

Was he being serious? Or maybe he was playing her so he could spy like Finn had suspected?

Everyone seemed to be waiting for her response—her mother and Aunt Bernice especially, on wide-eyed pins and needles.

"I'd be happy to help." He couldn't fake that deer-in-the-headlights vibe, could he? Maybe. She'd have to proceed with caution. Preferably without an audience. Melody directed a glance at her mother over her shoulder. "Weren't you two on your way out?"

"Nope." She held her ground by the counter.

"We have nowhere to be." Aunt Bernice at least wandered into the women's section. "I needed to do some Christmas shopping myself."

Uh-huh. She'd already bought half the merchandise here.

"Wonderful idea." Her mom scooted in that direction as well. "I can help you pick some things out."

At least they would pretend to be distracted. "So you need a Christmas present for your daughter?"

Mr. Braxton seemed to hesitate, glancing from her mom to her aunt. "I can come back if this is a bad time."

"Oh no. Now is fine." Having other people around was better than being alone with him. After the cookie swap she didn't know how to act. They'd gone from disagreeing to working together to almost flirting. They weren't friends, exactly. But he wasn't just the boys' principal anymore either.

Whew. Someone must have turned up the thermostat in here. Melody resisted the urge to fan her face. "We don't have any other customers yet, so I'm all yours." Nope. That didn't come out right. "I mean, I'm not *yours.*" Dear God, bail her out of this conversation now. Melody shed her cardigan and tossed it onto a nearby chair. "I just meant, um . . . so what kinds of things does Ainsley like?"

"She seems different every time I see her, you know?" He peered around at the dresses and sweaters and racks of pants surrounding them like he didn't know where to start. "She's fifteen and she's really into clothes. Usually I give her a gift card, but I figured since you know so much, maybe I can actually get her something decent this year. It's more fun to wrap up presents so she can open something." He still looked unsure.

"I totally agree." Melody was already going over ensembles in her head. This she could do. "Do you know what size she wears?"

"Her mom sent me her measurements." He held out his phone so she could read the screen.

Melody did the calculations in her head. "It looks like she'd be between a four and six." She flipped through a few hangers. There were so many good options. "Does she like to dress up? Or is she into more comfortable, casual clothes?"

"She likes to dress up." He started tapping on his phone again. "And she can take hours getting ready to go out for dinner. Here are some pictures from when I saw her last month." He held out his phone while he scrolled through a few candid shots of him with Ainsley.

"She's beautiful." And the girl had one of the biggest, brightest smiles she'd ever seen. Melody could see her father in her dark eyes, and she had that same small dimple in her right cheek when she smiled. Without meaning to, she also studied him in the pictures. In one of them they were both laughing. He looked so happy.

Melody noticed that her mother and Aunt Bernice had worked their way to the juniors section too. "You and Ainsley seem close." She moved to another rack near the wall, as far away from their prying ears as she could get.

"We are." Jonathan didn't elaborate, instead scrolling through the pictures again himself. "She's growing up," he finally said. "I can't believe she'll be driving herself around in six months."

"That's terrifying." She couldn't imagine. Watching her boys give up on Santa Claus had been traumatic enough. She had no idea what would happen to her when they drove away and left her at home.

"I know she'll be a good driver." Jonathan pocketed his phone. "But I still can't quite get my head around it. She's growing up too fast."

"I know the feeling." Melody spotted her boys, who were now refolding the jeans. When she caught sight of her mom watching her and Jonathan while she elbowed Bernice, Melody killed the small talk and got back to business. "We just created this new line." She pulled a black embroidered sweater off the rack and held it up for him to see. She was especially proud of the brightly colored flowers along the hemline. "It's been selling really well for us with the teens." And from the pictures she'd seen, she already knew it would fit his daughter perfectly.

"That looks like something she'd like." Jonathan took the hanger from her and inspected the garment. "She's a lot different than me. She's outgoing and fun and . . . vibrant."

"You're . . ." She absolutely couldn't call him vibrant. "*Fun* too." Probably. Just not at school. She'd seen some promising glimpses past his dryness at the cookie swap, though. He had a playful side. He just didn't show it very often.

Anyway.

She needed to stay focused on clothing here. "If you want to get her a whole outfit, we can pair the sweater with these pants." She rummaged through a rack until she found a four in the bright red wide-leg pants she'd just unpacked last week and held them up next to the sweater.

Jonathan stared at them, his eyes wide. "Those are . . . colorful."

"She'll love them," Melody assured him. Yes, they were loud but they made such a statement. "Oh!" She veered into the women's section. "And this will bring the whole outfit together." She selected the plaid pashmina with fringed edges. "I think this will be perfect for her." She took everything she had bundled in her arms and laid it all out on the table outside the fitting room.

Jonathan took his time looking the ensemble over, a thoughtful crease running through his forehead. "It looks nice together. I think she'll like it." He sounded surprised. "Did you design all of this yourself?"

"I did." She gathered up the clothes under her arm and led him to the checkout counter before he could change his mind. This might very well be the best gift a father had ever gotten for his teen daughter. She almost wished she could be there to see Ainsley open it on Christmas morning.

"How do you get your design ideas?" He dug out his wallet and removed his credit card.

"They just come to me." She carefully selected their branded tissue paper and wrapped the sweater first. "I'll see colors or textures or art and just get these images in my head." In fact, she could see about ten different ensembles that would work much better for him than the sweater vests and sensible button-downs. "Would you like a sneak peek at what you'll be wearing when you lose the Cookie Contest?" she asked sweetly.

"I'm relatively confident that won't be necessary." Jonathan turned his credit card between his fingers, eyeing her. "You've been working on your cookie, I take it?"

"Somewhat." She could feign confidence as well as anyone. "But I can't share any details, I'm afraid. The boys have sworn me to secrecy." She wrapped up Ainsley's fun new pants. "What about you? What're you making for the contest?"

Jonathan leaned an elbow into the counter. "I'm doing a gingersnap this year," he murmured after a sideways glance.

"A *gingersnap*?" A laugh snuck past her better judgment. Maybe she didn't have to worry so much after all.

Jonathan straightened and glared. "What's wrong with a gingersnap?"

"I don't know." Melody quickly wrapped up the scarf and then added up his total. "For a contest a gingersnap seems a little . . . basic. There's nothing special about them."

"Exactly. But everyone loves a good gingersnap," Jonathan insisted. "Trust me. This cookie I'm making won in three different magazine competitions my grandma submitted to." He straightened his collar. "So maybe there's nothing wrong with the basics. Maybe people even *like* basic because it's familiar."

"Or maybe people will want to try something new this

year." She wasn't in the principal's office now. She could argue with him all she wanted.

"I guess we'll see." He craned his neck to look at his total before he handed over his credit card.

"I guess everyone will see." Melody couldn't help herself. "Now that we're doing a live competition." She was fully aware that her tone bordered on sardonic but she didn't care.

Mr. Braxton studied her in his methodical way. "You didn't want to do the live competition?"

Was he really surprised? "It'll just be way more stressful baking in front of everyone like that." She scanned his credit card and handed it back to him.

"Why didn't you say something?" He'd frozen, and clear regret outlined his mouth. "I thought it would be fun—that people would enjoy watching. I didn't mean to force you into it."

"You didn't force me into anything." She'd agreed, after all. "Never mind. It'll be fine." She placed the wrapped garments in one of her signature red bags and handed it to him. "We'll still beat you."

"Good luck with that." Something sparked in his eyes. "Thanks for the help." He slipped his coat back on and peeked in the bag. "I never would've picked out something like this for her. But I think she'll love it."

"I hope so." She knew so, but that sounded arrogant. Melody walked him to the door.

Mr. Braxton hesitated before stepping outside. "I guess I'll see you at the contest."

"We'll be there."

All they had to do was beat a gingersnap cookie.

How hard could that be?

Six

OREOS? WHERE DID THE OREOS COME FROM?

Melody plucked the package of double-stuffed cookies out of the cart and set it on a nearby shelf. This was what happened whenever she brought Finn and Tate with her to the grocery store. If she left the cart unattended even for fifteen seconds while she evaluated the price differential between the generic flour and the unrefined, unbleached, organic variety, all of a sudden she had a cart full of Oreos.

Melody set a ten-pound bag of flour in the cart. There'd sure as heck better be some magic dust mixed into it for that price. Hopefully ten pounds would be enough to cover all the test batches they'd have to make of what she'd come to refer to as the Great Miracle Cookie.

"Hey, Mom!" Her boys galloped into the aisle, both with armloads of stuff she had no intention of buying. "Look at this!" Finn slam-dunked a box of some sugary *Star Wars*–themed cereal with marshmallows into the cart.

Melody fished it out and handed it back to him. "We're only here for the cookie ingredients. Remember?"

"Yeah but this is *limited edition* cereal." He held up the box and presented it like he was a model on *The Price Is Right*, pointing out each feature. "It's made with whole grains. There are *no* artificial flavors. And it might not be here next time we go shopping," he warned.

"I'm willing to take our chances." She ruffled his hair. "We can talk about getting a box during our next grocery run if you want to pay for it."

"What about these?" Tate slipped past her and added a box of protein shakes to the cart. "These help you get ripped."

She folded her lips so a laugh wouldn't sneak out. "I'm afraid they're not on the list for today, but, like I told your brother, you're more than welcome to bring your allowance money next time we go grocery shopping." Using their own money tended to make them think twice about whether a purchase was truly necessary. They had a much easier time spending her money.

"Okay, but, Mom . . ." Finn set the cereal box on the wrong shelf and showed her the bag of candies he had tucked under his arm. "We need these to help us think while we make the cookies." He held the caramels out to her. "I mean, look—*sea salt* caramel. I bet they'll be very inspirational."

Well, she'd give the kid points for using one of his vocabulary words for the week. She should make him spell *inspirational* while they were at it. "Sorry, bub." She kept her smile as sweet as the candy. "I think we have all the inspiration we'll need." She gestured to the full cart. Between a million of the best—and most expensive—organic, top-of-the-line ingredients and the twenty-eight online videos she'd watched all about making eggnog and crème brûlée cookies, she couldn't handle any more inspiration. "Now go put all of that back. We still need to get the eggs—"

"Melody Monroe?"

The voice behind her triggered a fight-or-flight response, but there was no way she'd make it down the aisle fast enough to get away from Charlene. So she steeled herself, turned, and invoked the *sorry I'm in a hurry* smile she reserved for . . . well . . . mainly Charlene. "Hey there, stranger." Melody started to ease the cart past her. She didn't have much to say to the woman after the cookie swap. "I'd love to chat, but—"

"How did the cookie swap end up?" She angled her cart to block the aisle. As usual, she had on a sensible navy pantsuit with a cream blouse, and her black hair was smoothed back into a bun.

In contrast, Melody wore tie-dyed leggings and an off-the-shoulder bright pink sweatshirt. "It was good." She shifted her cart to the left but couldn't quite squeeze past. Now was not a good time for her to get trapped in a confrontation. Especially with the boys still standing there. "Sorry, but we have to run—"

"I guess it was a good thing I had a rehearsal in the gym, or you all would've totally missed your fundraising goal." Charlene wore the smile she seemed to reserve for Melody too—complete with a condescending wrinkle in her nose. "It sounds like attendance was way down this year."

"All that matters is saving the STEM club, since that's the first extracurricular that would get cut." She kept her voice chipper for the boys' sake. They didn't like Blake or his mother, but she had to set the example here. "I just want to pitch in and do whatever's best for the school." You'd think they'd be on the same side, since Blake also participated in STEM.

"Right. Sure." Charlene eyed her cart like she was cataloging every ingredient there. "It looks like you're getting ready to do some baking. For the contest?" The nose wrinkle deepened into a crevasse. "Good luck. I'm sure you remember that I've won second place against Jonathan every year."

"Mr. Braxton's not gonna win the contest this year," Finn said with all the conviction his ten-year-old body could hold. "Nobody's gonna believe the cookie we're making."

"There's no way we won't win," Tate added.

"How about you two go put back that cereal and stuff?" Melody shooed her boys in the opposite direction before they could tell Charlene about the bet they'd made. She didn't need yet another opinion on the matter.

"Honestly, I'm surprised the contest is even happening." Charlene exaggerated concern. "From what I hear, you don't exactly have the numbers on the committee to pull off some of those large events. I hope you don't end up having to cancel."

"Oh, we won't have to cancel. We're doing a live competition this year. The contestants will be baking right up in front of everyone." For the first time, Melody saw the brilliance of Mr. Braxton's plan. People would be too curious to miss it. "The committee is looking to update everything. You know, to make the same old boring events a little more exciting? And there's already a lot of excitement about the new format." At least on their social media event. They had sixty-seven people interested.

"So *you're* going to bake up in front of a crowd?" Charlene chuckled. "That'll be something to see. I may have to clear my schedule."

She refused to let Charlene make her feel small. "You really should come by. The committee has so much momentum right now. It's a whole new era. We're letting a lot of different kinds of people participate," Melody said breezily. "Not just the bakers." Or the Type A personalities. "I honestly think this will be the best fundraising season the school has ever had."

"We'll see," Charlene said. "Good luck at the contest. I

hope that goes better for you than the cookie swap did." Her gaze swept over Melody's cart again. "It would be a shame to waste all those quality ingredients."

Before Melody could think of a comeback, Charlene sashayed away.

"Merry Christmas," she muttered, gripping the cart so she didn't give her the bird.

Finn and Tate met her at the end of the aisle.

"Hey, Mom." Her younger twin stepped onto the back of the cart. "I can't wait to see the look on Charlene's face when we win the contest."

"I'll take a video, and we'll show everyone." Tate took over pushing for her.

She let herself picture that shining moment. She and the boys standing on the stage in the school gymnasium holding up the trophy while everyone cheered. Even Mr. Braxton would cheer. And then he'd have to admit that he'd completely underestimated her. But they had a long way to go before they'd get there. "We can't focus on Charlene." Melody directed them to the dairy section. "We need to focus on making the absolute best cookie we can make and then we'll be happy, no matter what happens." Even if they lost. They couldn't really win the Cookie Contest, could they? "If we try our hardest, we can be proud of ourselves no matter what."

While the boys reassured her yet again that they weren't going to lose, she selected two dozen cage-free eggs.

Tate steered the cart while Finn rode on the back all the way up to the checkout lines.

People packed every station. It was going to take a half hour to get out of here. Melody's heart sank. "Is there a snowstorm tomorrow?"

"Maybe everyone's getting their ingredients for the Cookie Contest," Finn suggested, rifling through a nearby candy display.

"I doubt that."

They inched forward little by little and Melody caught sight of a *Better Homes & Gardens* on the rack. "Five Quick and Easy Christmas Desserts" read a headline. Lies! All lies. Instead, she picked up a *People* and started to flip through.

"Hey, there's Mr. Braxton." Before Melody could stop him, Tate stood up on his tiptoes and waved his arms. "Mr. Braxton! Hi!"

She went to shush him, but it was too late. The principal strode to their line, toting his shopping basket that contained only eggs, bread, and milk.

Melody slammed the magazine back onto the rack. She really needed to start shopping at the market in Evergreen so she didn't keep running into people.

"Is it supposed to snow tomorrow or what?" Jonathan asked as he got in line behind them.

"That's what Mom said." Finn cocked an eyebrow. "Are you spying on us?"

"I bet you are," Tate said before Jonathan could get a word in. "I bet you're here to see what ingredients we're getting for our cookie."

"Actually, I ran out of bread and milk, but now that I'm here . . ." He leaned over to peer into their cart. "Hmm . . . egg-nog. Interesting . . ."

Finn and Tate moved to block his view. "Our cookie is a secret," her younger twin told him.

"Top secret," Tate echoed.

Yes, the Great Miracle Cookie was a mystery, even to her.

"I respect that." Smiling, Jonathan took a step back. "You're smart to get an early start. I baked my test batch yesterday."

"I'll bet they were gross." Finn had assumed his argumentative stance—hands on hips, shoulders tensed.

"Finn!" Ugh. She never should've made that bet. "You apologize—"

Jonathan waved off the comment. "It's okay. I can assure you . . . my cookies are *not* gross." Amusement lit his eyes.

Huh. She'd never noticed that twinkle there before.

"Maybe you'd like to try one of mine?" Jonathan offered. "I could bring some by later tonight so you can get a taste of the competition?"

Finn and Tate looked at each other, completely baffled by the offer. But Melody wasn't confused. She knew exactly what Jonathan was up to. He was so confident he had the winning cookie that he wanted to psych them all out before the competition. Once she tasted his cookie, she'd want to give up altogether.

"No thanks—" she said at the same time Tate said, "Yeah, that's a good idea."

"Please, Mom," Finn begged. "Then we'll know what we're up against."

She didn't want to know what they were up against. And she definitely didn't want Jonathan anywhere near her first attempt at the Great Miracle Cookie.

"It's no trouble." Jonathan could not be as innocent as his expression claimed. He had a strategy here—some endgame. "I have two dozen of those cookies, and I'm not going to eat them all myself. So you'd be doing me a favor. Good cookies shouldn't go to waste."

"That's true." Finn had his father's same imploring gaze—

THE CHRISTMAS COOKIE WARS 🍪 87

the one that had gotten her to say yes to heliskiing and para-gliding and trying mayonnaise.

"Sure. Fine." She battled the sudden tension in her neck with a shrug. "If you want to drop off your leftovers, I won't stop you." She also wouldn't eat one. She wouldn't let Jonathan Braxton get into her head right now.

"Yes!" Tate high-fived his brother while she turned and started to load her items onto the conveyor belt.

"Hey, Ms. Monroe." Jeff, the teen cashier who lived down the street from them, greeted her with a big toothy grin. He'd always reminded her of a golden retriever.

"Hi, Jeff. How are you?" She pushed her cart to the end of the station and made it a point not to peek at the principal once. "All ready for Christmas?"

"My mom's getting all the decorations up, but I haven't been around much to help her." He scanned the sugar and flour.

She already knew how that went. Finn and Tate's social calendars had gotten far busier than hers already. She couldn't imagine what life would be like when they were sixteen.

"Oh, hey, Mr. Braxton." Jeff must've just noticed him standing behind them. "My mom brought home a bunch of your cookies from the swap. They were the *best*."

"Good to hear."

Melody didn't look at him in case he was gloating. His tone sure *sounded* gloating. She didn't have to peek at him over her shoulder to see his self-satisfied smirk.

"My whole family is already talking about the contest." Jeff finished bagging her groceries, thank goodness.

"Should be fun." She didn't want to talk about the contest at all. Melody quickly paid, but not before Finn said, "We're going to win this year."

Jeff frowned at her son. "You're entering the contest?"

"We are," Tate confirmed. "And we're going to have the most epic cookie you've ever tasted."

"Wow." The kid's grin more closely resembled a grimace. "Good luck."

If she heard that one more time . . .

"Thanks, Jeff." Melody stashed the bags in her cart. "Come on, boys. We'd better get going." They had a Great Miracle Cookie to make.

"Don't forget to leave the butter and eggs out until they're room temperature," Mr. Braxton called behind her.

"She knows that." Tate patted her shoulder. "Don't you, Mom?"

"I do know that." But only because he'd already told her.

Seven

LEAVING THE EGGS AND BUTTER OUT UNTIL THEY WERE room temperature did not make one iota of a difference.

Melody inspected the snickerdoodle dough, which, according to the recipes, should've been smooth and thick but had turned into a dry crumbling sandcastle in her bowl.

Maybe Jonathan had sabotaged them.

"Something's not right." She leaned into the counter and went over her full page of recipe notes again.

Next to her, Finn reached into the bowl and grabbed a chunk of dough, popping it into his mouth. "Tastes good to me."

Good was not enough. Melody walked back through each step in the plan she'd built from about ten different recipes. She'd measured everything meticulously. She'd even weighed the eggs!

"We're supposed to roll up the dough into balls." Tate took a handful and started to roll it between his hands, but the crumbles cascaded to the floor. "Oh." He frowned. "Yeah. Something's definitely not right."

"I know." Melody wiped perspiration off her forehead with the back of her hand. It was nearly eight o'clock and they hadn't even gotten one batch into the oven yet. The sense of panic she'd kept at bay by humming Christmas carols and teasing the boys swelled. "It needs something else." But what?

"More sugar?" Finn's voice had increased about five decibels because of the sugar he'd already consumed.

"Or what about more eggnog?" Tate held up the container.

"Maybe?" The dough seemed too dry, so adding liquid might help. "We'll start with a few tablespoons."

"On it." Tate found the measuring spoon and added the eggnog while she stirred. "That's helping, I think. Maybe." She didn't know. "Let's add a few more."

Tate tipped the carton but ended up spilling nearly a full cup into the batter. "Uh-oh." He offered her a repentant frown. "Sorry, Mom."

"That's fine. No biggie." Melody set down the spoon. Tate always took himself too seriously, and he happened to be much harder on himself than she ever was when it came to making mistakes. "Don't worry, honey, we'll add more flour." She dumped in three fourths of a cup and stirred, but the liquid still sloshed around the bowl.

"I ruined it." Tate's lips quivered. "Now we're gonna lose. All because of me."

Whoa. She hadn't seen Tate this close to tears since he'd accidentally broken his favorite *Star Wars* model a few months ago. "We're not going to lose." But it wasn't like they could win either. *Ugghh.* Why had she done this to them? If he was this upset now, wait until they lost the contest.

"Forget it. I quit," Tate muttered, turning to walk out of the kitchen.

"Wait." She couldn't let him walk out. "Nothing's ruined." Baking together was supposed to be fun, and now she had about ten seconds to save this night from becoming a bad memory. After a quick scan of the kitchen, Melody grabbed a handful of flour and smeared it across Tate's face right as he turned back to her. "Ha ha! Got you!"

His mouth gaped open but then he grinned—his real, caught-off-guard grin that so rarely appeared these days. "Oh yeah?" Her son scooped out a handful of flour and threw it at her.

The powder covered her face. "Hey!" She wiped her eyes with a dish towel.

"I'm gonna get both of you!" Finn stole the bag of flour and poofed them on his way to the other side of the table.

"Come back here!" Melody lunged in one direction while Tate lunged in the other, but Finn slipped between them, giggling the way he used to when Thomas would throw him up in the air.

"Oh no you don't!" She followed her younger twin past the sink and captured him in her arms. The bag of flour flew over their heads.

"I've got it!" Tate caught the bag, engulfing all of them in a powdery spray.

The boys' eyeballs grew wide, standing out against the white covering their faces.

"Look at you two." She laughed so hard her ribs ached.

"*Us?*" Tate could hardly get the words out past his own guffaws. "You should see *your* face!"

"It's about to get worse too!" Finn sent another poof of flour in her direction, and so she was now covered in the stuff, looking like the abominable snowman.

"You'd better run!" Her sons squealed while she chased them around the table.

Tate stealthily jumped over a chair and both boys collapsed onto the floor, the flour falling like snow between them. They were laughing so hard they couldn't even breathe.

This. This was why she'd taken over the cookie committee—so she could spend time with these two, laughing and playing and making memories together the way they always had this time of year. This was why they were doing the contest together. Not so they could win. Not so they could beat Mr. Braxton.

So they could be together.

Joy radiated straight from her heart, filling her up with a warmth that had been too elusive with all of the stressing and worrying. She wanted to press the pause button, to savor this—

The doorbell rang.

Melody froze. Oh no. No, no, no. She'd completely forgotten about Jonathan's promise to deliver his contest cookies.

"That must be Mr. Braxton!" Finn scrambled to get up, and just the sight of him all powdery made Melody start to giggle again. She grabbed her phone and snapped a picture to document this moment. Of course their principal would show up *now*. When they'd made a huge mess of their kitchen and themselves. They didn't even have any cookies to show for the chaos. Though, at this point, who even cared? He likely couldn't think much less of her than he already did.

"I'll get it!" Finn bolted out of the room before she could even shake the flour out of her hair.

"What a mess." Tate swiveled his head, glancing around them like he couldn't believe what he saw.

Melody could only giggle again as she did her best to swipe the flour off her face with a towel. She wasn't even sorry. She hadn't laughed this much in too long.

"Wow."

She heard the principal before she saw him. There was no hiding now. She tossed the dish towel onto the counter.

"Everything okay in here?" he asked, openly staring at the flour on the floor.

"Everything's great." Finn sounded jovial. "We had a flour fight, and you can't even give us detention or anything because we're not at school." There was a pause while her son's gaze shifted nervously. "Right?"

"Nope. No detention. I don't have any jurisdiction here." Mr. Braxton was still looking around at the mess with wide eyes. He probably didn't like messes, but she was used to them with two boys in the house. In fact, maybe Mr. Braxton needed more mess in his life.

"We were having a little fun." Not that she needed to explain herself to him. "Baking *should* be fun, right?"

"It always was for me with my grandma." His polished black loafers cut a trail through the flour. "In fact, back in the day, we got in a few flour fights ourselves."

Huh. She had a hard time picturing him covered in flour. Or laughing hysterically. Or making a mess.

"Did you bring the cookies?" Tate had become hyperfocused on the plate in his principal's hands.

"I did." Jonathan held out the goods. "They're *just* gingersnaps." He shot Melody a pointed look. "So I don't expect you to be wowed or anything."

Finn took off the plastic wrap. "They *look* pretty good."

Melody caught a glimpse. Okay, she was wowed. Those

cookies didn't look good, they looked fabulous. They were poofy and half dipped in what looked like white chocolate. "They turned out better than ours so far," she admitted. She might as well start preparing the boys for certain defeat. They couldn't even get their cookies in the oven, and Jonathan's appeared to be perfectly decadent.

"What happened to your cookies?" The principal directed his attention to the counter, where she'd abandoned the bowl.

"Nothing." Tate put himself between Jonathan and their cookie dough, his mouth full of another gingersnap.

"It's okay." Finn nudged his brother out of the way. "Mr. Braxton's cookies are *so* good. Maybe he can help us."

They might be beyond help. Melody scanned her kitchen. A teetering mountain of dirty dishes sat in the sink while ingredients and spills littered the counters. Everything seemed to be coated in flour too. Maybe they should raise the white flag on this whole endeavor. "The dough came out too crumbly. I don't understand it. I followed the recipes exactly, but we must have done something wrong."

"I can take a look." Jonathan peered into the mixing bowl. "Hmmm. You do know the flour is supposed to go *into* the mixture, right?" The wry grin he shot her over his shoulder could only be described as teasing.

Hold the phone! Mr. Braxton was teasing her? She couldn't miss this opportunity to get him back. "Oh. That's where we went wrong, then." Cue the eye roll.

"It's all my fault. I accidentally dumped in too much eggnog." Tate helped himself to another one of Jonathan's gingersnaps. His third? Fourth? Melody didn't know. She was dying to try one too, but pride held her back.

"It was my fault to begin with." She joined Jonathan at the

bowl. "The batter was too dry and got all crumbly. So we decided to add more liquid, but things got a little out of hand." Now here they were. Embarrassing themselves in front of this man once again. This time in their own home.

"I think we can salvage this." He rolled up his shirtsleeves.

For a second she was transfixed by the sight of his forearms. She'd never seen Mr. Braxton's forearms, what with all the button-up shirts he wore. But they were nice forearms. Muscular and toned.

"Why would you help us?" Finn screwed up his mouth all tight and skeptical. "We're your competition."

Ha! Jonathan knew they weren't his competition. Especially after tonight. Though she didn't want to tell the boys that.

"What can I say? I like a challenge." He found a measuring cup in the sink and started to wash it. "The better my competition is, the more satisfying my victory will be."

Who was this man and what had he done to Mr. Braxton? Melody threw a towel at him. "Don't egg them on."

The words came too late. Tate had already grabbed the flour bag. "I think you mean *our* victory!" Her son threw a handful at his principal, leaving a white circle blotching his navy blue sweater vest.

A gasp sucked all the air out of Melody's lungs. "Tate!"

But the man only laughed. He laughed! Loud and deep. "You'd better watch yourself, kiddo. I don't get mad. I get even." He scooped out some flour and lightly sprinkled it over Tate's head and then Finn's, which they thought was hilarious.

Melody had to blink a few times. Was Jonathan Braxton really standing in her kitchen having a flour fight with her children? A trail of warmth snaked through her, starting low in her abdomen and then traveling up to encircle her heart.

Warmth? Whoa. Where had that come from? She couldn't feel any warmth when it came to *Mr. Braxton* . . .

"What'd you say, boys?" The principal floured his hands and then put two handprints on his vest, making the boys fall all over themselves with laughter again. "You want some help?"

"Yes!" Finn and Tate cheered.

Melody watched from the sidelines while her boys gathered around the man who'd been their nemesis only minutes ago.

Was this even appropriate? What if someone saw his car there? Or what if her mother decided to make one of her impromptu visits? Oh God, the news would spread faster than word about a two-for-one sale on Christmas hams at the market. "You don't have to help us, Mr. Braxton." Melody rushed back to the bowl of doomed cookie dough. "We'll add a little more flour and everything'll be fine."

Then he could leave before someone got the wrong impression about him making a house call at eight thirty at night.

"I don't mind at all, Melody." He took the bowl out of her hands. "And you should call me Jonathan when we're not at school."

The warmth exploded into sparks now, crackling dangerously close to her heart. It was her! *She* was starting to get the wrong impression.

"Now, you can't only add more flour to the dough because the ratio of the flour and baking powder has to be perfect."

"That makes sense." Tate practically pushed her out of the way and joined his principal at the counter. "We learned all about ratios in math."

"Exactly." Jonathan—Mr. Braxton?—measured out a cup of flour. "Finn, you can dump this into the bowl."

Her younger twin was all too happy to comply, moving so quickly he spilled a little more onto Jonathan's fancy shoes. "There we go."

"Good. Now, Tate, you can add in a teaspoon of baking powder." Jonathan picked up the wooden spoon and started to stir the sloppy cookie dough while her older twin meticulously measured out the ingredient. "Perfect." The principal worked the dough with the spoon, and now his forearms were truly a sight to behold.

"Are you okay, Mom?" Finn asked. "Your face is red."

"I'm fine." She coughed. "It's warm in here with the oven on." And with this man in her space. How long had it been since she'd had a man in her space? Not since Thomas . . .

"See?" Jonathan held out the bowl in her direction. "The dough is coming together nicely now."

"Mmm-hmm." Likely because of that vigorous stirring. "Wonderful. Thank you so much for your help." She went to take the bowl away, but he whirled back to the counter, one of her sons on each side of him. "It looks like we need to add an egg too. The cookies will hold together better."

He could tell that by looking at the dough? "I'll get one." Melody stuck her head into the refrigerator and pretended to rifle around so the chill could take the color out of her cheeks. She shouldn't even have any color in her cheeks! Hello! This was Finn and Tate's principal. No matter that he was standing in her kitchen helping them make cookies. No matter that he was being so kind and sweet with her boys. No matter that his forearms could win an award.

This can't be happening. Not now. Not with *him.*

She was feeling things. Her body was starting to *do* things it hadn't done in years.

"The eggs are right there, Mom." Finn pointed to the shelf in front of her face.

"Of course." She took one and stood upright. "I don't know how I missed them." Likely because she'd found herself in a whole different dimension and now she wasn't sure how to function.

"Why don't you crack the egg into the bowl?" She held it out to Finn.

He backed away from her. "Heck no! Last time I tried to crack an egg, all the shells fell in too."

That was true. The eggshells had given their pancakes quite the crunchy texture.

"Here you go." Jonathan approached and held the bowl against him in one arm while he stirred with the other hand. "Crack away."

"Right." His close proximity set her nerves ablaze. Were her fingers tingling? She tapped the egg on the edge of the bowl and separated the shell, somehow getting all the liquid in the right place.

"See?" Jonathan gave the dough another good stir and tipped the bowl toward her. "Now you'll be able to roll out these cookies no problem."

"Thanks." Hopefully he didn't detect the squeak in her voice. Melody quickly turned around and threw the eggshell in the garbage. Things were getting out of hand. Her pulse had escalated and she was too warm and her knees were threatening to buckle. All very bad signs.

"Wow," Tate mused. "How do you know so much about baking?"

"I used to bake with my grandma." Jonathan set down the bowl and washed his hands, drying them on the towel next to her.

He smelled as delicious as her kitchen right now. What, did the man bathe in cinnamon and cloves every morning?

"Grandma taught me everything she'd learned from her grandma." He sprinkled some flour onto the countertop and then dumped the dough on it, kneading with his hands. "My parents weren't around much so I spent a lot of time with her."

As much as she tried to distract herself with tidying up, Jonathan held her attention.

Her younger twin gazed up at his principal in awe, as though seeing him in a whole new light.

Melody could relate. Everything he revealed clicked a piece of the Mr. Braxton puzzle into place. Maybe he liked order and control so much because he hadn't had any as a child . . .

"Where were your parents?"

"Finn, that's really none of our business." She glanced at Jonathan and their eyes found an instant connection. "You don't have to answer that." *Please don't answer that.* While her brain fought the sudden attraction, her heart had started to unfurl, one fragile petal at a time. She couldn't let it open all the way. Not for anyone.

"It's fine. I don't mind sharing." Jonathan continued to work the dough, rolling sections between his hands to form the cookies. "They were both very focused on their careers in academia. They didn't have much time to take care of a kid." He took another large section of perfect dough and handed it to Tate. "But I loved being with my grandma. I mean, imagine getting cookies like that all the time." He pointed to the gingersnaps.

"That'd be so awesome!" Tate carefully set the dough balls on the cookie sheet. "Not that your cookies aren't good, Mom."

"Right." Her specialty was flour fights.

"Good job on those, Tate." Jonathan nudged Finn to the counter. "Your turn."

"I've done this tons of times," her younger twin told him proudly. "We've made cookies ever since I was a baby, right, Mom?"

"That's right."

"Our dad was good at baking too." Tate said the words matter-of-factly, and Melody was glad. She'd encouraged them to talk about Thomas often so he was a part of their lives, so they could acknowledge their father and also what they'd lost. But hearing him say that now, in the context of Jonathan in her kitchen, made her throat tighten.

"I think I would've liked your dad." Jonathan used a spatula to place the cookies carefully on the baking trays sitting next to the oven.

"He was awesome." Finn snuck a piece of cookie dough into his mouth.

"He must've been to have sons like you." Jonathan held up the oven mitts. "Ready to do the honors, boys?"

"Yep!" Finn took one cookie sheet and slid it into the preheated oven while Tate handled the other.

Melody had become a bystander in her own kitchen, watching Jonathan's beaming smile. She wasn't sure she'd ever seen him smile this way. So . . . unguarded.

Because of the baking. Because he loved baking. Not because he was happy to be here in her kitchen. Not because a trail of warmth snaked through him too. His knees weren't weak. His pulse hadn't picked up. Nope.

"Now we set the timer for eight and a half minutes."

Jonathan pulled out his phone. "And then the taste testing can begin."

The twins cheered and high-fived each other.

Wait. Melody swam through the emotions back to the surface. That couldn't be right. "The recipe said we should bake them for ten minutes." She went to the kitchen table and flipped through her notes.

"Oh no." The principal waggled his finger at her. "Trust me. Eight and a half minutes is exactly what you need for cookies this size. They'll come out perfectly chewy on the inside and the slightest bit crisp on the outside."

"He knows, Mom." Finn poured himself a glass of eggnog and then offered one to Jonathan. "We always have eggnog when we're baking Christmas cookies. It's a tradition."

Yes, *their* tradition.

"I like eggnog." Jonathan pulled out a chair and sat down at the table. At *her* kitchen table, sipping eggnog with her boys, telling them all about his life and laughing with them and making them like him. Making *her* like him. Except, she didn't want to. She didn't want her heart taking sharp drops whenever she saw Jonathan. She didn't want the sparks crackling through her or the longing that crowded her chest.

She didn't want to long for anyone.

"It's getting late." There was no controlling her tone. Emotions were clashing—irritation and longing and a rising panic she didn't fully understand. "Mr. Braxton should probably be getting home."

He froze, the cup of eggnog suspended halfway to his mouth. "Oh. Right." His wise somber eyes met hers and completed a lengthy study before he quickly stood. "Yes, I should be going."

"But we haven't even gotten the cookies out of the oven

yet." Finn hopped out of his chair as though ready to block the door.

"Yeah." Tate stood at his brother's side. "Mr. Braxton helped us, so he should be able to try the cookies too."

"I can't stay," Jonathan said apologetically. "Sorry, boys. I have a lot to do at home." He scooted past Melody but wouldn't look at her now. "I'll see you at school tomorrow, though. And I expect a full report on the cookies."

"Yes, sir." Finn was hanging his head.

"Thanks for the eggnog," Jonathan called over his shoulder.

The front door opened for a few seconds before slamming shut, leaving the room too quiet.

"Wow, it was pretty awesome of Mr. Braxton to help us with our cookies, huh?" Finn downed the rest of his eggnog.

"Sure." Melody shrugged off the heartache that had pinned her back to the wall and grabbed a broom so she could clean up the mess they'd made. "But we can do this. The three of us together."

They didn't need to let anyone else in.

Eight

THERE HAD TO BE SOMETHING ELSE SHE COULD DO.

Since arriving at the boutique, Melody had already dusted every nook and cranny of the space, gone through all of the inventory, and helped eight customers find the perfect Christmas gifts, and she'd even resorted to cleaning the toilet to keep herself busy.

Yet she still couldn't shake the memory of kicking Jonathan out of her house. More accurately, she couldn't shake the image of the perceptive dawning in his eyes when he'd realized she didn't want him there. She hadn't been able to face him since. Each day, she'd dropped the boys off at school—fifteen minutes early—in the car pool line so she wouldn't run into him.

But she couldn't avoid him forever. The contest would start in two hours. Melody peeked into the break room, where the boys were playing video games next to their cooler of supplies.

Her stomach squeezed. Instead of being nervous about the contest, she was nervous about seeing Jonathan after their last awkward exchange. Was he upset? Embarrassed? Had he written her off?

Why did she care so much? That was the hardest question to answer.

Melody pulled her phone out of her pocket and studied the screen. She should text him. Break the ice. A good president would check in with the school contact to make sure things were all set for a big event, right?

Before she could overthink it, Melody fired off a text to Jonathan's personal number. *Everything all set for today? Need anything else from me?*

She went to put the phone back into her pocket but it dinged. He'd already replied?

All's well. Don't think so.

Hmmm. If her sister had sent that text, she'd know Kels was mad about something. Every text they exchanged had at least three emojis. But Jonathan wasn't overly effusive, so she shouldn't read into anything. Her fingers hovered over the keyboard. Should she say something else? Like *See you soon?* Or *I'm looking forward to—*

The phone dinged again.

BTW—I'm sorry for barging in on you three the other night. I hope I didn't upset you.

Oh geez. Guilt dislodged her nerves. He probably thought she hated him, when in reality the ache of Thomas's absence had caught her off guard. That happened less frequently these days, but there was still no predicting when it would come. *I'm the one who's sorry. I was tired. What a lousy excuse. Not to* mention a flat-out lie. Grasping at courage, she typed, You did nothing wrong. It was nice of you to help. As much as I love the holidays, this time of year can be really hard for me, that's all.

A pause stretched on, deflating her heart, but then those three promising dots appeared. He was typing.

It can be hard for me too. A rose emoji. A rose emoji! Her pulse kicked up, heat spiraling through her chest. She opened the emoji menu to find something she could send back to him. Definitely not the eggplant she'd sent to her sister last night! Kels had given her a hard time about that one when all Melody was trying to say was that they needed to go out for eggplant parmigiana at their favorite Italian restaurant soon. Of course, her darling sister had taken the conversation to a whole different level. (Insert rolling eyes emoji.)

Her eyes scanned the others she'd used recently. She couldn't send Jonathan the fireball or the horrified face or the heart eyes or the crying emoji she'd sent to her mom when she'd texted pictures of her flour fight with the boys. Hmmmm . . .

How'd the cookies turn out anyway? came in before she could settle on something appropriate.

Perfect. That was an easy answer. Actually really good. Thanks to you. He had rescued them from certain disaster and now she could thank him properly. You definitely saved the day.

Nah. You were close. You would've figured it out on your own.

Ha! Little did he know. Grinning at the phone, Melody leaned into the checkout counter to reply. I can assure you I wouldn't have figured it out. Not without your help. So thank you. I really appreciate . . . No, no, no. She deleted those last three words. As the boys always told her, texts were supposed to be short and simple.

You're welcome. I'm still going to beat you today, though. This time he included the man shrugging emoji.

She laughed out loud. Are you serious right now?

I'm just saying . . . I hope you like working in the cafeteria. Might want to bring some earplugs. It's loud this time of year. Big smiling face emoji.

Oh, this man. He knew exactly how to bait her. They might not have a shot at winning but he wasn't the only one who excelled in the art of trash talking. Whatever! She added a thoughtful emoji. You're going to look GREAT in polka dots.

Jonathan sent back six horrified face emojis in a row. You said nothing too wild.

Melody giggled again. Sheesh. He had her *giggling*. Can't help it. I'm pretty wild. She waited, her eyes fixed on the screen, a breath suspended in her lungs.

One of your best qualities IMO.

Her heart took a sharp dive. In his opinion? Jonathan had *opinions* about her? *Good* opinions? Or maybe she was reading too much into their banter. I thought you didn't like wild.

The seconds ticked by too slowly. Did he think she was fishing for compliments? She wasn't. She simply wondered if he could ever see her as anything other than a harried single mom who was always running late.

Wild has grown on me a lot lately, Jonathan finally typed. You're expanding my horizons. Do you really think I'd look good in polka dots?

Another giggle snuck out. You'd look good in pretty much anything. Her fingers tapped out the words automatically, but she couldn't send that! It might be true but it was too flirty. Too forward. What had come over her?

"Hey, Mom."

Tate snuck up behind her and Melody nearly dropped her phone. "Oh no, whoops." Her hands fumbled with it.

"Whatcha doin'?"

"Um. Uh." She stared at the screen in horror. The message had sent! *You'd look good in pretty much anything.* Not only that . . . somehow she'd added *three eggplant emojis* onto the end of it!

Her lungs churned out panicked breaths. "How do you recall a text?" She snapped up her head to implore Tate. "*Can* you recall a text?"

"Yep. Lemme see your phone." Her son held out his hand, but Melody kept it out of reach.

"No! Just tell me how to do it. Please!" Did Tate even know what an eggplant represented to a certain segment of the population? She'd never even used it except in the context of talking about real food!

"Okay," her son said calmly. "First, you have to make sure the text hasn't been read."

She squinted at the screen. *Read* was displayed loud and clear. "It says 'Read.'" Oh God. Jonathan had read that?

Tate shrugged. "Then it's too late."

"Yeah. Thanks. I got that." Melody couldn't seem to swallow. Her throat was too dry. She continued staring at her phone but there were no dots. No replies. She'd sent three eggplant emojis to Jonathan Braxton and now he had nothing to say to her.

"Are you okay, Mom?" Tate gazed at her with measured concern. "What was that text about anyway?"

"Nothing!" She switched her phone to airplane mode and

shoved it into her back pocket. She couldn't deal with this right now. She'd simply pretend it hadn't happened and she'd never look at her texts again. She'd tell everyone that she no longer believed in texting people and that they needed to call her from now on. She was clearly not qualified to text anyone. Ever.

"Hey, look." Tate pointed to the windows. "There's Nonna and Aunt Kelsey. That means it's almost time to go!" He bounded away, calling for his brother.

Melody slipped behind the register. She wasn't going anywhere. She couldn't. She'd have her mom tell everyone she'd gotten appendicitis or something . . .

"Who's ready to win a Cookie Contest?" her mother called as she made a grand entrance, all decked out in her Christmas finest. Melody swore her mother had owned that tinsel-laden sweater since the early nineties. The sweater, along with her Christmas light bulb necklace, had a certain vintage charm.

"Remember, it's not about winning," Kels said, shooting their mother a look. "It's supposed to be all in good fun."

"Right. But my grandboys are destined to take home the crown today." She frowned at Melody, who hadn't moved yet. "Come on, sweets. We've gotta hit the road now or you won't have time to set up."

"I can't go yet!" The shock of what had just transpired still had her volume up. "I'm having a crisis." She searched the space around her. "It's an . . . inventory problem. You should head over with the boys, and Kels and I will be there as soon as we can."

Kels hurried to the counter. "What kind of inventory problem? I checked the online system this morning and everything was fine."

"Something just came up." She raised her eyebrows sharply to stanch any more questions.

"Fine, fine, fine." Their mother scurried to the back of the space. "Oh, boys!" she sang in a high C. "Pack up! You get to come with Nonna, and your mom will meet us there!"

"Yes! Cookie time!" Finn dragged the cooler out of the break room, followed by Tate, who had the box of bowls and utensils.

"Bye, Mom!" Her older twin stopped to give her a hug.

"Get us a good station." Preferably one far away from Jonathan's. Like on the other side of the gymnasium so she wouldn't have to talk to him . . . or even look at him.

"Don't worry, Mom. We're on it." Finn dragged the cooler out the door.

"Toodles." Her mom waved and ushered Tate out behind him.

"What in the actual hell is wrong with you?" Kels examined her face. "You're all flushed and nervous. Good God. It's only a stupid contest, and you're probably not going to win anyway. So get it together."

If only the contest were all she had to worry about. Melody faced her sister. "If you were a man, what would you think if I texted you three eggplant emojis in a row?"

"I'd think you wanted to get some, of course." Kels laughed. "Is this about the text you sent to me last night? I was kidding around. I knew you were talking about eggplant parmigiana—"

"No. This is about what I accidentally texted to Mr. Braxton." Melody handed over her phone and buried her face in her hands. How could she have let this happen?

Kels's gaze ran over the screen, her eyes growing wider by the second. "Oh my God. You were sexting Jonathan?"

"No!" Melody wailed. "It was a total accident!" She paced, her hand on her forehead to quell the sudden headache. "We were having this nice conversation . . . I was going to delete that part about him looking good in anything because it seemed like too much, but then Tate walked in and I almost dropped the phone. The next thing I know, the message is sent with three eggplant emojis on the end of it!" Humiliation washed over her anew.

Her sister let out a guffaw, her upper body collapsing over the counter. "I'm dying." Kels sucked in a few breaths and then started to convulse with laughter again.

"What am I going to do, Kels?" She shook her sister by the shoulders. "I can't show my face in front of him. Ever again."

After a long, giggly exhale, Kels stood upright again. "Did he did say anything back?"

"I don't know." She tapped the screen unlocked and put her head down on the counter. "I switched to airplane mode so I wouldn't have to see."

"Hmm," Kels murmured, studying the screen. "No reply has come in yet."

"See?" Melody resumed her pacing. "I can't even imagine what he thinks. He might assume I was putting out some kind of booty call or something."

That set her sister off again. This time, tears ran down Kels's cheeks. "Maybe he thinks you want to take him out for eggplant parmigiana."

"This is not funny." Melody sat on the stool to pout.

"I know it's not." Her sister let out another giggle but quickly cleared her throat. "Come on. Let's head over to the school. You can always tell him you're sorry. You meant that text for someone else." She elbowed her. "Then maybe he'd say he was hoping it was for him."

"Not likely." Jonathan didn't exactly seem like an eggplant emoji kind of man. Melody stood and pushed in her stool. Kels was right about one thing. She couldn't keep hiding. She'd have to face him eventually and she might as well get it over with. This dread had to be worse than actually seeing him.

Melody pulled on her coat and grabbed her purse and followed Kels out the door.

"Do you think you actually have a shot at beating him today?" Her sister paused to lock up.

"Not a chance." She led the way to her car, which she'd haphazardly parallel parked along the curb, and they both climbed in. "Those cookies he brought over were like a bite of heaven." She might've eaten them all if the boys hadn't begged her to put some in their lunches. "I had no idea gingersnaps could be so good."

"Looking at Mr. Braxton, you'd never guess he had a hidden talent for baking." Kels turned up the heat.

"There're a lot of things you'd never guess about him." Melody eased the car along the icy roads, going well under the twenty-five-miles-per-hour speed limit. "Like, did you know he has a dimple? Oh, and he's pretty strong. I mean his forearms are all muscly—which you'd never know with all those layers he wears. I'll bet he spends some time at the gym."

A long silence prompted her to glance at her sister, who was staring at her with her mouth agape.

"What?" Melody directed her gaze back to the road, heat flashing across her face. Maybe that last tidbit about Jonathan's arms had been overkill . . .

"Nothing." Amusement played in her sister's tone. "It's just that I've never noticed any of those things about Mr. Braxton.

But maybe he smiles at you differently than he smiles at me." Her grin turned devilish. "And I'm really curious to know how you learned about his forearms."

"He rolled up his sleeves." So Kels could drag her mind out of the gutter right now.

Melody found a parking spot near the back half of the school lot and quickly bailed on the conversation. She should *not* be noticing little details about Jonathan and she definitely should not be sharing those tidbits with her sister. Right now, she had to save face. Play this cool.

She stayed three steps ahead of Kels as they joined the crowd streaming in through the gymnasium doors.

"Wow, it looks great in here," someone nearby said.

The compliment kindled a warm glow. She and her mother and Aunt Bernice had opted to buy new decorations for this event, and they'd gone with a North Pole theme. Each baking station had a cardboard cutout that made it look like a little shop you might find in Santa's village.

"There's Finn and Tate." Kels had caught up to her. "Oh . . . and Jonathan too." She slid a gaze in her direction, but Melody was careful to hold her expression neutral.

"Huh." Why was she not surprised that the boys had chosen the station right next to Jonathan's? While the principal's ingredients appeared to be organized on the table in the order he was planning to use them, Finn and Tate had seemingly not managed to get anything unpacked.

"Look, Mom!" Finn called as she approached. "We got the spot right next to Mr. Braxton!"

"Then we can see his face when we beat him," Tate added, smirking at his principal.

"That's great." She snuck a peek at Jonathan and then did a double take. He wasn't wearing a sweater vest? And no formal button-up shirt either. Instead, he'd dressed in a nice hunter green V-neck sweater. Possibly cashmere.

The boys saw a friend and drifted away to chat.

"Wow, Mr. Braxton. Don't you look nice?" Leave it to Kels to break the ice freezing the air between them. "Changing up the wardrobe for the Cookie Contest, huh?"

"Oh." He looked down at his sweater like he'd forgotten what he was wearing. "Yes. I figured there was no need to dress up when I'd only be wearing an apron anyway."

This from the man who'd dressed up to attend the basket-ball team's tournament?

"What d'you think, Mel?" Kels nudged her. "Nice sweater, huh?"

All of her blood instantaneously rushed to her face. And she'd only just gotten rid of the last blush. "You promised to help Mom, right?" She made sure Jonathan wasn't looking and then tightened her mouth at her sister—the same threat-ening expression she used to use when Kels spied on her when they were teenagers.

"That's right." Kelsey smiled sweetly. "Have fun, everyone! I know I will." She traipsed away with one final glance over her shoulder at Melody.

Avoiding Jonathan's gaze, she skirted behind their table and started to unpack the ingredients in the cooler. All she could think about were those three eggplant emojis lighting up his screen. Heat closed in on her again, and she quickly shed her cardigan.

"Our cookies are gonna be so good!" Finn bounded to Jon-athan's table. "That test batch we made when you came over turned out amazing!"

"I heard." Jonathan's tone hit a playful note, but she still couldn't make herself look at him.

"Yeah, thanks for your help, Mr. Braxton." Tate had wandered over too.

"It was nothing." Jonathan shook the flour dust off his sifter and set it carefully next to his measuring cups. "I owed your mom one."

Melody finally looked at him. Her expression must've registered the confusion clouding her thoughts.

"You helped me shop for Ainsley. So I owed you one." He smiled at her like he normally would've—like he would've last week, before the text conversation gone awry. Maybe the phone was wrong. Maybe he hadn't read it. She couldn't tell. Jonathan was totally preoccupied reordering his spatula and teaspoons and whisks. The man's assortment of baking utensils was every bit as impressive as his forearms.

Melody started to bring order to the supplies that the boys were unloading haphazardly onto the table. That was all the other night had been, then—him repaying a favor. And maybe she'd read into the flirty text thread too? "Good. We're even, then." He hadn't come to see her or to drink eggnog with the boys or to spend time with them at all. He was simply repaying a favor. And she'd gotten carried away and had blown everything out of proportion. "Then I won't feel bad about beating you today." Nothing like a little trash talk to shield herself from the slight disappointment edging in. Either he hadn't seen the last text or he was ignoring it—which would be worse?

Jonathan looked up in surprise, a slow grin taking shape. "You really think you have a shot at winning, huh?"

That dimple. Honestly. Where was Kelsey when she had the proof he had a dimple? "I mean, these cookies are the best I've ever made." Technically true, though the bar was low.

"I can't wait to try one." For the first time he faced her fully and he looked so good, relaxed and casual and broad in that sweater. Her sister had been right. It was a very nice sweater. Especially on Jonathan.

Microphone static buzzed through the speakers.

"Welcome to the twenty-third annual Cookeville Cookie Contest!" Her mom waved from the platform, the light bulb necklace blinking. "This will be the first time we see our bakers go head to head on a live stage. We have quite the competitors here today, which means you all are going to get a taste of some of the best cookies ever made."

Finn and Tate joined the cheering from the crowd.

"Don't forget, we have to focus more on *making* the cookies than *eating* them," Melody admonished.

"Competitors will have four hours to make, bake, and decorate five dozen of their best cookies," her mom went on. "Our volunteers will keep the ovens hot and running in the kitchen, but contestants, you are responsible for getting your cookies in and out."

Oh boy. Here they went. She had to completely tune out any thoughts about Jonathan and focus. Nerves churned in her stomach. Had she remembered everything? Her eyes ran over the supplies strewn across their table. Why did their station look like such a mess?

The microphone crackled again. "At exactly three o'clock the cookies must be ready for tasting at your stations. Ready? Set . . . Go!"

Melody lunged toward the measuring cups at the same time Finn reached for the flour, and they collided in a poof.

"Don't forget," Jonathan said smoothly. "The flour goes *in* the bowl."

Ha. "Real bakers aren't afraid to get dirty in the kitchen." She froze. Wait. That didn't come out the way she'd intended.

"I'm definitely not afraid." Jonathan's lips folded on a sexy little smirk.

Maybe he had seen her text after all!

"Come on, Mom!" Tate measured out the baking soda. "We've gotta get moving. We're already behind."

Right. No flirting with the competition. She settled into a chaotic routine with the twins, bumping into each other while they added ingredients and sifted and stirred. People gathered to watch Jonathan work in his ordered methodical fashion.

"You'd better watch out, Mr. Braxton!" Tate yelled. "We've got some tricks up our sleeve today."

"Yeah." Finn could never be outdone by his brother. "You won't even recognize our cookies when they're all done. They're gonna rock!"

"I bet they will," their principal called. "But they're not gonna rock as much as mine."

"All right, you two. Focus," Melody scolded. Their cookies would bomb if they didn't start paying attention. "Whisk those eggs, Finn. Tate, cream the butter."

"Yes, ma'am," they said in unison.

"Say cheese!" Kels appeared with her phone raised.

The boys both obliged, but Melody ducked. This would not be her finest moment for a picture—her bangs were sticking to her forehead. Hopefully Jonathan was too busy baking to look at her right now. Not that she wanted to look good for him.

"It appears everyone is moving right along," her mom said into the microphone. "So far we have two teams already loading up their cookie sheets."

"What?" They were still stirring. As tough as their dough was right now, they might be stirring for an hour.

"How's it going over there?" Jonathan didn't even sound out of breath.

"Everything's perfect." She wheezed before continuing. "How about you?"

"These might be my best gingersnaps ever. You're not adding too much eggnog, are you?"

She shot him a look and then noticed he'd already placed all of the gingersnaps on his cookie sheets. And he was by himself!

"Let's roll, Mom!" Finn put on gloves and then started to form the dough the same way Jonathan had.

They worked while other contestants passed by, pushing their carts toward the kitchen. Finn rolled balls of dough. Tate dipped them in cinnamon sugar and put them on the cookie sheet.

"You're doing great, boys." Her heart hadn't raced this fast since she'd tried the spin class at the local rec center. This could be a whole new workout craze—cardio baking. "That's it. Keep it going."

"This one's done!" Tate transferred the cookie sheet onto the cart.

"So's this one!" Finn's went next.

Two more to go.

"Need some help?" Jonathan leaned against his table, at leisure.

"No," Melody said at the same time Finn said, "Yes."

"We've got this," she told her sons. "We can win all by ourselves."

They nodded, their expressions determined, hands working fast, and then they loaded the last cookie sheets onto the cart.

"Woo-hoo!" She high-fived them while they rushed the cookies into the kitchen.

"This oven's open." Ms. Sanderson waved them over.

"Hi." Finn's eyes lit up.

"Look at these cookies," the object of his affection gushed. "They look like winners to me."

"Thanks," he said somewhat shyly.

So adorable. Melody leaned against the wall to catch her breath and set the timer on her phone. Some people were already pulling their cookies out of the oven, but they were in good shape. They should still have plenty of time to decorate the way they'd planned.

"How's it going?" Kels snuck up next to her.

"It's going." At least she could breathe normally again.

Her sister leaned closer. "Interesting that Mr. Braxton wore something different today, don't you think?"

"I guess." He must've gotten an early Christmas present or something.

"I've never seen him wear anything but a sweater vest." Kels gave her a meaningful look. "Have you?"

"No." Though she hadn't exactly spent much time with him outside the context of school either.

"But today—when you sent him a particular text he changed up his look—"

"Mr. Braxton, are your cookies done?" Finn called.

Melody snapped her head to the right. How long had Jonathan been standing at the oven next to them?

"They'll be done in thirty seconds."

Was he frowning? Melody didn't want to stare too long, but she did murderously squeeze her sister's hand.

Kels only smiled. "I'd better go help Mom."

Sure, she could escape while Melody had to stand here and wonder if he'd heard everything her sister had been suggesting.

"That's time for me." Jonathan suited up with oven mitts and briskly pulled the cookie sheets out of the oven, lining them up on his cart before disappearing.

"My goodness, this is exciting." Aunt Bernice walked around the kitchen fanning her face with a napkin. "And the smells in here. I can't wait to try all of these delicious cookies." She snagged Melody's elbow and pulled her aside. "Don't worry. I've been campaigning for your cookies the whole time. Now, Jonathan's got the looks, but you've got the story, honey. You should hear the sympathy when I remind people you're a widow."

"Bernice!" She wriggled away from her. "I don't want sympathy votes."

Her aunt scoffed. "Well, that's the only way you're going to win."

"Time!" Tate called.

Thank. God. She slipped away from her aunt and helped the boys load up. "Careful now." They couldn't sprint back to the gym and lose all the cookies in the process. When they reached their station, she found the piping bags in the cooler and got everything ready for decorating. After giving the cookies a while to cool off, they took their time creating the swirls of frosting before Melody used the kitchen torch to caramelize the tops, and then they dusted everything with the gold glitter.

"Wow. Those are stunning," someone said as they passed by.

"Beautiful," another spectator commented.

"Hear that, Mom?" Tate shot her a priceless grin. "We're gonna win."

Her heart clenched. It might be time to start preparing them for defeat. "Even if we don't win, look at what we made together." She started to arrange the cookies on the platter.

"I'm really impressed."

Melody hadn't realized Jonathan was looking over her

shoulder. "You're so talented." His expression was startled. "Uh, er, I mean all three of you. What a great design."

"Why, thank you." Finn wiped his hands on the apron he'd insisted on wearing.

"There are two minutes until three o'clock," her mom announced into the microphone. "Everyone, please make sure your cookies are plated."

The noise level in the room seemed to rise.

"We're done!" Tate raised his hands in the air while Finn cheered.

Melody wanted to collapse onto the floor. But a line formed at their station and she politely greeted everyone who took a cookie, graciously accepting the compliments.

"Wow, Melly." Her sister took a bite of the caramelized frosting. "These are delicious."

"Really?" They'd truly done it? They'd managed to make a cookie people actually wanted to eat?

Kels nodded, looking as surprised as she felt. "Really. Nice job."

She turned to high-five Finn, but he was staring at Jonathan's station with wide, disbelieving eyes.

A woman was spitting—literally spitting—a bite of Jonathan's cookie into a napkin. "These are *awful*." She threw the cookie into the trash can. "Sorry, Mr. Braxton. I can't finish that."

Melody waited to see if this was some kind of joke.

"Are you serious?" Jonathan picked up one of his cookies, examined it, and then took a bite. His expression immediately warped. "Whoa. Salt. They're way too salty." After tossing the cookie into the trash, he took a pinch of the sugar from the container at his station and dropped it into his mouth. "This is salt. Someone replaced my sugar with salt."

"You're sure?" one of the many women lined up at his table asked.

"Who would do that?" another groupie demanded.

Melody shook her head. Someone had sabotaged him? That was a first for the Cookie Contest . . .

"I heard Finn say earlier they had some tricks up their sleeve." That came from Mrs. Altman, the grumpy science teacher who'd busted the boys for setting her ants free.

"What?" her older twin screeched. "No! We didn't cheat! We're gonna win this contest fair and square!"

"All right." Melody rested a hand on his shoulder. "No one's accusing you of anything."

"Who else would it have been?" Mrs. Altman elbowed her way to the table. "All your boys have been talking about for the last week was how they're going to beat Mr. Braxton. They've even made bets with other kids at school."

A headache started to pulse in her temples. That would be her fault. She never should've made a bet with Jonathan.

"Okay, folks . . ." her mom said into the microphone. "I'm getting word that we have a situation. Please bear with us as we work through this." She set down the mic and jumped off the stage with surprising agility for someone who'd recently had a knee replacement.

"What's happening?" she asked Melody.

"We're not sure yet." Jonathan still seemed to be in a state of shock. "Somehow, my sugar was replaced with salt."

"And everyone's blaming us," Finn complained, crossing his arms tightly over his chest.

"Are you sure you didn't accidentally bring salt instead of sugar?"

Melody had to appreciate her mother for trying, but this was Jonathan Braxton they were talking about. Mr. Meticulous.

"I'm pretty sure." He was staring at Melody, as though trying to work out whether her boys truly might've had anything to do with his predicament.

A mama's fury burned in her chest. She quickly led her boys away from the crowds by the hands. "Finn, Tate . . . I need to know. Did either of you even touch any of the ingredients on Mr. Braxton's table?"

"No, Mom. I swear." Tate was on the verge of tears.

"We'd never do that." Finn's fair cheeks blazed. "Mrs. Altman just hates us, that's all. She hates us as much as she hates ants."

"I believe you." Leaving them standing there, Melody marched back to her table, mainly addressing Jonathan. "Finn and Tate had nothing to do with this. I've been standing with them the whole time."

"No, you weren't." The science teacher wore a snide grin. "You got here late. I saw you walk in."

"We didn't do it!" Finn yelled from behind her.

"Like they'd ever admit to sabotaging the principal," Mrs. Altman muttered loudly.

"Okay, that's enough." Jonathan took his entire platter of cookies from the table and dumped them all into the trash. "I'm officially withdrawing from the competition. You all might as well go around and try the other cookies."

A collective groan went up from the crowd.

"That's not fair!"

"You can't withdraw."

"Someone sabotaged him."

Why did they all seem to stare at Melody?

"I'm not sure what to do," her mother said. "This is *unprecedented*."

All Melody wanted to do was take her boys and walk out to make a point, but she was the committee director. She had to take charge. "We'll have a quick cookie committee meeting in the library to figure out what to do—"

"You can't be involved." Mrs. Altman clearly had an agenda here. "You're in the competition."

"She's right, Mel." Her mother squeezed her hand. "Don't worry. I'll get everyone together and we'll discuss." She turned to the mob. "In the meantime, everyone, please walk around and taste all of the cookies currently entered in the contest so you can fill out your ballots."

While the crowd dispersed, her mother started waving for all the committee members in the vicinity—including Jonathan—to follow her out the doors.

Tate was crying now, angrily swiping at the tears rolling down his cheeks. "Everyone thinks we cheated."

"I know, hon." She wouldn't dare fuss over him in public so she simply handed him a napkin to blow his nose, her heart aching. "Everything'll turn out okay. Why don't you two go try some of the other cookies while we wait?"

"I don't even want to." She'd only seen that stony expression on Finn's face a handful of times.

"Then go get some hot chocolate from the coffee cart." She dug some cash out of her pocket. "With extra whipped cream."

That perked them both up. They walked away together, lamenting about Mrs. Altman.

Keeping her head down, Melody started to clean up their station. No one stopped by to try any of their cookies. Not even one person. Finn and Tate were going to be heartbroken.

Finally, the cookie committee members paraded back into

the gym and Melody cornered Jonathan before anyone else noticed. "You know Finn and Tate didn't do this, right?"

The slightest hesitation flickered in his expression. "I don't see how they could've." But that wasn't a straight-up denial. That comment left the door open on the possibility. And she shouldn't be so wounded from it, but these were her children.

"The point is, they *wouldn't* cheat." She imagined her expression was ten times harsher than even Finn's had been. "You know them better than that." He saw them every day. Yes, they occasionally got into mischief, but they weren't liars, and they weren't cheaters.

Regret gripped Jonathan's mouth. That dimple was nowhere to be seen now. "Listen, Melody—"

"Okay, everyone." Her mother had made it back to the stage. "Thank you for your patience. Right now there's no evidence that anyone purposely switched ingredients, so the show will go on. Taste those cookies and cast your ballots within the next ten minutes."

"Everyone vote for Mr. Braxton's cookie," Mrs. Altman called to the crowd.

"But that's not fair!" Tate marched to the table, hot chocolate in hand. It would've been easier to take him seriously if he didn't have a whipped cream mustache. "The best cookie should win, and his wasn't the best cookie!"

"Enough." Jonathan moved to stand in front of Tate. "Everyone move on. Go cast your ballots. There's no need for accusations."

Yes. There was no need to make accusations. And there was no need for her and the boys to be here any longer.

"You okay?" Her sister rushed to give her a hug.

"No." All she'd wanted was to hear Jonathan say he knew Finn and Tate hadn't cheated. She didn't know why that was so important to her, but it was. "Would you mind packing up all of our stuff, Kels? We're leaving." She made sure Mr. Braxton heard.

"You bet." Her sister escorted her and the boys to the doors. "Don't worry, honey. I'll take care of everything."

Nine

THEY HADN'T EVEN GOTTEN ONE VOTE.

"I can't believe this." Melody sat across the kitchen table from her mother, nursing a lukewarm cup of coffee that her mom had brought in a travel mug to soften the blow. Thankfully, the boys were both still asleep and oblivious to the fact that they'd been blacklisted from the contest. If only she were still asleep too. If only all three of them could hibernate for a few weeks and sleep this catastrophe off.

As it was, she'd hardly gotten any rest last night, her emotions alternating between anger on behalf of Finn and Tate and disappointment that Jonathan hadn't stood up for them.

"The whole thing is ridiculous." Her own mother still had some mama bear growl left in her too. "I mean, how on earth could anyone possibly think those two boys had anything to do with replacing Jonathan's sugar? The nerve!" She bit into a homemade chocolate donut—with extra sprinkles—that Melody's dad had sent over. "Jonathan probably made a mistake. He *has* seemed distracted at school lately, if you ask me. In fact, on Wednesday he was fifteen minutes late to his own staff meeting. That's never happened. Something's going on with him."

"No." Melody helped herself to another donut. The familiarity helped take the sting out of her heart. Her dad had made these same donuts when Melody had gotten dumped the first time, when she hadn't made the volleyball team junior year, when her two best friends had gone on a spring break trip without her in college. These donuts had gotten her through many of life's disappointments.

"Jonathan wouldn't make a mistake like that." No matter how distracted he'd been. "I wouldn't even make a mistake like that and I'm not half the baker he is." The fact was, he'd poured sugar into that container before leaving his house, and sometime during the contest, someone had dumped it out and replaced it with salt.

And no one, in the entire crowded auditorium, had seen anything?

"I can't believe someone would stoop so low." Her mother drummed her fingers against the table. "Finn and Tate would never even think about pulling a stunt like that."

"That's true." They knew how much trouble they'd be in if they did. She squeezed her eyes shut and massaged her temples. "They were so upset last night. They didn't even wanted to finish watching *The Santa Clause*."

Maybe that irked her more than anything. The only reason she'd entered the damn contest in the first place was to rekindle some holiday magic with her boys. Instead, they'd all ended up hurt and disappointed. Now they'd probably never want to bake cookies again. "All Jonathan had to do was stand up for them, and everyone would've listened to him."

But he hadn't.

Her mother scoffed. "He can't really believe Finn and Tate would do something like this." She thunked her mug down on the table. "Don't you worry, honey. I'll talk to him. I'll tell him—"

"No. I should be the one to talk to him." In fact, she'd go over to his house right now and have a little chat with him before she lost the nerve. That was what she should've done last night anyway. She'd thought about texting him but she didn't trust herself.

Melody stood up and rinsed out her mug.

"You're going right now?" Her mother followed her to the sink. "Like *that*? I mean, maybe you want to throw on some jeans and a nice sweater, put on a little makeup."

By the time she did that, indignation wouldn't be flowing out of her like molten lava. "I don't need makeup to tell Mr. Braxton that he ruined our whole contest experience when he stood by and let everyone publicly accuse us of cheating." She stepped into her boots. "I don't need to be wearing a nice sweater to tell him how disappointed the boys are that he didn't say one word in their defense." She was on a roll now!

Melody marched to the garage door. "You stay put in case the boys wake up," she called over her shoulder. "This won't take long."

WHEN SHE PULLED up in front of Jonathan's Craftsman-style house seven minutes later, she'd replayed the whole ugly scene in her head ten more times, only amplifying the hurt and the anger. She and Jonathan might not be all that close but they'd had a few intriguing moments, at least in her mind. Clearly she'd misread the connection. That should make this easier.

She stomped up the porch steps, knocking on the heavy wooden door with authority.

It took a minute for footsteps to thump on the other side. The door swung open, and Jonathan appeared, visibly startled to see her. "Melody." He stared at her for a few silent seconds, his gaze seeming to take all of her in, making her keenly aware of her frumpy sweats stuffed into her snow boots. Meanwhile, Jonathan looked like he could've been going to work. No sweater vest, but he had on a crisp gray button-up shirt that accentuated his nice broad shoulders.

Once again, her mother had been right.

"Hey. Come on in." He stepped aside and some delicious gooey cinnamony smell—quite possibly a homemade cinnamon roll—wafted out to tempt her, but she couldn't go in his *house*. Especially with it smelling like that. Next thing she knew, she'd be sitting at his kitchen table stuffing her face with a cinnamon roll instead of defending her children's honor. "No, thanks." She purposely did not inhale the aroma too deeply, lest it soften her tone. "I just came to tell you how upset the boys are about this whole situation. They worked incredibly hard on those cookies and they were hurt that you allowed people to believe they had something to do with—"

"Jonathan?" a woman's voice called behind him.

Melody's mouth hung open. A woman. Jonathan had a woman at his house on a Sunday morning.

The owner of the voice appeared in the foyer behind him, and she wasn't only a woman. She was a beautiful woman— model beautiful. Tall and elegant with flowing black curls and flawless skin. She was dressed casually but nicely in jeans and—you guessed it—an elegant sweater. Yep. She looked exactly like someone Jonathan would belong with.

"I'm so sorry." The woman offered her a warm smile. "I didn't mean to interrupt." With that voice, Melody would bet she was a good singer too. "The timer went off, and I wasn't sure if the cinnamon rolls were done."

"They should be." Jonathan didn't glance away from Melody, and she wished she could disappear—beam herself back home. What had she been thinking showing up on his doorstep like this—in her sweats and snow boots with her hair unbrushed and righteous indignation splotching her face?

"I'll go take them out of the oven." The woman acknowledged Melody with a nod and then disappeared again.

"I feel awful about what happened at the contest," Jonathan said earnestly, as if Melody hadn't just rudely interrupted his romantic cinnamon roll baking date.

It had to be a date, right? She must've completely misread the flirting over their text thread yesterday. Oh God. Their text thread! She'd sent him three eggplant emojis when he had a girlfriend!

"I was going to text you last night but I misplaced my phone, right before the competition." He stepped closer to her.

Before the competition.

"Oh. Good." She shook her head. "I mean, that stinks." For him, but definitely not for her. She couldn't be sure he'd lost it before he'd seen the text she'd sent, though. And now, knowing he had a girlfriend, she had to clear the air. "Um, I'm not sure if you saw the last text I sent with the uh . . . well . . . the *vegetables*."

The first hints of a smile twinged the corners of his mouth. "I saw it. Didn't you get my response?"

His response? He'd *responded*? "Uh, no." Now it wasn't anger that had her all hot. Nope. There were other things happening in her body. Blood rushing, a craving simmering, butterflies flapping. But she couldn't have butterflies for Jonathan. "I was going to tell you yesterday—that text was totally meant for someone else," she blurted.

His smile flatlined. "Really?"

"Yeah." She pretended to be very interested in a hangnail on her thumb because she could not look into his eyes and lie. "I was texting my sister at the same time and my signals got crossed and I accidentally sent it to you. See, we have this favorite Italian place where we go out for eggplant parmigiana all the time, and I had a hankering, so I texted her to tell her she could wear anything she wanted . . ." *Stop. There.* Actually, she should've stopped before she started. Now she sounded pathetic.

"Oh." Jonathan's expression had gone neutral, resembling the one he usually wore during a lecture. "Then I guess it's a good thing you didn't see my response. It must not have sent. I don't get great reception in the gym."

"I guess that *is* a good thing." No, it wasn't! Now she'd never know what he'd typed back. She would have to wonder until she died! What could he have possibly responded to that? There was no way to find out now. She'd botched this entire conversation. "Um, I should probably be going." She spun and stumbled down the steps.

"I'm going to make this up to Finn and Tate." Jonathan had followed her down to the sidewalk. "And to you, Melody. I promise. I know they're not responsible and I didn't mean to imply I thought otherwise."

"Okay. That's great. Um, thanks," she said before quickly ducking into her car. She might have peeled out, thanks to the surge of adrenaline he'd fired up in her. Instead of going home, she veered to the west and parked in front of her sister's two-story house in the newer part of town.

She slipped and slid her way up the walk and rushed in through the front door.

"Bwoof!" Turk met her in the living room, nudging his massive head right into her crotch. "Easy, boy." She fended him off as best she could and continued to the kitchen, where Kels and Doug and Gen were sitting around the breakfast table.

"Hey, Melly." Her sister jumped up. "Is everything okay?"

She didn't even know how to answer that question.

"Auntie Mel!" Genevieve hugged her.

"Hey, hon." She gave the girl a tight squeeze. "I'm so sorry. I didn't mean to interrupt your breakfast."

"Your timing is perfect, as always. We're done." Doug came over and swept Gen up onto his shoulders. "Let's go finish our game of Ping-Pong in the basement." He galloped out of the room with his daughter giggling.

"What happened?" Kels was at her side. "Is it Mom? Finn or Tate?"

"No, no. Nothing like that." She accepted the mug of tea her sister offered. "I just came from Jonathan's house."

Kels gave her attire a good once-over, her face scrunched. "Really?"

At this point, Melody no longer cared what she'd been wearing. She didn't know what to think about her encounter with Jonathan, and she needed Kels to make some sense out of it. "I went to confront him about not sticking up for the boys, and there was a woman there."

"A woman." Her sister slowly sank to the chair across from her.

"A gorgeous woman," Melody confirmed. "And elegant."

Kelsey considered the information. "Maybe she's his sister."

"They didn't look alike." And there'd been a certain awkwardness between them. Maybe they were newly dating. "Why wouldn't he have introduced me if she was his sister?"

"Did Jonathan make it seem like you interrupted something?" Kels still looked skeptical.

"Not really." In fact, she hadn't even realized anyone else was there at first. "He invited me in."

"And you said no?" Her sister threw up her arms in disbelief. "Well, maybe he would've introduced you to the woman if you'd gone in with him."

"I couldn't go in. I was mad." And the cinnamon rolls would've distracted her. "It was supposed to be a confrontation, but then the woman appeared and I got all weird." She rubbed her forehead, trying to erase the memory. "I told him I meant that text I sent for you, and he said it was a good thing I didn't get his response, then."

"He actually responded?" Kels leaned halfway over the table. "Are you kidding me? What did it say?"

"I'll never know now." But she would wonder every time she saw him. "He said it must not have gone through because he was in the gym."

"The reception really is terrible in there." Her sister drummed her fingers on the table. "We have to find out what that text said. There has to be a way."

"Maybe he was telling me how inappropriate it was to send eggplant emojis."

"Or maybe . . . *maybe* he asked you out on a date or something! You two were totally flirting." Kels didn't give her a chance to shoot down that suggestion. "Let's say he did ask you out. Would you go?"

Ha! "Not if his model girlfriend was going to be there."

"Let's say that was his sister. Then would you go on a date with him?" Kels raised her eyebrows.

"I don't know. Maybe." She might be able to lie to herself, but she couldn't lie to her sister. "It's not going to happen anyway. He's taken." Which was just as well. "I probably read into his texts. That's maybe just how he texts with women." She didn't give her sister a chance to shoot down *that* suggestion. "Besides, I have enough complications in my life right now. Somehow I have to figure out how to convince the entire town we didn't cheat at the Cookie Contest."

"Yeah. About that." Her sister's grimace set her on edge. "I should probably let you know, as your deputy director and everything, that the cookie committee members want to hold an emergency session this afternoon."

Melody jolted to her feet. Was she serious? "A meeting *without* me?"

"No. They'd like you to be there too. But they want me to lead it."

"They're going to oust me, aren't they?" What had she lasted as the director? All of two weeks? "Unbelievable. And I won't even be able to defend myself or my kids."

"Don't worry, Melly." Kels tugged on her hand and prodded her to sit back down. "Mom and I and Aunt Bernice and Joan all have your back. We won't let them oust you."

"Is Jonathan going to be at the meeting?"

Her sister pulled out her phone. "It looks like he responded yes."

"And I'm a yes too." She was not about to let them to run her out for something she didn't even do.

Ten

THE LIBRARY HAD ALWAYS BEEN MELODY'S FAVORITE ROOM at the boys' school. It was the one space in the whole building that didn't have such an institutional vibe. The librarian, Mr. Ponder, had won grant money to turn the space into a whimsical storybook land where the kids could not only check out books but also immerse themselves in make-believe worlds.

Finn and Tate had spent a lot of hours in the reading corners with vibrantly colored beanbags and chairs, and the vast displays of some of the more popular series had fueled their love for the adventure and science fiction genres.

Most of her recommended parent volunteer hours had been spent right here, reading to children, shelving books, consulting on the displays. Now, though, she had a sense of foreboding as she walked through the doors.

A circle of hard plastic chairs had already been positioned in the group reading area, replacing the colorful chairs and beanbags, which were now stacked gloomily in the corner.

"Melody." Aunt Bernice met her by the circulation desk

with outstretched arms. "How're you doing?" She hugged her tight, obstructing Melody's ability to answer. "How're Finny and Tate? The poor boys. I don't know if I've ever seen them so upset."

"They'll be okay." Finn and Tate were resilient. They'd been through far more than most kids their age, and she liked to think they'd developed some wisdom and perspective along the way. Melody extracted herself from the embrace. "Papa was going to take them sledding this afternoon." A distraction until she could get this situation cleared up.

"Practically everyone is talking about the whole fiasco." Aunt Bernice cast a suspicious glance around them, but only Joan hovered nearby, listening in.

"Don't worry." Her mom's friend huddled in with them. "We have your back."

Thankfully, the other committee members—Tracey, Deb, and Nancy—seemed to be too engrossed in their own hushed conversation at the center of the chair circle to notice she'd walked in. It appeared Jonathan hadn't arrived yet.

"Do you know who did this?"

Bernice had a habit of asking questions she already knew the answer to.

"I don't think we'll ever know." As acting president, she might be making a suggestion to install surveillance cameras in the gym before next year's contest.

"We've got our money on Mrs. Altman," Mom whispered. She'd snuck in behind them.

"Oh yes." Aunt Bernice's head bobbed in a confident nod. "That would make the most sense."

"She's a real grump," Joan agreed.

"She couldn't have physically pulled it off," Melody re-

THE CHRISTMAS COOKIE WARS 🎄 137

minded them. With two arthritic hips she wouldn't have been able to move fast enough.

"What about Charlene?" her mother suggested. "She's given you nothing but trouble."

"I thought about her too, but she wasn't around." Which was strange in and of itself. Melody couldn't believe Charlene hadn't come to watch her fail.

"She could've hired someone else to do it," Aunt Bernice mused.

"Well, we can't publicly name any suspects without proof." Kels completed their little band of misfits. "But I'm going over there right now to start planting seeds for your innocence." She swept past them and greeted the others.

"We can do that too." Bernice pulled on her mom's and Joan's hands and dragged them to the circle too.

Melody hung back, drawing in a breath and holding on to it. This was probably how the *Survivor* contestants felt going into Tribal Council. She fully anticipated that those three members would try to make a case for her dismissal, and now she was contemplating letting them. This whole gig had been way more trouble than she'd bargained for—

"Melody."

A shiver ran through her at the depth of Jonathan's voice. Did he say her name differently than everyone else's, or did she only hear him differently? She turned, her footing shaky, and fought to stand strong beneath the wave of panic or anticipation or hope or whatever it was that crashed over her. "Hey." No one else might have heard the tremor in her voice, but she felt it rock through her.

"Hey." True concern creased his forehead. "Are Finn and Tate feeling any better?"

Based on the worry evident in his expression, he already knew the answer. "No. They're really not." And she wasn't either. "Excuse me. I should find a seat." His gaze followed her; she could feel the weight of it, but she didn't look back at him.

Melody opted for the spot between her mother's and Aunt Bernice's purses. She sat watching her family members carry on heated discussions with the other committee members until Kels whistled. "Why don't we all sit down and get started?"

Jonathan made it to the circle last and ended up sitting directly across from her. The only way for her to avoid his gaze was to stay hyperfocused on her sister.

"Okay, so apparently since I'm the deputy director and our director is involved in the dispute, I'll be running the meeting." Kels seemed to direct the words at Tracey, Deb, and Nancy. "But for the record, I think this whole thing is ridiculous. For one thing, Jonathan still won the contest, even though he got sabotaged. And, for another, there is absolutely no proof that Melody and her boys were involved in the alleged switching of the ingredients."

"Someone compromised the integrity of the contest," Deb said. "I mean, Melody only just took over and we're already having issues. I, for one, am not convinced this is a good leadership change."

"Agreed. Let's not forget too that Mr. Braxton spent his hard-earned money on those ingredients." As Jonathan's assistant, Nancy was always protective of him. "Nothing like this has ever happened in the history of the cookie committee."

Tracey also glared at Melody like she was a pariah. "Is it true you and Mr. Braxton made a bet?"

"That was a joke." Anger steeled her spine. "Come on. We all know that no cookie the boys and I make could *ever* beat his cookies." She slashed a hand in Jonathan's direction. "I was planning to volunteer in the cafeteria anyway." Exaggerating had never hurt anyone.

"Exactly." Nancy had been scolding children in that tone for at least twenty years. "You knew you couldn't beat him. The boys knew that. So maybe they decided to give themselves the best chance."

Deb nodded. "You have to admit, it doesn't look good."

"At this point there may be no alternative but for you to step down." Tracey looked to the other two for support.

"If she steps down, then we're stepping down too." Kels gestured to their mom and Aunt Bernice and Joan. "And then there is no way you'll have the numbers to pull off the Cookie and Cocktail Crawl and Cookie Daze."

"We'll have to disband the committee for good," Nancy said. "Maybe Charlene was right in the first place. That might be the best option."

"No." Melody stood. "We are not disbanding. I haven't done anything wrong, but I'm happy to step down if—"

"Can I say something?" Jonathan interrupted.

Oh, now he had something to say? Melody spread out her hands in a silent invitation and took her seat. She could resign when he was done talking.

"The whole thing was my mistake. I grabbed the wrong container before I left my house." Somehow he uttered the most perfect self-deprecating chuckle. "I thought I had packed the sugar container, but I switched them." His innocent shrug didn't fool her. "So Melody and Finn and Tate had nothing to do with it. I made the mistake."

He was totally lying.

"Oh. Well, that explains it, then." Kels smiled brightly,

clearly seizing the opportunity to wrap this up. "The whole thing was simply a big misunderstanding."

"Exactly," Jonathan continued with a dimple-less smile. "I was embarrassed to admit my mistake at the contest, but there you have it. No one sabotaged me. I sabotaged myself. And I promise to set the record straight in the school newsletter this week."

Silence fell while Nancy, Deb, and Tracey all exchanged skeptical glances.

"I don't understand," Tracey said politely. "You keep a whole container of salt in your house? That looks like your sugar container?"

"Yes, as a matter of fact I do."

Melody watched his face intently, picking up on a flicker of amusement.

"The salt container looks a lot like my sugar container. Everything in my kitchen matches."

Now that part she could believe. He likely had all of his ingredients and spices alphabetized too.

"You're sure?" Deb didn't seem to believe him either, but no one would question Jonathan too much.

"I'm positive. Sorry for the confusion. I'll make it up to everyone with some gingersnaps that have sugar instead of salt." His good-natured tone had every woman in that room smiling, including Melody.

Unbelievable. She evened out her expression before he saw.

"Great! Don't worry about it, Jonathan. No harm done." Her sister's jovial tone brushed the whole thing off. "Since we now know the truth, I expect you all to set the record straight when you're discussing the situation with your neighbors and friends," Kels said to Deb, Nancy, and Tracey. "Now, Mel, why don't you take the floor so we can discuss the Cookie and Cocktail Crawl?"

She waited for another argument, but everyone seemed to have accepted Jonathan's tale. Even if no one believed it. Now they were all staring at her, waiting. So that was it? One sentence from Jonathan and this whole inquest was over? Without an apology from anyone?

"Melody?" her mom prompted.

Oh, for crying out loud. "Everything's on track for the crawl." Her grumpy tone couldn't be helped. "We have commitments from all the shops on Main Street. Each establishment is planning to offer a specialty cocktail and cookie while people browse around." She'd spent the last week making the rounds to get all of her neighbors at the boutique excited about the event. Because she was actually good at this director stuff. "This year, I also asked everyone to offer mocktails and hot chocolate for the under-twenty-one crowd."

"What a great idea." Judging from Nancy's overly enthusiastic praise, she was back in the woman's good graces.

All because Jonathan had lied for her.

"Perfect!" her sister chirped. "Now we just need to get the word out."

"I'm working on that part." Deb waved a hand. "I brought flyers to hand out after the meeting."

"Alrighty, then." Kels stood up. "I believe we've taken care of the business. So I'm officially ending the meeting. Let's go home, people."

Everyone stood up and started to put away their chairs, but Melody went right for Jonathan, cornering him near the reference section. "You didn't have to make up a story to protect us," she half whispered.

He peeked around the shelf as though making sure no one would see them. "I couldn't let them force you into resigning. Especially when I know you and the boys weren't responsible."

Uh-oh. The magnetic force field of his eyes had drawn her in. She couldn't look away. "You didn't seem sure at the contest." That was what had hurt the most. He'd hesitated. She'd seen him hesitate . . . kind of like he was now—gaze darting around, mouth twisted in the slightest indecision.

"You misread the situation." He shuffled a half step closer. Close enough that she could detect the scent of his fresh, clean laundry soap.

"But you didn't say anything." Her mouth seemed to be moving in slow motion, which was weird given the erratic state of her heart.

"I never know what to say to you." He gave a frustrated shake of his head. "I mean, I never feel like I say the right thing to you. The things I *want* to say."

The world seemed to come to a screeching halt. All she could see was Jonathan looking at her—looking into her eyes—with a sort of desperate longing.

Melody ached to find a breath. He wanted to say something to her? Something important? "Wh . . . what about your girlfriend?"

"Girlfriend?" Jonathan shook his head slowly.

"She was at your house this morning—"

"That was my ex-wife," he murmured. "She brought Ainsley up, and we were all having breakfast together." His face drew even closer to Melody's, and those eyes. She couldn't look away. They were luring her in, head over heels, and she was losing herself in the midst of the pull. He didn't look like Principal Braxton right now. He looked like a man. A man who had every pulse point in her body throbbing. Oh mama, she was in so much trouble.

Jonathan's lips quirked. "There's only one person I'm interested in right—"

"There you are!" Deb broke the spell, barreling up the narrow aisle between the shelves. "Melody, what do you think about this for the Cookie and Cocktail Crawl flyer design?" She moved between them and held up a paper in front of her face.

The images blurred together in blobs of color. "Uh." She blinked but couldn't straighten out her vision. Jonathan was only interested in one person? "Looks great."

"Good." Deb shoved a whole stack of papers into her hands. "Now, I'm going to need you to distribute at least twenty copies to each of the businesses on Main Street so they can hang them in the windows."

"Sure. I can do that." She looked down at the flyers, trying to see past the pure wonderment working through her and, when she lifted her head again, she realized Jonathan had disappeared.

Wait. She sidestepped Deb and bypassed her mother and Aunt Bernice, and Joan, finally locating Kels by the door. "Have you seen Jonathan?"

"He left. Said something about having to go pick up his daughter." Her sister's eyes narrowed, going on high alert. "Why? What's wrong? What happened?"

Melody shook her head. She couldn't talk about this now. Deb, Tracey, and Nancy were on their way out.

"Bye, girls." Nancy scooted past them, her posture the slightest bit repentant. "Be sure to turn off the lights when you leave."

"Will do." Kelsey's stare bored into Melody's forehead.

"I'm glad that unfortunate business is settled." Bernice put one arm around each of them. "Why don't we all go out for a celebratory cocktail? I'm buying."

"We can't." Kels seemed to grasp that Melody couldn't exactly speak for herself right then. She was too busy trying to figure out if Jonathan meant her. He had said he was interested in someone, right? She hadn't imagined that?

"We have to, uh, go Christmas shopping." Kels linked their arms together. "For you three. So clearly we can't be with you right now." She flicked off the lights and half dragged Melody down the hall and out the front doors to her car. "Get in." Her sister clicked the unlock button.

Melody's hand fumbled with the door handle and she slid into the passenger seat, completely oblivious to the freezing temperatures.

Kels turned on the car and blasted the heat. "What happened in there?"

She relayed the scene as best she could, leaving out the part about her heart going ballistic.

A smile took shape on Kelsey's face, growing bigger with each word Melody spoke.

"I mean, he didn't come out and say he was interested in me." Could he be? Could regal, organized, put-together Jonathan be interested in *her*? She didn't know what to do with the hopes that were rising inside her.

"He didn't have to come out and say it." Kels clapped and squealed, throwing her own little party right there in the front seat. "Honey, Jonathan Braxton is totally in love with you."

Eleven

"SO WHAT HAPPENS NOW?" KELSEY'S SQUEALS AND GIG-
gles and exclamations of *I knew it!* and *He has a crush on you!*
had finally tapered off.

"I have no idea." Her sister might not have noticed, but
Melody hadn't exactly been celebrating alongside her. After
emerging from her grief over Thomas's death, she'd spent the
last few years content and safe and comfortable. She wasn't
supposed to fall for her kids' principal. Or anyone, for that
matter. "I'm pretty sure Finn and Tate would never forgive me
if I made any kind of move on Mr. Braxton."

"Oh. Come. On." Kels grabbed the lapels of her coat and
shook her. "You have a crush on him too. It's *so* obvious."

Instead of denying, she redirected. "The boys are my sole
focus this holiday season. We still haven't done most of the
things on our holiday traditions list—picking out their ornaments, our big ice skating night, our gingerbread house, a visit
to Santa . . ." Although that last item would be a tough sell this
year. She'd have to find a pretty epic bribe . . . er . . . reward.

"Why can't you do all of that and have a secret romance

with Jonathan?" Kels whined. "The boys would never have to know. You two could meet up in Denver for a weekend—"

"I'm getting out of the car now." Melody pushed the door open and scrambled to stand before her sister could plant any fantasies in her head. "I need to pick up the boys at the park and cross at least one thing off our list today."

"But you know you'll be thinking about Jonathan while you—"

Melody slammed the door on the words and cut a path through the fresh snow to her own car, where she could redirect herself in peace.

As she climbed in, Kels drove past her, honking and waving.

She shook her head and started up the engine. Did Kels have any idea how hard it was to keep secrets from Finn and Tate? She had to store their Christmas presents at her parents' house. Besides, if she ever did have someone special in her life again—a big *if*—she'd want to share that with them, not sneak around like she was doing something wrong.

Something told her they wouldn't exactly be thrilled about sharing her with Mr. Braxton.

As if on cue, "I've Got My Love to Keep Me Warm" started playing on the radio. Melody hit the button to play her Bluetooth instead, but it happened to be cued up to "All I Want for Christmas Is You."

"You've got to be kidding me." She skipped to the next song—a nice safe version of "Deck the Halls."

To keep her thoughts from drifting into forbidden territory, she spent the drive to the park considering how she might convince the boys to visit Santa for a picture. It wouldn't have to be a big deal—they could snap a quick picture at the Cookie and Cocktail Crawl event since Santa would be all set up near the end of the route. Then she'd reward them each with some money to spend while they walked around. Yes, that was a good plan. She'd tell them they could eat as many cookies as they wanted along the way too.

Cars crammed the lot at the park, and colorful parkas dotted the sledding hill. Her boys weren't hard to spot when they were with her six-foot-five father. In true Papa fashion, he wore his red plaid trapper's hat. She got out of the car in time to see them all load up on the same toboggan she'd ridden down this same hill with her dad back in the day.

She hurried to capture the moment by snapping a few pictures and waved as the three of them sailed past her on the sled, the boys squealing and her father laughing.

They came to a stop in a poof of snow.

"These two are running me ragged." Her dad rolled off the sled and pushed to his feet, cheeks ruddy and smile singing. He couldn't fool her. He loved sledding every bit as much as Finn and Tate.

"Thanks for taking them, Dad." She hugged him, this big bear of a man who'd been everything to them since they'd lost Thomas.

In those first few months, her dad had shown up every evening, usually bringing along a dinner her mom had made, and he would quietly walk the three of them through their nightly routine—getting the boys bathed, reading them a story or five—and then tucking them in.

Afterward, Melody would collapse on the couch, completely drained of both energy and emotion, and her dad would sit in the recliner thumbing through the newspaper he'd brought along. *You can go home*, Melody always said to him. But he'd just stay put and turn to the next page. At some point she would fall asleep and then she would wake up the next morning to find him gone and a blanket tucked in around her. His quiet and consistent presence had gotten her through those months.

"How'd that stupid cookie meeting go?" Finn had snow crusted in his eyelashes.

Ugh. She hated that word. But she let it slide since she understood his anger. "It wasn't stupid." She reached into her pocket and handed him a tissue for his runny nose. "Actually, Mr. Braxton shared with everyone that he thinks he made the mistake."

Her dad snorted in blatant disbelief. "He switched out his own sugar with salt?"

"He *thinks* he maybe got mixed up." She winked at her dad so he wouldn't blow Jonathan's cover.

Tate gasped. "Then everyone knows we didn't do anything wrong? No one's gonna hate us!"

"Right. Now everyone will know we had nothing to do with the mistake." Watching the clouds lift off the boys' expressions, she understood even more why Jonathan had lied. And she was grateful. He'd saved the boys from having a very tough week at school.

"He's gonna tell everyone in the whole town, right?" Finn pulled off his hat, and instantly he was five years old again with those curls sticking up all over.

"I'm sure word will get around." Melody shared a smile with her dad. "So now we can all move on. We don't have to worry anymore."

"Isn't that nice?" Her father scrubbed Finn's hair.

Meanwhile, Tate's eyes ruminated. "I can't believe Mr. Braxton would switch his sugar with salt."

"Well, he said he did." For them. Warmth enveloped her heart. But no. She couldn't allow any warm fuzzy feelings for Mr. Braxton. She had to redirect. "Hey, I thought we would go shopping, so you two could pick out your new ornament for this year."

"But Papa promised us hot chocolate." Her mission to distract Tate from analyzing the situation had worked.

"Why doesn't Papa come with us?" Though she'd likely have to bribe her father too when it came to shopping. "We can get hot chocolate at the coffee shop and look around in Rudy's place?"

Her father could never resist a trip to the antique store. Rudy had collected all kinds of treasures from estate sales over the years, and the two of them went way back.

Sure enough, her dad shrugged. "I guess I could be persuaded."

"How long do we have to shop?" Finn was the only holdout.

"Until you find an ornament you'd like to add to your collection." For their very first Christmas, she and Thomas had picked out ornaments for them, and then they'd continued the tradition every year until the boys had turned four and could pick out their own. The hope was that someday, when they grew up and started their own families—sniff, sniff—they'd have a whole bunch of ornaments to hang on their Christmas trees.

"So I can pick out an ornament in like a minute and then be done shopping if I want?" Finn put on his angelic smile.

"That would defeat the purpose of a fun tradition." And spending time together. "You probably want to take a little more time to look for the *right* ornament. It'll be fun."

"Shopping is never fun," her dad muttered, making the boys giggle.

"Oh, come on. You love browsing around Rudy's place." She elbowed him in the ribs. "And we'll even *start* with the hot chocolate."

The boys let out more grumbles, but her dad waved them to the parking lot. "Why don't all three of you monkeys ride with me? Then I'll drop you back here after we're done?"

"Works for me." She caught each boy under an arm and swept them along the sidewalk. Before long, they'd be too tall for her to capture so easily.

Whistling behind them, her dad hauled the sled and tossed it into the back of his truck. Once she was settled in the passenger seat, she changed the radio from his typical talk radio to Christmas tunes, earning a grunt from her father. But by the end of the drive to the coffee shop, he was humming along with "Jingle Bells" too.

They all piled out of the truck—the boys first, of course. Finn and Tate bolted into the coffee shop before she'd even shut her door.

Inside her coat pocket, her phone dinged. Melody paused outside the coffee shop windows and checked the screen. It was from Jonathan! Luckily no one heard her gasp.

I found my phone.

A warm pulsing sensation thrummed in her chest. She looked around, spotting her dad waiting for her by the entrance. Good news, she quickly typed.

I thought so. Because we didn't get to finish our conversation earlier.

You disappeared. She started to move, shuffling her feet in the direction of her dad, but dragging them as much as possible while those three dots bounced.

Sorry about that. I had to pick up Ainsley from a friend's house. Didn't want to be late. Can you talk now?

Talk? Jonathan wanted to talk to her? Melody stopped a few feet away from her dad, fully aware he was watching her closely. I can't, actually. Her heart deflated. Sorry. We're out shopping.

Another time, then. I'm sure I'll see you soon. He added a winking emoji.

Melody desperately scrolled through the emoji list and then fired back a thumbs-up. Thumbs-up? Really? At least it was better than an eggplant.

Her dad held open the door for her. "Who were you texting?" He kept his voice down. Not that the boys could hear him, they were too busy gawking at the baked goods in the glass case.

"Um." She removed her beanie before her face got too hot. "No one important." The blush creeping up her neck begged to differ.

"So it would seem Mr. Braxton lied to get everyone off your back, huh?"

She raised her gaze to her father's. He'd always been too damn perceptive. She never could pull one over on him. "He did it for the boys. He was trying to protect them."

According to his smile, he still saw through her. "That's a good man there. Don't you think?"

"Mr. Braxton is a wonderful principal. He'd do anything for his students." She walked to meet the boys before her dad could detect any of the other feelings she had for Jonathan.

"I want the white peppermint hot chocolate," Finn was telling the cashier.

"Yeah, me too." Tate bumped his brother out of the way. "With extra whipped cream."

The girl behind the counter grinned at them. "And extra sprinkles?"

They both nodded, likely playing it cool because she was a teenager and she happened to be cute. At least Melody thought so.

"And I'll take the salted caramel with no whipped cream. Dad?"

"Dark chocolate—don't tell your mom."

Melody laughed. Ever since he'd turned sixty, her mother kept on him about his blood sugar.

Before she could dig her credit card out, her sweet father had told the cashier to put it on his tab, and then they all gathered at the pickup station.

"Do you two have any idea what kind of ornament you're going to look for?" she asked the boys. Last year, they'd both gone with hockey ornaments, since playing on the town pond had become their newest obsession.

Tate shrugged. "Depends what we can find in a store full of old stuff."

"Vintage," her father corrected. "That stuff in Rudy's place isn't old. It's vintage. And, trust me, they don't make things like that anymore. Those ornaments you pick out'll last forever."

"That's true." She'd had to glue at least half of the new ornaments in their collection back together at one point or another.

The drinks came up, and Melody grabbed a bunch of napkins to stuff in her purse on the way out of the store.

Snowflakes drifted along on the chilly breeze, twirling

and glittering under the light of the streetlamps. Melody inhaled the frosty air, closing her eyes for a second to breathe it all in—the boys' chatter ahead of them, the snow, the cold on her cheeks. Now *this* felt like Christmas.

And Rudy's shop *smelled* like Christmas—evergreen and gingerbread.

"Hey, Artie. Melody." Rudy sat behind the counter where one of those small box televisions was positioned. "What're you lookin' for today?"

"We're looking for Christmas ornaments," Tate answered for them.

"You're in luck, kid. Got a whole section of 'em there in the back." He turned the volume down on his television. "Some real neat ones too. One of a kind. You won't find any like that in a Hallmark store."

"Don't I know it." Her father leaned into the counter.

While the two older men exchanged words about how cheaply everything was made these days, Melody wandered from shelf to shelf, giving the boys some space to explore on their own. Rudy had curated the most eclectic collection of dishes and ancient appliances and beautiful crystal accents. She picked up a large milk glass bowl and found a treasure hidden behind it. The most unique copper mixing bowl she'd ever seen. She picked it up, turning it over.

"Quite the piece, huh?" Rudy called from the counter. "I had to do some cleanup on it, but now she really shines."

"It's lovely." She turned it over and over in her hands. An intricate scrolled pattern lined the outside and somehow it didn't have one dent or scratch.

"Came from an estate sale." Rudy walked over, followed by her father. "Best I can tell, it's from the 1960s. Pure copper, I believe."

"Sure looks like it to me." Her dad took it from her and examined the surface.

"The wife swears it's the best for making eggs fluffier, whatever that means." Rudy always took pride in his rarer finds.

"I'm sure." Melody accepted the bowl back from her dad. It sat heavy and solid in her hands, cool to the touch. It would be the perfect gift for—

Redirect.

Such a specific gift might be too intimate and thoughtful for the boys to give to their principal. They typically stuck to the usual school themed gifts for the staff—pens, candy, gift cards . . .

She set the bowl back on the shelf and continued wandering, her father now ambling by her side.

"Somethin' on your mind?"

Kels had been right. Melody could try to distract herself as much as possible, but that didn't stop her thoughts from drifting to Jonathan. He was the first person she'd thought of when she'd seen the mixing bowl.

She hesitated, checking around them to make sure the boys were still perusing ornaments in the back. Maybe the reason her dad had been so wonderful after Thomas had died was that he'd lost his own father. He'd been fourteen, not four like her boys, but he still grasped the absolute shock of having a parent alive one moment and gone forever the next.

"How long did Grandma wait to go out with Jimmy after your dad died?" Strange that she'd never asked him that question before.

"She met Jimmy a few years after, if I remember right," he answered after a long pause.

"And you were okay with her dating again? As a kid?" If her

grandmother had met Jimmy two years later, that would've made him sixteen when his stepfather had come into his life.

"I wouldn't say I was *okay* with her dating." Her dad picked up an old hammer and examined the handle. "I liked Jimmy. And I wanted her to be happy. But I had my moments of hating the whole thing. Why d'you ask?" He set down the hammer and glanced at her.

Yes, why was she asking? "Just curious."

His chin tilted up as he studied her, those wise eyes seeming to take it all in. He knew why she was asking. Or at least he had an inkling, but he didn't push. "There was this one time when I told your grandma I didn't like her dating. I was mad that Jimmy had come over for dinner on my birthday, and I told her all about it." He chuckled softly. "I'll never forget what she said back to me."

Melody picked up a music box and let it play while she waited. Dad talked about his mom frequently enough that she knew what a wise woman her grandmother had been. She wished she had gotten to know her better, but she'd had a stroke when Melody was six years old and had deteriorated rapidly after that.

"She said, 'Arthur, I know you're spittin' mad about losin' your daddy, but I only have two choices here.'" The way he made his voice higher to mimic his mother made Melody smile. "'One choice is to stay where I'm at for the rest of my life. And where I'm at right now is sad and lonely. And the second choice is to take a risk so I can get out of this rut I'm stuck in.'"

"That's a good way to put it for a kid." It had been a few years since she'd felt sad and lonely, but she could relate to being stuck in a rut.

"After she said that, I got it." Her father stopped at a shelf crowded with old leather wallets. "I didn't want her to be sad and lonely. And she told me she couldn't grow without letting new people into her life. That made sense."

Melody let the words sit. Growth wasn't quite the wisdom she'd been expecting to glean from her grandmother's experience. She'd thought her father was going to say something about his mom telling him she needed to find her own happiness again. And that was the thing . . . Melody was happy. She missed Thomas and what they'd had, but she'd worked through the grief and she had a full life.

But she couldn't say she'd grown much in the last few years. She'd kept her circle small, her life simple. She worked and she took care of the boys and she spent time with her family. That was all. And it had been enough. But now . . .

"Jimmy was real different than my dad." Her father opened up a worn black leather wallet and studied the inside. "But my mom was different too after losing him. And they were happy. Every bit as happy as my parents had been, if not more." He set the wallet back on the shelf. "He'd lost his wife too, so I think they appreciated what they'd found together more than most people."

The nostalgic smile on her dad's face warmed her. She linked her arm through his as they continued shopping. "The boys and I are so lucky to have you."

He squeezed her against his side. "I think I'm the one who's lucky."

"Look, Mom." Finn raced to them holding up a snowy owl made from feathers. "Isn't this the coolest ornament ever?"

"Very cool." She refrained from saying *I told you so.* "Is that the one you're going to choose?"

"I don't know yet." He was already en route to the back of the store. "We can't decide. There's a lot to look at."

"Take your time." It seemed shopping in a store full of old stuff wasn't so boring after all.

"You know . . ." Her father changed directions, heading back the way they'd come. "Mom and Jimmy were friends before they were anything else. No harm in being friends with someone." He stopped her in front of the copper mixing bowl.

Shaking her head at him, Melody picked it up again, her heart beating the way it only seemed to for Jonathan. He would like it. He'd use it, most likely. Maybe it would remind him of baking with his grandma. "I suppose having friends is a good thing." She and Jonathan had become friends. And she kind of owed him one for taking the blame for the salt. "Hey, Rudy, how much do you want for this?"

The man behind the counter turned down his television again. "You can take it for twenty dollars."

"That's not enough." He'd probably paid more than that at the estate sale he bought it from.

"Merry Christmas." He waved her off and turned up the television again.

"Thanks, Rudy. It'll make the perfect gift." She couldn't wait to see Jonathan's face when she gave it to him.

MELODY LINED UP THE TEACHER GIFT CARDS ON THE kitchen table—each one neatly wrapped with a scarf she'd selected from the boutique and secured with red and silver foil ribbon.

And then there was the mixing bowl.

She'd wrapped that too—in festive red and green paper. You could still tell it was a bowl though, so it wouldn't be some big surprise when Jonathan opened it. When would he open it? At school? In his office? Would everyone know she'd given it to him? The gift had seemed like a good idea at the time, but would it make her feelings for him too obvious?

She slumped into a chair at the table. Oh, how quickly she'd forgotten the complications that romantic feelings could introduce into daily life—the wondering, the analyzing, the questioning.

"Hey, Mom." Tate bounded down the stairs and went straight for the breakfast sandwich she'd made him.

"Good morning, sweets." She assessed his outfit with a wince. Track pants and a Marvel sweatshirt? He'd clearly missed the memo for his big fifth-grade choir concert after their holiday party today.

"Why aren't you dressed?" One by one, she picked up the gifts and put them in the box she had waiting. "Come on, Tate. We're going to be late for school."

"I *am* dressed." Her cherubic son shoved half of the egg sandwich into his mouth. Like her, he was definitely not a morning person, and normally she could let his choice in apparel slide, but not today.

"You can't wear that outfit for the holiday concert." She poured him some orange juice to soften the blow. "There's a dress code. Remember? Your shirt has to have buttons on it." She'd gotten a text from his teacher to remind her. In her parenting philosophy, her kids should have autonomy when it came to getting dressed—they were the ones who had to take ownership of their own appearance, after all. But today her hands were tied.

"I don't see why we've gotta dress up to sing some songs," Tate mumbled with a full mouth.

"Because all of the loving parents and grandparents and aunts and uncles will be taking pictures of you and your classmates singing those songs." She kept her voice light and sweet, even while she had one eye on the clock. "That's why I brought you that awesome outfit from the boutique."

"The shirt's itchy." He downed the juice.

"So wear a shirt under it." She knew for a fact that the shirt was a pima cotton blend, but she didn't argue. "Go back upstairs and change, please. Pronto."

Little did Tate know that when he looked at her with such a grumpy furrow in his forehead he reminded her exactly of his sweet four-year-old self. If only she could hug him to her and smooch his cheeks to make him giggle the way she used to.

"I don't even like singing." He did, however, enjoy stomping out of a room.

"Thanks, honey," she called as he disappeared.

And now, back to the mixing bowl.

Maybe it didn't have to be a big deal. Since she'd be staying at school to help the boys' teacher with the holiday party, they could secretly leave it in Jonathan's office without a tag. Like an anonymous gift from Santa. As far as he knew, it could be a gift from anyone. Even Santa. Smiling to herself, Melody added the package to the box.

"Hey, Mom." Finn bounced into the kitchen dressed in the pants, button-up shirt, and vest she'd laid out for him last night. He'd even combed his curly hair away from his forehead.

"Wow. Lookin' sharp." She almost reached for her cell phone to snap a picture but then thought better of it. There'd be a whole lot of pictures today. She didn't need to waste her few chances at the breakfast table.

"Why, thank you." Finn took a bow before settling in at the table. "Do you think Ms. Sanderson will like my outfit?"

Melody hid her grimace underneath a smile. She'd totally forgotten to discuss the Ms. Sanderson crush with him after the cookie swap. "Oh. Yeah, sure. I bet she'll think you're *adorable*." Seeing as how the woman could probably be his grandmother. She'd always hated to burst any of the boys' bubbles, but this one would have to pop sooner than later—preferably without too much heartache or embarrassment. "Um, so is there anyone in *your class* you want to impress?" Hopefully . . .

"Nah. All the girls care about are their clothes and their hair." Finn tucked a napkin into the collar of his shirt. "And they also tell on me when I do something they don't like. But Ms. Sanderson and I talk about *real* stuff."

"Oh?" It was pretty cute how he got all starry-eyed when he talked about Ms. Sanderson. She poured him a glass of juice. Her younger twin had always been quite the conversationalist. He'd spoken his first word six months before Tate and had then proceeded to talk for his brother as much as he talked for himself.

"Yeah, we talk about *Star Wars*," he said around a mouthful of food. "She's seen all the movies and she knows *everything*. Plus, sometimes she gives me a couple extra chicken nuggets."

"Wow." No wonder he was smitten. What fifth grader could compete with chicken nuggets and *Star Wars*? She'd developed a swallowing technique to assist her when she needed to hold back a giggle so the boys wouldn't think she was laughing at them. But this crush thing was simply darling. Melody turned to put the juice back into the refrigerator.

"I'm ready," Tate grumbled behind her.

She faced him and resisted the urge to straighten his collar. "You look very nice." And so grown-up. A trapped sigh tightened her chest. The urge to press pause on the time button kept getting stronger and stronger. "We need to be on time. Can you grab the box of gifts for me?"

She grabbed her coat off the rack and slipped it on before following the boys out to the car.

"Why'd you get Mr. Braxton a bowl again?" Tate shoved the box of gifts onto the back seat between him and Finn.

"*I* didn't get him the bowl." Her cheeks warmed while she waited for the garage door to open. They slipped most of the way down the driveway. "*We* got him a bowl. For Christmas.

Because he likes baking. We always buy Mr. Braxton something."

"But no one gets Mr. Braxton *real* gifts." Finn was still working on his breakfast sandwich. "Everyone gives him pencils and candy and stuff. He's the *principal*." He said the word like he was talking about Darth Vader. "It'll be *so embarrassing* to give him something nice."

Melody's shoulders tensed. Maybe he was right. Maybe the copper relic had been a mistake. "It doesn't have to be a big deal. I was thinking we'd leave the bowl in his office and he won't even know who it's from." Then there'd be no analyzing anything on either side. No rumors would start about the lavish gift they'd given the principal. And Jonathan wouldn't know how much she was thinking about him.

"Like a secret Santa gift?" Finn held up the bowl, examining the packaging.

"He'll probably like it," Tate muttered, still stewing about the wardrobe change. "Since he likes baking and stuff."

That was what she'd thought, but she should've left well enough alone and found a nice pen and notepad instead. "Remember, it's a *secret* Santa gift, so don't tell him where it came from. It'll be more fun that way." Not to mention safer.

"Okay." Finn set it back in the box and started humming "The Twelve Days of Christmas."

Melody joined in and the tension in her shoulders instantly loosened. It would be fun to do a secret Santa gift. They should do more of that—giving gifts anonymously. Maybe she'd bring that up at the next cookie committee meeting. They could start a new tradition in town.

Cars already packed the school parking lot, so Melody headed for the back forty. "We're going to have to hustle inside." They had approximately five minutes before the bell rang. "Finn, you grab the gift box. Tate, you get the party games box out of the back. Come on, boys, let's move, move, move!"

They exited the car in a flurry of chaos, her grabbing her purse, them grabbing backpacks and boxes, and then booking it across the parking lot, rushing through the doors with two minutes to spare. She could officially consider her morning workout done.

Dodging frantic kids and parents, she followed the boys to their classroom. "Once we get inside, I'll grab Mr. Braxton's gift and—"

"Good morning, boys." Jonathan greeted them at the classroom door. "Ms. Monroe." His gaze swept over her before refocusing on the boys. "You made it just in time."

"Mmm-hmm." It was half murmur, half throat clearing, because the shock of seeing him standing there crushed her windpipe. "What're you—" She coughed. "Um, what're you doing in the classroom?"

Jonathan always started out the day in his office. Always.

"Both of my fifth-grade teachers are out with strep throat." He used his authoritative principal tone, definitely not the same voice he'd spoken in when they'd had their exchange in the library. "So I'm subbing in here, and Nancy is subbing in the other class."

"Great." Her smile felt all wrong. "Okay. Well. This'll be fun, then." She'd get to spend the whole day awkwardly interacting with him in front of the boys and twenty other kids.

"Can I put the box down now?" Finn shifted his weight side to side.

"Yes, yes." She nudged him away from Jonathan before he could look at the gifts too closely. "We'll pass those out later."

"Is that a bowl?" Jonathan asked.

Too late. His secret Santa gift had been spotted. "I don't know," she said mysteriously, this time steering Finn and the box to the table at the back of the classroom. "Can't ruin any surprises." And Jonathan could not open their gift in front of all these kids. They'd talk! Parents would find out. She could hear the rumors now.

Melody helped Tate set down the box of party games, and then both boys trotted away to hang up their backpacks.

"That sure looks like a rather large bowl." Jonathan approached and picked up the wrapped package. "And it feels pretty solid . . ."

"That's for you, Mr. Braxton. It was supposed to be your secret Santa gift," Finn said behind her.

Melody closed her eyes so she couldn't see his reaction. "It was supposed to be a surprise," she half whispered. Not to mention completely anonymous.

Finn stepped in front of her. "You should open it." Her younger twin had always loved giving people gifts.

"How do you know it's for me if it's a secret?" The principal's dimple peeked out at her.

"Because my mom picked it out for you at Rudy's store."

Melody looked around them to make sure none of the other fifth graders had picked up on this conversation. Thankfully, the typical first-thing-in-the-morning chaos was in full swing, kids hanging up their coats and backpacks. "I didn't exactly pick it out," she said too loudly. "We all were doing some Christmas shopping together—the boys and my dad and I. And I came across the mixing bowl. It's so unique. I thought it would be a shame to leave it on the shelf. I know you bake a lot so it seemed like you could use it." She stopped

there. Overexplaining might lead him to believe she was trying to cover her tracks because the gift meant something
deeper than it should.

Jonathan's smile widened, reaching for the corners of his
eyes. He carefully peeled the paper away from the bowl.

Why had anticipation started to thump through her heart?
She gave her collarbone a little tap to settle it down.

"What d'you think?" Tate had joined them now, a look of
hopefulness gaping his mouth. "Do you like it?"

"Are you kidding? I love it." Jonathan let the paper fall to
the floor as he studied the copper surface. "Really." His eyes
rose to hers, and they were filled with something she'd never
seen there. Almost like wonder. "It's exactly like one my
grandma used to have."

"Okay. Good." Her voice had gone hoarse. "Hopefully you
can use it." His whole face had come alive—like this was the
best gift he'd ever been given . . .

"I'll use it for sure." He stared at her like they were the
only two people standing there—even while twenty-two kids
milled around. "I have a lot more cookies to make for Cookie
Daze."

"Is this where the party is?"

Melody's stomach curdled. What was Charlene doing here?

The woman carried her own box of games and activities
to the table.

"Good morning, Charlene."

It was amazing to watch the transformation in Jonathan's
expression take place. His cheeks went stiff and his smile
evened out into a polite curve. "We're just getting ready to
start class. The party will start in about a half hour." He
stooped to pick up the wrapping paper he'd dropped and

quickly set it onto the table, along with the mixing bowl. "We have a math quiz to do first." There was his principal voice—the one Melody had grown so accustomed to hearing. Not the same soft velvety tone he'd used seconds ago.

The kids were groaning as they took their seats, and Jonathan quickly dodged Charlene to move to the front of the class, instructing them all to take out a notebook.

"I saw that you signed up to take the lead on the party this year." Charlene set her bigger box down next to Melody's. "But I figured you could use some backup. Being the party mom is a big job, so I decided to be your co-hostess for the day."

"Actually, I think I have this covered." She didn't even want to give her the satisfaction of looking offended.

"Well, since I'm here . . ." Charlene started to unpack an assortment of festive plates and napkins—which Melody had brought too. "Mr. Blaire called me last night to tell me he just got a positive strep test so Jonathan would be stepping in for him today." She leaned closer. "He thought the more help Mr. Braxton had today, the better off everyone would be."

So Mr. Blaire didn't think Melody could handle the party either? She straightened her posture. "I'm perfectly capable of handling this myself."

"Of course you are." The woman rested a placating hand on her shoulder. "But the more the merrier, right? Especially this time of year."

Right. This time of year should be about goodwill and generosity and giving and harmony. She really shouldn't be eyeing the copper mixing bowl like it could be used as a weapon right now. That in mind, Melody carried *her* box of supplies to a different table along the far wall. "We can make this the food table. I'll set up over here while you take care of the crafts." They would divide and conquer, and then no one would have to witness her not-so-festive side.

While she spread the tablecloth, Melody listened to Jonathan give a math review. He was good up in front of the kids, authoritative but also patient and funny. She'd never thought of him as funny before. But she found herself smiling when he told the kids he always tried explaining fractions to people at parties, but it really divided the room.

A collective groan rose up, but the students were also smiling and giggling. When Jonathan glanced her way, she realized she was staring at him and probably smiling too much. So she turned back to the table and set out the plates, napkins, and silverware, arranging and rearranging so she wouldn't get distracted by a certain sweater-vest-clad principal again.

"Plates should really go over here." Charlene crowded in and moved the stack of paper plates to the other side of the silverware. "I brought some too. I wonder if mine would be a better color for this tablecloth."

Melody counted out a ten-second inhale before answering—a technique she often used with the boys. "Let's just use what's out and add yours if we need more." She made sure her tone didn't leave room for negotiations. She'd already lost out on the activities she'd brought. Charlene had taken up the whole table with what looked to be an intricate glass ball ornament craft. There went Melody's pet-snowman-in-a-jar idea.

"Sure. We can use my plates for the parents since they care a little more about presentation."

Melody wanted to iron those condescending wrinkles out of Charlene's nose.

"I've never heard Jonathan make so many jokes," Charlene murmured, arranging the napkins into a fan pattern. "He's really lightened up lately. There're rumors going around that he's dating someone."

"Dating?" Melody's mouth went dry. "Why would people think that?"

"Maybe you haven't spent much time with him lately, but he's off his game." Her knowing expression matched her tone perfectly. Charlene loved being the bearer of gossip. "I mean, can you believe he accidentally used salt in his cookies instead of sugar?"

"No. I can't." She'd continued to wonder if Charlene had anything to do with that ingredient switch, but her surprise about Jonathan's "mistake" appeared genuine. So who had sabotaged him?

"He's also been late to meetings," Charlene went on. "And apparently he's not being nearly as strict as he usually is."

Melody snapped a quick glance in the principal's direction. He was going over instructions for the quiz. "That doesn't mean he's dating someone. Maybe he's stressed about the holidays or something."

"But he seems happier." Charlene crossed her arms, not even hiding the fact that she was staring at the poor man. "I mean, look at him right now. Have you ever seen him smile so much at school? And he was making all those cheesy jokes earlier."

They weren't cheesy. Melody clamped her mouth shut. Charlene was already sniffing around, and, if something did happen between her and Jonathan, Charlene would be the last person on earth Melody would share it with.

The woman tsked. "I wonder who's gotten to him. I mean, there've been many who've tried."

And she would know this how? Charlene had been married to the president of the bank for fifteen years.

"Have you heard anything?" Her arched eyebrows gave her a villainous look. "He'd better not be dating someone from the school. That would be completely inappropriate. I mean, talk about a conflict of interest."

"No. How would I have heard?" The words came out too defensively. Melody moved to the end of the table so she could straighten the edge of the cloth. "I have no idea who Jonathan could be interested in, er, dating. Besides, it's really none of our business." It shouldn't be anyone's business what Jonathan did on his own time.

"Hi, ladies," the man himself said behind her. "Thanks for getting everything set up."

Melody's knees weakened. She didn't turn to look at him in case Charlene noticed something amiss.

"Don't worry, I brought some other plates we can use for the parents who attend," Charlene said.

"I like these plates."

Melody could *feel* him looking at her. But what would Charlene see if she looked back? She was losing the ability to act indifferent when Jonathan got this close to her.

"This whole table looks great. What a nice setup."

"Mmm-hmm." In times like these, it was best to stick with business. Melody straightened the napkins. Again. "Parents will be here in an hour to join the party." The room would be crowded with a lot of people, so she'd never be caught alone with him and hopefully Charlene wouldn't pick up on anything.

"That'll be perfect." Jonathan checked his watch. "I gave them a half hour to complete the quiz, and then I'll have them put their stuff away and get ready."

"Sounds good." She knelt to hide her box of abandoned activities under the table.

"Mr. Braxton, let me show you the activities I brought." Charlene turned all sugary sweet. "Wait until you see how fun the craft project is."

Melody stood up to the sound of them walking away.

For the next half hour she kept herself too busy to talk to Jonathan or Charlene. Instead, she focused on greeting parents, instructing them on where to set out the food they'd brought, and setting up the Minute to Win It Games. Once the party was in full swing, she stayed in the background and snapped pictures on her phone.

See? She could host a successful classroom party. Except they were running low on punch. After snapping one more picture of Finn and Tate doing the reindeer balloon race, she snatched the punch bowl and made her way to the cafeteria, where she found Ms. Sanderson washing dishes.

"Hey, Melody." She dried her hands on a towel. "Can I make you more punch?"

"I've got it." Ms. Sanderson likely had enough work to do. She found the sodas a parent had brought in the refrigerator and started mixing the magic potion that had gotten an entire classroom of kids hopped up on sugar.

"That Finn is such a sweetheart." Ms. Sanderson stashed a large bowl on a high shelf. "He gave me a *Star Wars* Pez dispenser with a sweet note for Christmas."

"He thinks pretty highly of you too." Melody found a spoon and stirred the punch. "In fact, I think he might have a little crush on you."

"Are you serious?" Ms. Sanderson broke out in a belly laugh. "Well, that just made my day. No one's had a crush on me in a very long time."

"I know the feeling." Until recently. She continued to stir

the punch, something in her heart stirring too. Maybe her feelings for Jonathan were a conflict of interest, but they'd also brought a new energy to her daily routine. It was fun to have a crush on someone. "All right." She rinsed the spoon in the sink and handed it to Ms. Sanderson. "I'll see you next week when I have the honor of being your cafeteria volunteer."

The woman laughed. "You must've drawn the short end of a stick, huh?"

"I lost a bet." But now that bet made her smile. She didn't mind losing to Jonathan much. And how bad could working in the cafeteria be anyway?

Carefully, she carried the punch bowl back down the hall. She was just about to refill the pretzel bowl when her phone chimed in her back pocket.

Melody scanned the room as she pulled it out, finding Jonathan in the opposite corner. He was gazing down at his phone with a smile.

Thank you for the gift. It's been a while since someone has surprised me with something so thoughtful. A single red rose emoji punctuated the text.

Her heart fizzed as much as the punch. She crossed to the bookshelves so she could shield her phone screen from the crowds around her. I kind of owed you one for making up a story to bail out the boys and me. I guess we're even.

I don't think we are. He added a sad face emoji. I wish we were alone right now.

Melody laughed out loud and then quickly covered her mouth. Why is that? she teased.

"Melody? Melody!" Charlene waved to her. "Can you be a doll and run to the supply closet and grab more paper towels for me?"

"Happy to!" Normally she wouldn't have let her co-host order her around, but she shot out of the room with her phone suspended in front of her face.

If we were alone, we could finish our conversation.

Maybe we can find a way to be alone soon . . . As she typed, she swore her heart started to spin in dizzying circles. What was she *doing*? She had no idea but she couldn't stop.

Yes, please. Begging hands. Just tell me when.

When? She had no idea! When would she possibly be able to sneak away for a secret rendezvous with her kids' principal?

Melody inhaled deeply, opening the supply closet doors to find a roll of paper towels. Staying hidden in the closet, she typed back, We may have to get creative.

I'm more creative than people give me credit for came right back at her.

Before she could answer, another message chimed in. I have to know . . . was that text really meant for someone else?

Melody froze in place, grasping at the courage to be honest—to take a risk. To tell him the truth. To admit she had feelings for him. She didn't know if she could, so she turned to move out of the closet.

And there he was. Jonathan. Standing two feet away. He said nothing, only waited for her to make a choice.

Fear threatened a coup, but a sudden overwhelming strength suppressed her doubts. It almost took more effort to be afraid. "I wasn't texting my sister." She gambled with a step closer to him, meeting his gaze. "The eggplants were a total texting mishap, but I meant the other part—"

"Did you find the paper towels?" Charlene squawked from halfway down the hall.

"Yep! Here they are!" Melody raised the roll in the air and then fled from Jonathan before she could say another word.

Thirteen

"THE COOKIES MIGHT BE A DISAPPOINTMENT, BUT THIS mulled wine could win best cocktail of the evening." Kels poured another ladleful into her insulated cup.

"I think you've probably sampled enough now, sis." Melody turned up the Crock-Pot a notch, inhaling the spicy cinnamon aroma. They'd set up their cookie and cocktail station along the wall closest to the boutique's checkout counter—the best place to encourage those extra purchases.

The sparkly red tablecloth and silver plates and napkins looked quite festive, in her opinion. And the best part was she hadn't had Charlene looking over her shoulder rearranging everything. "I don't know what you're talking about. These cookies might be my best effort ever." She'd taken a rule out of Jonathan's playbook—keep it simple and go with a classic, which also happened to be her specialty—sugar cookies made from store-bought dough. No stress, and they'd been done in a half hour.

After the contest debacle, she'd given up on trying to win the cookie queen crown. She was happy to let Jonathan remain the champion forever. A lovesick sigh slipped out. They'd been texting constantly over the last few days, but between her spending time with the boys and preparing for this event and Jonathan getting in as much time as he could with Ainsley, they still hadn't actually seen each other.

"We are going to be *so* busy tonight." Kels restocked their shopping bags.

"You're sure you don't mind if I walk around with the boys?" She had to ask one more time. Even though her mom and Aunt Bernice would be helping Kelsey cover the registers and hand out cookies and cocktails, she still felt guilty about leaving.

"Are you kidding?" Her sister carried her cup to the checkout counter and turned on the music. "Genevieve is home with a sore throat, so it's not like I can walk around with my fam anyway. I'm happy to stay here and party while I hand out cookies. And drink mulled wine." She raised her glass a little higher.

"I'm sure we won't be out the whole time." Melody glanced at her watch. Customers would likely start arriving in less than a half hour.

"Don't worry about it." Kels had focused on the computer, getting it all fired up for a big night. "You go have fun with the boys. I know how much you love the crawl."

Yes, the Cookie and Cocktail Crawl and Cookie Daze were her absolute favorite events of the entire holiday season. "Remember how Thomas used to wear his light-up suit and glasses?"

"He was always the favorite of the entire cookie crawl," Kels said fondly. "I loved how the tourists would make him stop to take a picture with them."

Melody laughed. "He loved it too." And, while the first couple of crawls after his passing had been difficult, now walking through the shops at night sampling cookies and cocktails with almost everyone in town made her feel close to him again. Those memories brought warmth and laughter. "I'm just glad the boys and I can continue the tradition." As a surprise, she'd found them all Christmas light bulb necklaces to wear in honor of their dad. "It's going to be a great night."

"Why don't you three get all bundled up, and I'll take a couple pictures before you head out," Kels suggested.

Melody practically skipped to the break room, where Finn and Tate were playing their video games. "Are you boys almost ready to go?"

"Go where?" Tate didn't look up from the screen of his device.

"We're going to walk around the cookie crawl like we always do, silly." She dug their coats and hats and gloves out of the bag she'd brought.

"And I'm going to take some pictures before you leave, so no complaining." Kels had followed her into the room.

Finn turned off his device and stuffed it into his backpack. "Mikey and Noah and Jett asked if we could walk around with them. Doesn't that sound awesome?"

A pain stabbed her chest right at her heart's center. "I thought we'd walk around together." They always did the cookie crawl together. And she had those lighted necklaces in honor of Thomas . . .

"Noah and Mikey and Jett's parents said they could go on their own." Tate stood by his brother. "Can we? Please, Mom?"

No teetered on the tip of her tongue. But she wouldn't be making that decision for them. It would be selfish. So she could spend the evening with them and not have to walk around alone. So she could feel closer to Thomas and relive a memory, when they were ready to grow and move on.

Tate held his hands in prayer. "We'll all stick together and just do the crawl and then we'll come right back to the store."

"We promise," Finn added. "You can trust us."

"I know I can." And it wasn't like she worried about them. She knew almost everyone in town. She also knew she had to start giving them these moments of independence if they were ever going to become functioning adults someday.

"So that's a yes?" Tate's posture teetered on the edge of an exuberant leap. "We can go?"

"Sure." That was all she could say without her voice cracking. She bit the inside of her cheek to keep tears at bay while the boys jumped around cheering and high-fiving.

A throat-clearing beat the emotion out of her tone. "But you'll need to bundle up. Wear your hats and gloves the whole time."

"We promise." They started to pull on their winter clothes while she trudged back to the checkout counter.

"Aw, sweetie. Come here." Kels pulled her into a one-armed hug. "You're such a good mama."

"Do I have to be?" Melody let herself whine. Sometimes it felt good to whine. "Would it be wrong to follow them at a distance?" They wouldn't even have to know she was there.

"Here." Her sister hurried to the Crock-Pot and ladled a small cup of the mulled wine, setting it in front of her. "We'll stay here and drink together, you and me. We'll have our own party."

"That sounds dangerous." Her sister could outdrink her any day of the week. Melody had always been a lightweight.

"Did they have to start giving up everything all at once this year? I mean, first writing letters to the North Pole and then visiting Santa, and now I don't even get to do the crawl with them." She'd get all of the whining out now, before the boys emerged and heard her going on like a four-year-old.

"It sucks," Kels agreed loyally. "We give birth to them. No big deal. And then they ditch us."

The camaraderie took the edge off the ache under her breastbone. At least she could always count on Kels for company.

"We're going, Mom!" Finn appeared first, beanie not even pulled down over his ears.

"Thanks for letting us go!" Tate didn't have his coat zipped up.

"Stick together." She marched to Finn and pulled down his hat and then gestured for Tate to zip up his coat as she made her way to the drawer where she'd hidden the light bulb necklaces. "I got these for you." She took out two, leaving hers in the drawer so they wouldn't see it.

"Like Dad used to wear!" Finn bounded over and grabbed his, switching it on before pulling it over his head.

"Cool." Tate grinned, pushing the button on his until the lights blinked. "Thanks, Mom."

She opened her arms. They were still required to give her hugs, darn it. "Call me if you need anything. And have fun." She shouldn't forget that part.

"We will," they said at the same time, both offering her the mandatory goodbye embrace.

Only two years ago, she might've kissed their sweet heads, but not tonight. Tonight she stepped back and waved them out the door, only snapping one lone picture on her phone.

Rather than allowing herself to wallow, Melody made the

rounds through the store, greeting crawlers and offering her assistance with picking out clothing to any browsers while her mom and Aunt Bernice and Kels offered cocktails and cookies and checked out customers. Within a half hour, their scarf rack had been picked through, so she found the stock in the back and worked on refilling the shelves.

"Hey, Melody."

Jonathan's voice stood her up straight and she bumped her head on the arm of a nearby mannequin. "Oopsie. Jona—Mr. Braxton." What was she supposed to call him in public these days? "Hey." The sight of him made her knees instantly weak, but she had to hold herself together. It wasn't like they could talk about anything important. Here. With all these people around.

Besides, a teenaged girl stood with him. His daughter, Ainsley. She recognized her from the pictures he'd shown her. Wow, talk about a resemblance. They had the same dark eyes with thick lashes, and she had a dimple in the exact same place, except hers seemed to show all the time.

"This is Ainsley." Jonathan put his arm around his daughter. "I told her all about the boutique, and she was dying to do some shopping."

"I *love* shopping." Ainsley stuck out her hand. "Nice to meet you, Ms. Monroe. My dad has told me a lot about you."

He had? The best kind of heat clouded her face. "It's lovely to meet you too. I love that top you're wearing."

"Thanks!" Ainsley looked around. "I like your store. There's so much fun stuff! Can I look around for a while, Dad?"

"Take your time." Jonathan grinned as she walked away. "She wasn't too sure about coming to the cookie crawl until I told her about your store. Then she couldn't wait."

"I'm glad you brought her." She picked up the empty box that had held the scarves, but Jonathan quickly took it out of her hands. "I thought you were supposed to be out walking around with the boys tonight."

Just last night she'd told him over text how excited she was to spend the evening with them. But she also didn't want to cry in front of the man when they hadn't even been out on a date yet.

"Oh. Uh, no." She did her best not to let her face fall and directed him to the break room, pointing out where he could set the box. "Turns out I'm pretty busy here tonight, so Finn and Tate headed out with their friends."

"We're not *that* busy." Kels poked her head into the room at the most opportune time. "She could go out on a walk, if she wanted to. Or if someone else wanted her to. I'm *just* saying."

"Why don't you *just* add more oranges to the mulled wine?" Melody mumbled with the same look she used to serve up when her sister used to tease her and her high school boyfriend.

Kels giggled mischievously and disappeared.

"Sorry." Melody took the plastic wrap off another platter of her very special cookies. There was no way she wanted to intrude on Jonathan's time with Ainsley. She knew how much it meant to him. "Kelsey's been sampling our cocktail this evening." She slipped out the door to place the platter on their table with Jonathan at her heels.

"Is everything okay?" he asked when she turned back around.

The kindness in his voice caught her off guard. She'd purposely kept a distance from him, a shield up since there were so many people around, but now all that protection fell away. "Why?"

He simply gazed at her for a few seconds before answering. "Your eyes . . . they just aren't as bright as they usually are."

A weight fell off her. Why was she even trying to pretend? He saw through her anyway. "You know how much I was looking forward to hanging out with the boys . . . Only they weren't as excited about going with me. They wanted to go with their friends instead." Melody ladled him a cup of wine, then walked away from the table, away from everyone else with Jonathan at her side. "It doesn't matter." Maybe it wouldn't matter if she kept telling herself that. "They're getting older and they *should* be walking around with their friends. That's what's supposed to happen."

"But you miss the time with them." His gaze found Ainsley across the room. "Trust me. I know. If my wife hadn't found someone else she preferred to be with, I probably would've stayed in a not-so-great marriage so I could be with Ainsley all the time." He watched his daughter hold a sweater up and grin into one of the full-length mirrors.

In fact, the same sweater Melody had helped him pick out for her gift last week.

"We all know they're supposed to grow up and need us less," Jonathan went on. "But that doesn't make the process any easier. There's no good way to prepare for those moments when they start to choose other people over you."

"No. There's not." But somehow commiserating with him was making it a tad easier. If only she could move closer to him. Maybe he'd put his arm around her, hold her close . . .

"Look, Dad." Ainsley rushed over. "Isn't this gorgeous?"

"Stunning. It's Melody's own creation." He beamed an appreciative smile at her. "She's a talented designer."

Was she blushing? That seemed to happen a lot in Jonathan's presence.

"You designed this? Are you serious?" Ainsley started to inspect the garment. "So you don't, like, order things that are already made?"

"I prefer to come up with my own designs and then work with a tailor shop to produce them. That's why we have kind of a limited selection." She'd never dreamed she'd open her own store. In college she'd gotten her design degree, but then she'd landed a job in California. Once she'd married Thomas, they wanted to be close to family so they moved back, and she did some freelance work, but Thomas had always encouraged her to open a place on Main Street. If only he could see her now.

"That's the coolest job in the whole world," Ainsley said. "I'd love to be a fashion designer. Hey, maybe I can interview you for my school paper in Denver! I'm one of the reporters."

Melody had to laugh. No one had ever looked at her like a celebrity.

"I'd love that." She didn't get to talk design nearly enough. Finn and Tate had never been interested in hearing about styles and fabrics. She'd probably bore the poor girl half to death, but it would be fun to share her hard-earned wisdom with someone else.

"That'd be awesome!" Maybe her own children didn't want to be with her, but Ainsley couldn't seem to wait. "I'll be here the whole break."

"Perfect. You just let me know what works." Her schedule seemed to be opening up, whether she wanted it to or not.

"Can we get this sweater, Dad?" His daughter held up the Christmas gift he'd already gotten her. "Please?"

Wow. That puppy-dog face would be nearly impossible for Melody to resist.

"Well. Um. The thing is . . ." He shot Melody a panicked look.

"You know what?" She pulled her mouth into an apologetic frown. "I'm so sorry, but I need that one for an online order. That's the last one we have in stock, and I totally forgot to take it off the rack this afternoon."

"Oh." Ainsley's smile dimmed but didn't disappear completely. "That's okay. I get it." She handed the hanger to Melody.

Now she felt bad. "Don't worry. We should be getting more in right after Christmas. I can make sure to set one aside for you."

"That'd be great!" Ainsley wandered to a nearby rack of belts. "I think I'll keep looking around while you finish your wine."

"Sounds good." When his daughter ambled away, Jonathan raised his cup in Melody's direction. "Thanks for the save. I really want her to be surprised when she opens her gifts."

"Don't mention it." She took a napkin and offered him a cookie from the platter. "I should be thanking you for making me feel better about getting ditched by my kids." It was nice to know she wasn't the only one.

"I'm glad I could help." He took a bite of her store-bought sugar cookie. "These are delicious."

"Really?" A laugh overpowered the word.

"Yes." He finished the cookie and dusted the crumbs off his hands. "Have you tried them?"

"Of course." She'd eaten a few right after taking them out of the oven. For a second, she thought about letting him believe they were an original recipe but . . . "That's store-bought dough," she admitted. "Definitely not as good as yours. The boys are still talking about the gingerbread puppies you brought to the party."

"Those are always a hit at school." He grabbed another cookie. "But maybe I should give up baking and start buying dough at the store."

Melody laughed again. He made it easy. "Please don't. I'm not above admitting that your cookies really are the best. I can't imagine never eating another Mr. Braxton cookie."

"That's good to hear." He tossed both his empty cup and his napkin into the trash can. "Ainsley's apparently cutting back on sugar this year? And it's more fun when you have someone to bake for." Did she imagine the change in his tone on that last statement? The timbre seemed lower, almost . . . suggestive.

"Okay." Ainsley marched back to them. "If I keep looking around, I'm going to want to take this entire store home with me."

Where had this girl been her whole life? Talk about a self-esteem booster. "I take that as the highest compliment."

"You should because she's pretty picky." Jonathan winked at his daughter and she shot him a smirk. He shrugged. "All I'm saying is that we had to make a lot of post-holiday returns last year."

"That's because he has no sense of style," Ainsley whispered loudly.

"Hey." He looked down at his attire. "What's wrong with my style?" He seemed to address the question to Melody.

"Welllll . . ." Um, how should she put this? "It's very . . . *traditional*?"

Ainsley giggled. "That's a nice way of saying old-fashioned."

"Not exactly," Melody protested.

"Maybe it is time for an upgrade." He aimed a wary glance at the men's section. "If you're still willing to be my fashion consultant, I could come in sometime. When it's less busy." There was that tone again—the one that melted her insides.

"Really?" Ainsley was gaping at her father. "I've tried to help you plenty of times, mister. And you wouldn't listen. I see how it is."

"You're not a professional fashion designer, are you?" Jonathan's face appeared to have flushed slightly too. And that only made Melody's heart beat faster. If anyone looked at them right now—really looked at them—they would all see how much she'd grown to like him. And no one could know. So she turned away.

There was a line forming at the checkout counter now. She really should help. "Well, I'm glad you two came in tonight. Hope you enjoy the rest of your evening."

"You're not doing the cookie crawl?" Ainsley asked before she could walk away.

"Oh. No. I wasn't—"

"Actually she was really hoping to." Why did Kels always have to be within earshot?

"You should totally come with us!" Ainsley elbowed her father. "Right, Dad?"

"Yes. Please come." There was a surrender in the quiet invitation. A hopefulness. As if he wanted her to come and he didn't care who knew it.

"Go. Have. Fun." Her sister appeared at her side. "Mom and Aunt Bernice and I have this place covered."

"Okay." She wanted to surrender too. She liked being with Jonathan. Even if she shouldn't. And anyway, it wouldn't be like they were walking around *alone* together. Ainsley was with them. So who cared if a few people saw them meandering down Main Street as friends? "If you're sure I'm not intruding."

"The more the merrier." Jonathan gestured for her to lead the way.

"Here're your coat and hat and gloves." There was nothing subtle about Kelsey's wide grin. "Don't hurry back."

Melody hushed her with a stern look.

Jonathan held open the door for her and Ainsley, and then they ambled down the crowded street together.

With the colorful twinkling lights strung from lamppost to lamppost and the trees wrapped in white lights, the entire Main Street glowed. Each business had a different display in the storefront windows—Christmas trees and beautifully wrapped presents and nutcrackers and quaint villages.

"Oh, hey." Ainsley sped up. "There's Claire." She waved at a girl on the other side of the street. "Can I go say hi?"

"Sure." Jonathan stepped out of her way and then frowned, watching her walk away. "I have a feeling I'm about to get ditched too."

Melody laughed. "I hope this doesn't sound bad, but I'm glad I'm not the only one."

"I don't mind so much either." His gaze settled in hers, and she couldn't look away.

"Ainsley has finally made a few friends in town. I put her in an art class at the rec center this summer and she really connected with a couple of the kids. That makes it more fun for her when she comes to stay with me."

"I'm sure." Her heart ached for him a little. She couldn't imagine spending so much time away from the boys.

"Hey, Dad!" Ainsley waved her arms. "Can I walk around with Claire for a while?"

He raised his eyebrows at Melody. A silent *See?* "Sure," he called. "Just check in a little later."

"Thanks!" She and her friend scampered off.

"You know what this means?" Jonathan held out his elbow and she took it, steadying herself on the slightly slippery sidewalk. "We're finally alone."

A group of teenagers pushed past them, nearly knocking Melody over. "Not really." She peeked up at him, an anticipation building deep in her core. "But we could be. We could sneak away and walk in the park." No one would be over there right now with the cookie crawl going on.

"I love that idea." Jonathan switched their direction and they quickly crossed the street, walking past the shops to the end of the block.

"Ainsley seems like such a sweetheart." She hadn't spent much time with her, but she could already tell how respectful and creative she was.

"She's the best," Jonathan agreed. "Smart and vivacious and thoughtful. She's a lot like her mom."

Her expression must've given away her surprise because he laughed. "Her mother and I have had our differences, but Liz is an extraordinary person. She's energetic and gregarious and a brilliant businesswoman. I couldn't appreciate her more for how much she's invested in our daughter."

Melody was still too stunned to speak. It wasn't every day that you heard someone talk about their ex-partner that way.

"I'm not sure Ainsley is much like me at all," he said.

Now that simply wasn't true. "In my experience, kids are the perfect blend of their parents." That was the hope, right? That they would inherit all of the best traits of the people who loved them the most? "I see some of Thomas and some of me in both Finn and Tate. Though it does seem like they got their best things from their father." Thomas had been every bit as creative and active and funny as the two of them. She paused and gazed up at Jonathan while they waited for the light to change. "I know they can be a handful at school sometimes."

"Every kid is a handful." He offered his arm again, and they crossed to the sidewalk that led into the park. "Finn and Tate are also honest and creative and hilarious. And they work hard. Thomas must've been a good man."

"He was." It used to be that she couldn't talk about him without the tears flowing, but that ache had faded. Now she loved to remember him. "I wish he were here to see them grow."

"I can't imagine what that's like." He slipped his gloved hand into hers.

Melody held on to him, on to the understanding and empathy. "I've had them all to myself, and they've been the center of my world for six years now. I know things can't stay that way forever." The boys needed to grow and change and embrace an independence that would lead them to find who they were. "But I don't feel ready to let go either."

"I can relate." Jonathan guided her to the gazebo at the center of the park, all lit up with colorful twinkling lights. "Since Ainsley became a teenager, it seems like I'm having to let go more and more. I don't like it. But I'm doing my best to respect her space so she won't resent me later."

"That's wise." She wasn't sure she was proactively trying to give the boys room to grow up. It was more like she was being forced to. But tonight . . . right now in this moment . . . she didn't mind so much. She stopped walking and turned to face him. "I guess there is a bright side of letting your kids grow up."

"What's that?" he asked softly.

"It means you can do something for yourself." Something

like taking a walk with a man who'd reawakened her heart. "This might be the most fun I've had with anyone besides the boys or my sister in quite a while."

"Really?" The word hardly hovered above a whisper.

"Yeah." She couldn't figure out why he sounded so surprised. Was it possible he hadn't picked up on her attraction to him? "I don't get out much."

"Me neither." He hesitated. "Honestly, there hasn't been anyone I've wanted to get out much with. Until now."

"I think I know what you mean." Melody's heart clenched hard, and she could only breathe in short gasps.

Jonathan closed the distance between them, his gaze locking on hers. "What I was trying to tell you the other day, after the meeting, is . . ." He eased out a sigh. "I mean . . . I don't know. I can stand up in front of the entire school and talk without getting nervous or losing my train of thought." He paused, his voice softening. "But when I try to talk to you, Melody, like this—just the two of us, my heart beats faster, and I lose myself in your eyes and I don't even know what to say or how to tell you how much I admire you or that I think you're artistic and funny and beautiful and you're such a good mom."

She laughed. "I always figured you thought I was a hot mess." What with all of the tardies and the fibs . . .

"No." Jonathan stepped close enough that she could've easily touched her lips to his if she hadn't lost the ability to move. She wasn't laughing now. She was reeling from the intensity of a hunger she hadn't even known was there.

"*No.* Clearly I'm the one who's a mess." He studied her, then sighed. "I think you're so . . . you're just . . . I mean, I'd like to stop talking now so I can kiss you."

"Okay." The simple utterance scorched her lungs. "Yes." Jonathan was going to kiss her? Really kiss her?

The dimple completed his smile, and he took his time, drawing his face closer to hers, watching her with an unhurried anticipation.

She braced herself, prepared to hold back—to not lose herself—but when his lips touched hers, something unlocked in her chest, opening her up from the very center. Melody melted into him, knees unstable and lazy, arms threading around his waist to bring him in closer.

Energy crackled inside her, shining its light into every dark neglected region of her body.

Jonathan's hand cupped her jaw and then his fingers skimmed down her neck, making her skin tingle. His hands slid over her shoulders and then he held her to him, his lips grazing hers as she tasted cinnamon.

Melody pulled back to catch her breath and found herself staring into his eyes, her lungs winded and achy. "So I've been wondering something . . ."

"Yeah?" Jonathan brushed another kiss over her lips.

Whoa. How was she supposed to talk when he kept stealing her breath? "That text I sent . . . you never told me how you responded."

"No," he breathed against her neck. "You're right. I didn't." Jonathan swept her hair behind her ear and kissed her again, deliberate this time instead of teasing, firmly, decisively, seductively, opening his mouth to hers.

Desire shivered through her—not gone like she'd thought. Still very much alive. Melody wrapped herself against him, following the rhythm of his lips on hers. Oh, dear God. She had missed this. Kissing. Breathing like this. Wondering if her heart would give out. Melody backed up against the gazebo wall so she didn't sink to the ground.

"You really want to know what I said back?" he murmured, moving his lips along her jaw and then to her ear.

Uhhhhhh, know what now? The sensations in her body had started to overpower her brain.

"My response . . ." he whispered. ". . . said—"

"Hey, Tate, go long!"

That was Finn's voice. Finn! She broke away from Jonathan, an icy panic dousing the heat that kiss had generated.

Jonathan's wide eyes stared back into hers.

"They're on the other side of the pavilion," she hissed. Probably on their way to buy some candy at the concessions.

"Okay." He exhaled loudly and straightened his coat. "It's okay. There's no way they saw us."

"No. They couldn't have," she squeaked. "I'm sure they didn't." She sure as heck hoped not!

"Hey. It's all right." Jonathan pulled her close again, sealing her into a safe space between him and the gazebo wall. "Why don't we walk over there to check on them? Say hello?"

As much as she didn't want this to end—the kissing and the talking and whatever that was he'd done to her ear—they had to go. "Okay." She stepped away from Jonathan, smoothing her hair underneath her beanie.

They rounded the corner, her a few steps ahead of Jonathan, and there were Finn and Tate with their friends playing football near the concessions.

"Hey, guys." Somehow, Jonathan sounded completely normal. How was that possible when her lungs had shrunk at least three sizes?

All of the kids involved in the game paused.

"Hey, Mr. Braxton." Finn squinted. "And Mom?"

"What're you doing here?" Tate asked.

"We came to check on you." She swallowed against the lump burgeoning in her throat. "Mr. Braxton's daughter is out with some friends too, so we wanted to see where everyone was."

"Well, you found us." Finn threw the ball to Tate.

"How many cookies have you two had?" Jonathan asked cheerfully.

"Six," Tate said at the same time Finn said, "Nine."

He laughed. "Sounds like you still have some work to do then. I'm sure there're at least twenty more kinds out there."

Both boys grinned.

"Let's go check out the coffee shop," one of their friends called.

"See ya, Mom!" Tate took off with a wave.

"We'll be back at the shop soon," Finn promised.

"See you then." When they were gone, she let her back rest against a tree trunk to take some pressure off her shaky legs. "Holy moly. I might've just had a heart attack."

"Sorry." Jonathan was keeping his distance now. "I shouldn't have kissed you. Not here. Not like that."

Melody took her time answering, gathering her breath, calming her erratic pulse, and she thought back to what her dad had said at Rudy's place that night. About how his mom explained she couldn't stay where she was forever. About how you had to take risks in order to really live.

"Please don't regret it." Every part of her softened when she looked up at him. "I don't. It was . . . lovely." That was the only word to describe the unfurling. That kiss had opened her up. It had made her feel something again.

"I don't regret showing you how I felt." He moved closer again but stopped short of touching her this time. "I know a relationship could be . . . complicated. But I want to spend time with you. However that works. As friends or as . . . more, if that's what you want."

"I'd like that." In fact, she'd like to march him back to the gazebo and pick up where they left off, but more people had started spilling over into the park. "Though I think we've moved past the friend zone." Her lips tingled. She likely wouldn't be able to spend time with him without giving in to the temptation to kiss him again.

"I was hoping you'd say that." Jonathan took both of her hands in his. "How about I take you out after the next cookie committee meeting? We don't have to tell anyone. It can be our secret."

Melody nodded, her smile growing by the second.

Forget secret Santa. She was going on a secret date.

Fourteen

MELODY'S PLAN HAD BACKFIRED.

She'd arrived four minutes late to the meeting so she didn't have to chat with Jonathan too much before it started or surely everyone would see. Everyone would see her cheeks get all rosy when she talked to him. Everyone would hear the slight breathlessness in her voice. They'd pick up on the change that had taken place in her ever since the man had kissed her senseless. For two days she hadn't been able to focus. She'd been smiling and humming—not Christmas carols but love songs.

Four minutes late was supposed to ensure that she could walk into the conference room in the school's office and simply start the meeting before she even had the chance to get flustered, but her darn sister was waiting in the hallway.

"Whoa, hot mama." Kels added a few whistles.

At least no one else was around to hear her sister's teasing tone. They must've all been tucked away in the conference room already.

"I guess I didn't realize we were supposed to look *hot* for this meeting." Her sister watched her take off her coat and hang it up on the racks outside the office. "Clearly I missed the memo."

"I have no idea what you're talking about." She smoothed her black velvet skinny jeans and straightened the off-the-shoulder deep green sweater with metallic threads running through it, pretending she hadn't obsessed over this outfit for two hours earlier that afternoon.

"I thought it might be nice to wear something other than our athleisure line for once." Though Kelsey's reaction had her questioning her choices. Was this outfit too obvious? She didn't need the whole room full of cookie committee volunteers wondering why she'd suddenly decided to dress up. "It doesn't hurt to do a little advertising once in a while."

"I'm pretty sure you're not advertising the boutique's clothes to Deb and Nancy and Tracey, given the fact that none of them ever shop there." Kels frowned, sizing her up. "Wait a minute. Are you wearing *eyeliner*?"

Well, shoot.

"Aren't the boys spending the night with Mom and Dad?" Her sister gasped. "Is something going on with you and Jonathan?"

Busted. Melody hadn't told anyone about her date with Jonathan. She hadn't told anyone about the texts they'd been firing back and forth since the cookie crawl, or the two late-night phone calls. She didn't *want* to tell anyone because then she would have to deal with the complications.

Right now, this was her and Jonathan's secret to share.

"We should get inside. The director can't be late for the meeting." And she couldn't risk looking directly into her sister's eyes or she'd crumble and tell her the whole story.

"You're holding out on me," Kels complained, following her into the office. "I tell you all my juicy secrets."

Melody paused before going into the conference room. "You don't have juicy secrets." She hadn't either. Until now. Her heart sparked the way it had every time Jonathan's name lit up her phone screen the last few days, skin heating, limbs weakening. She couldn't wait to see Jonathan but she was so nervous . . .

"Are you blushing?" Kels had her hands on her hips now. In that posture, her sister meant business.

"We'll talk about it later." Melody pushed in through the door, silencing any more arguments.

Everyone had already taken seats at the table—Jonathan was at one end, so she snagged a seat as far away as she could get from him and forced herself not to stare in his direction. Kelsey took the seat three down from her, a distinct pout rumpling her face.

"Sorry I'm late, everyone." She sounded winded, even to herself. "Why don't we get started?" The faster they got this over with, the quicker she and Jonathan could sneak off into the moonlight. She made the mistake of glancing at him. Jiminy Christmas, he looked good with a shadowed stubble on his jaw. She seemed to remember that stubble grazing her neck.

Jonathan's mouth softened into a smile at her, and there went her sloppy lovesick grin again. She really had to get a hold of herself. "Um, let's see." She couldn't seem to stop touching her hair. "So, everyone, how do we think the cookie crawl went this year?"

"Friends I've talked to said that was the best one in years." Nancy applauded. "Well done, Melody. I haven't heard one complaint. And I talk to a lot of people."

The rest of the group joined in, but Melody silenced them with her hand. "It was a group effort. We all put in a lot of work."

"But you led us through it." Even Jonathan's voice brought a cascade of tingles spreading down her neck. "I can't remember ever having such a good time at the cookie crawl."

A giggle slipped out. A giggle!

Kels's eyes popped open wider, but thankfully she didn't say anything. The boutique had been so busy when Melody had returned that night that she hadn't even talked to her sister. And then Doug had called Kels because Genevieve had a fever, so she'd left in a hurry. Thankfully.

Moving on . . . "With Cookie Daze right around the corner, I thought we should talk about adding a few new events." She rummaged through the notes she'd made with the boys last night. "One idea was to add an obstacle race course where you collect as many cookies as you can."

"That sounds like fun." Tracey was taking notes too.

"How would that work, exactly?" Deb asked.

She started to detail the plans she'd brainstormed with Finn and Tate, but her phone screen kept lighting up with incoming texts from Jonathan.

You look beautiful.

Melody cleared her throat, a smile creeping in. "Finn and Tate would like to call the event the Great Cookie Race . . ."

The phone snagged her focus again. I have a surprise for you. A surprise? Her gaze crossed Jonathan's. He was grinning . . . and melting her into a pile of mush right there in her chair.

"Um. So." Melody was determined to ignore him and at least finish the meeting.

I can't wait until this meeting is over.

Her heart took the brunt of that message, skipping and floundering to find a rhythm. What had she been saying again?

"The Great Cookie Race sounds fun." Kels saved her. Her sister knew something was happening between her and Jonathan right now. She always knew.

"Yes. The Great Cookie Race." She coughed. "Um, Finn and Tate would like to take the lead on the event, and they've already got the whole thing planned out. As far as the other events, I've assigned each committee member specific oversight responsibilities." She flipped to the next page on her notes and blitzed through the breakdown of her plan for Cookie Daze volunteers before Jonathan could text her again. "I think that's it. Does anyone have any questions?"

"Just to clarify, we're storing all the cookies and baked goods we collect in the concessions kitchen at the park?" Nancy asked.

"Yes. I think that's best." According to Tracey, they used to store the cookies they collected from volunteers at Charlene's house, but it simply made no sense to have to pack them up multiple times. "Then no one will have to be responsible for transporting well over two thousand cookies to the park. I've let our volunteer bakers know that they can drop off their cookies the day before. And then we'll lock them up safe and sound in the concessions kitchen overnight."

"Got it." Nancy added the note.

"And do we all need to be there when people drop them off?" Deb asked. "Because I have a hair appointment that afternoon, and you know how hard it is to reschedule around the holidays."

"I can be there." Melody stacked up her notes and shoved them into her purse. "So can the boys. It's only a two-hour block of time."

"I'm happy to help too."

Was Jonathan's tone suggestive or was it just her? "That would be, um, great. Thanks." She noticed her mother looking back and forth between the two of them with a perceptive slant to her eyebrows. "Anyway. I can't wait for next weekend. I think this'll be the best Cookie Daze we've ever had. Any other questions?" This time she hardly gave a pause. "Great. Then I'll see you all on the big day."

Tracey, Deb, and Nancy started to chat about their favorite cocktails at the crawl while her mother and Aunt Bernice discussed the cookies they were planning to contribute for the Great Cookie Race.

No one moved except for Kels. "Hey, I need your opinion on something." Her sister started to drag her out the door. "In the hallway. It's personal."

Sure it was. Personal for Melody. She stepped out the door with Kels.

"You kissed him, didn't you?"

"Keep your voice down," she hissed. "How did you know?"

"I didn't until right now." Kels clapped and squealed. "I was only guessing but you looked suspicious. Oh my God, your first kiss in how many years? Six?"

"Does it matter?" She prodded her sister away from the door so Jonathan wouldn't hear. "It's not that big a deal."

"Of course it is. This is huge." Kels hugged her and then let go, doing a little dance. "Come on. I'm happy for you, that's all. Jonathan is sooo amazing and you are too." Her jaw dropped. "Wait a minute. Are you going out with him tonight? So that's why you're dressed up!"

Melody wished she could see inside the conference room. Why was everyone taking so long to leave? "Hush, will you?"

"You are!" Her sister didn't wait for a response. "That's why the boys are spending the night with Mom and Dad."

"Yes, we're planning to go out, okay?" she relented. "If everyone ever leaves, that is." The rest of the committee seemed content to loiter in the conference room all night.

"I'm on it." Kels marched to the door of the conference room and threw it open. "All right, everyone. Time to go. The cleaning crew needs to get in here ASAP."

Melody wanted to shrink into the wall. Could she be more obvious?

"I didn't think they were cleaning the building tonight," Nancy mused on her way past Melody.

"This time of year, I'll bet they have to clean every night." Deb slipped on her coat.

"Those kids are tracking in everything on their boots," Tracey agreed.

Aunt Bernice, her mother, and Joan paraded out the door next. "Bye, you three." Melody hugged them. "Thanks for coming."

"Aren't you leaving with us?" Aunt Bernice asked.

"She has to go back and get her purse." Kelsey stepped between their mother and their aunt and slung an arm around each of them. "But we need to head out now. I was hoping you three could make sure I get home okay. I think something might be wrong with my car."

"Oh no," their mother clucked. "We'll follow you for sure."

Kels glanced over her shoulder and winked before they disappeared out of the office.

Were she and Jonathan truly finally alone? A thousand butterflies beat their wings against her rib cage, carrying her back inside the conference room. She found him looking through a file folder at the table.

"Are they gone?" He shut the folder and stood. "I was trying to stall. I thought they'd never leave."

She must've been floating toward him because she couldn't feel the ground underneath her feet. "They were taking their sweet time. But, yes, they're gone. Now what was this surprise you were texting me about?" She couldn't believe how differently she saw Jonathan now. Three weeks ago, she'd been sitting in his office nervous and now here she was, openly checking him out. Trying to flirt.

Boy, was she out of practice.

"You'll see." Offering his arm, Jonathan escorted her out of the office, pausing to grab their coats. "I'll drive and then I can bring you back to your car later." He helped her slip on her wool jacket, and she realized how much she missed thoughtful gestures like that. Not only being on the receiving end but also offering the same polite courtesies to someone else. Thomas and she used to do that all the time—little things without thinking like pouring creamer into each other's coffees and setting out each other's favorite mug in the morning.

"I can't wait to see where we're going." The words came out softer than she intended. Everything inside her had gone soft, especially her heart.

"We're leaving town so we don't have to worry about running into anyone." He opened the door of his dark SUV for her. The car smelled like him, like cloves and cinnamon and hints of leather from the upholstery. In contrast to hers, the inside of this car was immaculate and orderly. But she did notice an empty to-go coffee cup in the cupholder, so he wasn't a total perfectionist.

"I like the sound of that." Going away with him—alone— where they could both let down their guard and simply be together. No one else needed to know they were spending time together until they figured out what they wanted to be. Maybe this was a fling. Maybe it was more. They didn't need to know right now. "As long as I'm home by ten." Finn and Tate would call to say good night, and she had to make sure she had service.

"I promise." Jonathan turned on the engine and cranked the heat, but despite the twenty-degree temps outside she hadn't even noticed the cold. Everything in her hummed with warmth and light.

Christmas carols started to play low.

"What's Ainsley doing tonight?" she asked as he drove out of the parking lot.

"She's hanging out with her art friend." He turned left on the main road. "She knows we're going out, though. I get that it's different with your boys." Jonathan glanced at her. "They're younger, and hearing that you're going on a date with the principal might not exactly go over well."

Ah, yes. She'd had this exact same conversation with herself earlier this afternoon. "I don't know, actually." She'd almost told them but hadn't found the right opening. "I've never talked to them about dating." She never thought she'd have to talk to them about dating. Falling in love again had seemed like an impossibility. Melody glanced at Jonathan's profile, his structured jaw, the curve of his lips, the strength of his neck, and longing flooded her.

"I haven't dated anyone since my divorce," he said, reaching for her hand. "We can take our time figuring things out. I want you to know I'm okay with whatever you decide when it comes to Finn and Tate. Really. I know they're the most important people in your life and I wouldn't want it any other way. And this is only our first date. You never know. You might decide you don't like me after tonight."

Melody laughed. "I appreciate that." She glanced out the window and relaxed back into the heated seat. They were already on the outskirts of town. "What about you? Could this date get you into trouble at work?" She was almost afraid to ask. She didn't want to worry, not when spending time with him felt so new and exciting and . . . right. How long had it been since she'd let herself get swept away in something wonderful and surprising?

Jonathan took his eyes off the road to smile at her. "Nah. There's no official policy barring me from dating a parent of my students, but I know this could be a little complicated."

"And probably frowned upon?" she prompted. Because she knew how the town gossip mill could churn.

He shrugged, one hand on the wheel and one still holding hers. "I'm sure there are some people who wouldn't like it. But you can never make everyone happy anyway." He shot her a grin. "Someone is always complaining to me about something. I can handle it."

"I'm sure you can." Could she? That wasn't a question she needed to answer tonight. Tonight they would be alone and she was free to embrace everything—the warmth of his hand in hers, the anticipation pounding through her pulse points, the light and laughter he'd brought into her life. Right now going out with Jonathan felt like freedom, and her only plan was to take this one date at a time.

"I hope you love your surprise." He turned off the main highway and followed a winding road back into the forest.

"I can't even begin to guess what we're doing." She looked around them. It was completely dark, but the stars lit up the endless sky, winking like they were in on the mystery.

"We're almost there," Jonathan murmured. "Close your eyes."

No one had ever planned a true surprise for her. Not like this. Thomas had been terrible at keeping secrets. "Why not?" She let her head rest against the seat and kept her eyes closed until the car stopped.

"Let me come around and open your door." The note of excitement in his tone made her heart start to drum.

Where could they be?

Within seconds, the door had opened and the cold air engulfed her face.

"Take my hands." He helped her out of the car. "Easy. It's a little snowy here." Coming alongside her, he slipped his arm around her waist and they walked several paces, their boots crunching in the snow. "Okay," Jonathan murmured. "You can open your eyes."

Color. That was the first thing that filled her vision. So many sparkling colors. Twinkling lights covered every tree in the thick forest, spiraling all the way up the trunks and draping the branches. Lanterns of all different colors and shapes dangled from the branches around them, making the foliage glow. "This is incredible." She turned in a slow circle, taking it all in. There were blue trees and pink trees and red and yellow and green and white. Hundreds of trees surrounding them, all dressed up in light.

"It's called the Enchanted Forest." Jonathan's smile glowed almost as brightly as the display around them. "The landowners here do this every Christmas, apparently. And they only ask for a donation if you're able."

For the first time, she noticed a few other people milling around, but everyone spoke quietly, in reverence to this fairy-tale world. "It's . . . magical." So vibrant and alive. She laughed even as tears heated her eyes. "I had no idea this was here." Or you could bet this would've been another one of her holiday traditions with the boys.

"Ainsley saw it on Instagram." His arm came around her waist again and they left the parking lot behind, ambling down one of the well-packed paths into the trees. "We came last week, and I kept thinking about how much you'd like it—the colors and designs."

Melody leaned into him, peering up into his eyes. "You were thinking about me?"

"I think about you a lot." He stopped them in a grove of trees adorned in blue lights of all shades and turned to face her, pulling her closer by her waist. "When I see something lovely or when something makes me laugh, I wonder if it would make you laugh too." His face lowered closer to hers. "You don't think about me?"

"When I'm getting the boys ready for school for sure," she teased. "Mostly because I don't want to be tardy."

Jonathan pouted. "That's not exactly what a man dreams about."

She slid her hands over his shoulders. "But I also thought about you last night when I was sitting by the fireplace in my living room after the boys went to bed." Courage gathered, filling her chest, making her lungs pull at their seams. "I wondered if you like sitting by the fireplace too." She'd wondered if he had been sitting there with her, would he hold her in his arms and maybe kiss her again?

"I do like sitting by the fire." His face drew closer, his eyes reflecting the lights around them. "But I think I would like sitting anywhere with you."

Melody gulped the cold air, then touched her lips to his, because he was right there and it had been too long. Shock waves already rocked her, sending quakes all the way down to her toes. Jonathan scooped his arms around her, holding her close, and even through all those winter layers between them she swore she felt his heart pounding with hers.

"I think I would like sitting anywhere with you too," she murmured against his lips. God, his lips. They claimed hers again, firmly, decisively, urgently, and she leaned into him, afraid her legs would give out. Jonathan held her up, their bodies pressed together, their breath rising between them in clouds. His tongue sought hers, electrifying every nerve ending, bringing flashes of light behind her eyelids.

How had she gone without this so long? This fire burning up her body and soul?

Melody clung to him, kissing him from the very depths of her, tears stinging even while she smiled against his mouth. She kissed him until her breath ran out, until those happy tears started to glide down her cheeks. And then she paused to look into his eyes, seeing the same flickers of hope that flashed inside her. "I'm going to have to tell the boys soon," she uttered. Because how would she be able to hide her feelings for him after tonight? She didn't even want to try.

"Tell them what?" Jonathan's innocent smirk teased her.

"I'll tell them Mr. Braxton surprised me in more ways than one," she murmured, brushing a kiss across his lips. "I'll tell them I like Mr. Braxton a lot . . . that I might even have a secret crush on him."

Her lips found his again, her whole body sighing.

She could not, however, tell the boys how much she liked kissing their principal.

Fifteen

"ALL I WANT FOR CHRISTMAS IS YOOOOUUU . . ." MELODY quickly looked around to make sure the boys hadn't heard her singing along—with feeling. *Phew.* Nope. They must still be in the break room with their heads bent over their very detailed plans for the Great Cookie Race.

Even if they had heard, they might not think much of it. She'd been singing ever since her very own fairy-tale romance in the Enchanted Forest. While she made dinner, while she showered, while she got ready in the mornings. And while she restocked the green off-the-shoulder sweaters, apparently.

"Make my wish come true. Baby, all I want for Christmas is—"

The bells above the door jingled. Oh good. A customer. She set the sweaters on a shelf. The store had been quiet ever since she'd picked up the boys after checking on all of the Cookie Daze decorations and equipment they'd stored in the locked shed at the park. She didn't want another surprise like the one they'd gotten at the cookie swap. All the supplies had appeared to be in good working order but she planned to check again tonight. Nothing could go wrong with the biggest event of the season.

In the meantime, she'd worked on restocking shelves, singing to herself, letting her thoughts drift to a certain principal.

Jonathan's daughter crept past the checkout counter.

"Ainsley!" She hurried to meet her, heart soaring as she searched for Jonathan behind her. But he wasn't there. "This is a pleasant surprise."

"I hope you're not too busy," the girl said somewhat nervously. "I was running some errands downtown and thought I'd stop by."

"I'm glad you did." She ushered her to the coat rack and gestured for her to hang hers up. "The store is pretty quiet today. Can I get you some tea or hot chocolate or anything?"

"That sounds great, actually." She seemed to relax. "I'd love some hot chocolate."

"We keep a ton of snacks and stuff in the break room too, if you're hungry." Melody walked her through the door. There were the boys, sitting quietly at the table, focused on their iPads. "These are my two sons, Finn and Tate." She pointed them out respectively. "Boys, this is Ainsley. Mr. Braxton's daughter." She almost slipped and called him Jonathan but caught herself just in time.

"Nice to meet you, Finn and Tate." Ainsley wandered to the table. "My dad has told me a lot about you."

"Probably because we get into trouble sometimes," Finn mumbled.

Melody cringed a little. He was normally a lot friendlier, but occasionally he still seemed to be a little bitter about the whole Cookie Contest debacle.

Ainsley laughed. "Not at all. He told me about the Cookie Contest and how you two should've beat him."

"We totally should've!" Tate agreed, finally looking up from the drawing he was working on.

"We would've won fair and square if it hadn't been for that mistake he made," Finn added.

"That's exactly what he said." Ainsley leaned over the table and looked at Finn's iPad. "What're you working on?"

"We're gonna run a great cookie obstacle race at Cookie Daze." Her son proudly held up the screen.

"It's gonna be the awesomest event there," Tate insisted.

"It sure is." With how hard they'd been working on plans for the last several days, Melody had no doubt the new race would be a big hit.

"Sounds like fun." Ainsley pulled out the chair and sat between the boys, just like that. Jonathan's daughter clearly had a way with younger kids. Melody wouldn't be surprised if she babysat.

"See?" Finn traced the lines of the drawing with the stylus. "The race'll start at the top of the hill. Teams'll race down on sleds picking up as many cookies as they can on the way and then they'll crawl through this tunnel." He paused as though wanting to make sure she was following. "One person has to pull the other person on the sled the whole time. That makes it a lot harder."

"We're gonna make the tunnel with pool noodles." Tate slid his iPad to Ainsley. "This is the diagram for how we're going to build it."

Ainsley studied the drawing, and Melody had to hand it to the girl. She seemed very interested. "Wow. That's pretty cool."

Finn tugged on her arm to get her attention back on him. "Then, after the tunnel, they'll have to pull the sled around these candy canes."

"They'll be set up like the slalom course in the Olympics," Tate said helpfully.

"Amazing."

"They're still going to be picking up as many cookies as they can the whole time." Melody wished she could capture Finn's serious expression in a picture. He was very concerned about all the details.

"The cookies will be in baggies so they don't get wet in the snow," Tate explained.

"That's really good thinking," Ainsley said sincerely.

"So far, that's all we have." Tate frowned. "We're trying to think of a really cool way to end the race, but we haven't come up with anything good enough yet."

"Hmmm." The girl's eyes lit up. "I know! What if you had the teams build a snowman to finish the race?"

"Yes!" Finn started to draw again. "That's brilliant."

"Perfect," Tate agreed. "It'd be one more hard obstacle, and then the team that gets their snowman done the fastest would win."

"Or we could do points." Finn tapped the stylus against his chin exactly the way his father would've. "They could get points for how many cookies they collect and then points for finishing the snowman first."

Melody wished she could start filming right now. She loved it when the boys tackled a project like this together—using their creativity to bring an idea to life. It was so much better than playing a video game.

"I love the points idea," Ainsley told the boys. "You should totally make sure everyone has to do a three-part snowman. Lower, middle, and upper so it's more of a challenge."

"Good idea." Tate scrawled some notes on the screen.

"Do you wanna help us be in charge of the race?" Finn asked slowly, like he was in awe of this teen girl who'd just walked into their lives.

Quite honestly, Melody was a little bit in awe herself. She hadn't anticipated that Ainsley would be so good with the boys.

"I'd love to!" Jonathan's daughter looked truly delighted. "Thanks for including me."

Tate had on his thinking frown. "I guess one of us can be at the beginning and one can be at the bottom of the sledding hill and one can be at the end. Then we can keep a good eye on things to make sure no one is cheating."

"Great plan." Ainsley stood back up and pushed in her chair. "Let me know if you need help making the tunnel or the candy canes."

Based on her younger twin's gaping mouth, it looked like Ainsley had just replaced Ms. Sanderson as the coolest chick in Finn's book. "Really? You'd help us make stuff?"

"Sure." She peered at the screen again. "I love craft projects."

While Ainsley and the boys discussed ideas, Melody made her a mug of hot chocolate from the instant brew coffee machine. By the time she handed the girl her mug, plans were flowing.

"Maybe you and my dad would want to compete in the race as a team," Ainsley suggested a little too innocently. Jonathan had made it clear that his daughter knew the boys weren't aware of their budding relationship, so she wasn't too worried about her saying something Finn and Tate might pick up on.

"Maybe." Though they probably shouldn't be seen together in public in Cookeville. As much as she enjoyed his company, it was nice to get to know each other without all the drama. "But clearly you didn't only come here to help the boys with the Great Cookie Race. Is there something else I can do for you, my dear?"

"I'm hoping you can help me pick out some new clothes for my dad."

"Oh." Melody waved her out of the break room. "I don't want to force him to change anything." Truthfully, the sweater vests were kind of growing on her. They were so Jonathan . . .

"He *wants* some new clothes. Trust me." Ainsley dabbed at a smudge of whipped cream on her upper lip with the napkin. "He seems to care a lot more about how he's dressed lately."

"He does?" What a relief to know she wasn't the only one who rechecked her appearance before going to pick up or drop off the boys at school.

"Trust me." Ainsley glanced around surreptitiously. "I thought he was going to have a meltdown when he was getting ready for your date the other night. He couldn't find anything he wanted to wear in his closet. He kept talking about how he really needs to get new clothes."

"Then I'm happy to help." She'd be willing to bet she could guess his size. She'd spent plenty of time studying the man. "If this is really what he wants."

"It's what we all want." Ainsley wandered into the men's section, her gaze perusing the racks. "Honestly, after the divorce I think he stopped caring what he wore or how he looked. It was really hard for him."

"I'm sure it was." In the midst of her own loss, her appearance couldn't have mattered to her less. Their histories weren't exactly the same, but she'd seen Jonathan with Ainsley enough to understand how much he enjoyed being a dad. When he'd gotten divorced he hadn't only lost his wife, he'd lost the chance to be with his child all the time too.

"It's really good to see him care again," Ainsley murmured. She hesitated. "I mean I know you've only been on one date, but I love seeing him smile again."

"I'm smiling too," Melody admitted.

"I left him a note and asked him to meet me here when he got home from his meeting." Ainsley set her hot chocolate on the table displaying the folded sweaters. "But I thought we could start to put some outfits together, me and you. Suggestions for him to try on when he gets here."

"Sure." Ideas were already spinning and gathering. It had been a while since she'd gotten to play fairy godmother.

"My dad doesn't like shopping much," she warned. "So I'm afraid he'll have a pretty short attention span."

"I know some people like that." Namely her two children. She always had to offer a reward in order to motivate Finn and Tate to try on clothes.

Maybe she could offer Jonathan a reward too . . .

Thoughts like that would only get her into trouble right now. Seeing as how the boys were mere steps away, she would have to keep her distance. Unfortunately. "Let's take a look over here, shall we?" She guided Ainsley to the career section.

"Oh, what about this?" His daughter held up a gray alpaca blend polo sweater. "This would be perfect for him to wear to work."

And it would look mighty sexy stretched over his broad

shoulders and chest. Melody didn't offer that opinion. "Yes, I think that would look really good on him. Maybe with these?" She held up slim cotton blend pants that could be dressed up or down, depending on the situation.

"For sure." Ainsley held up the sweater to the pants. "And then we can add that blazer right there if he wants to dress it up even more." She snatched the navy sport coat off the rack and put all three articles of clothing together. "This is so much fun! I love being a personal shopper."

"I have to agree." That was why she spent so much time on the sales floor while Kels handled a lot of the behind-the-scenes business stuff. "Here, let's start a dressing room for him." Melody took the three hangers from Ainsley and hung them up in the empty dressing room near the back of the store. "You have a good eye for fashion."

Ainsley positively glowed in the light of the compliment. "You really think so?"

"I do." And she seemed so passionate. "If you're ever looking for an internship or anything, I'd love to have you here."

"Really?" She picked up her mug and took another sip. "Because I've been thinking about spending all of next summer with my dad. I haven't told my mom yet, but I really love it here. The city is so big and chaotic compared to Cookeville." Her expression became guarded. "I just don't know how my mom would feel."

That had to be so difficult, always trying to appease both parents. "If there's one thing I know about moms, it's that we all want what's absolutely best for our kids. I'm sure you and she can figure out what that is together."

"Yeah." Her smile made a comeback. "And she's pretty cool about everything. I'll let you know after I talk to her."

"No rush." She'd be happy to have the help over the summer. Maybe it would give her some time to actually sneak away with a certain principal . . .

Thoughts like that were still catching her off guard, but she could see sitting on a beach with Jonathan for a weekend.

"What're you guys doing?" Tate poked his head out of the break room.

"We're picking out clothes for my dad to try on," Ainsley said happily. "He needs a new wardrobe."

"That's *boring*." Her son ran to Jonathan's daughter. "How about we go look for supplies for the race instead?"

"Yeah!" Finn darted out of the break room too. "We don't have much time to get everything ready."

"Boys, Ainsley came here to shop with her dad." Melody added a suede trucker jacket and a denim shirt to the dressing room. "You'll have to wait—"

"Actually, I'll bet the corner store has a bunch of the things we'll need." Ainsley abandoned the clothing racks, already heading for the door. "We can run down there real quick and be right back."

"Yes!" Finn raced her to the door, plowing it open.

"Whoa." Jonathan stepped inside the shop. "What's happening?"

"We're gonna go to the corner store with Ainsley real quick," Tate called over his shoulder, already sailing past his principal. "Be back soon!"

"Did we get ditched again?" Jonathan was wearing her favorite smile.

"I think we did." Not that she was complaining this time. Stealing moments alone had proved to be quite the challenge. Melody hurried to meet him, all cylinders inside her body firing at once. She stopped a good three feet away, lest she lose herself in the magnetic pull and kiss him right then and there.

"Hey." He simply looked her up and down appreciatively for a few seconds, his smile growing slowly. "Ainsley left me a note to tell me I'd better get my butt down here right after my meeting to buy some new clothes."

"I hope that's okay." A telltale warmth snaked through her. "Because if you're not interested in new clothes, we don't have to—"

"I came right away," he interrupted, closing the distance between them. "And I may have even broken the speed limit the whole drive here."

"And why is that?" Melody moved her arms up around his shoulders, drawing him closer. Yes, they were on display in front of the big picture windows, but who cared? It was snowing too hard to see much anyway.

"Because you're here." He lowered his mouth to hers, his lips light and teasing. "And I've missed you."

A long contented sigh melted her into him. "I've missed you too." She couldn't stop herself from glancing outside to make sure the kids wouldn't see them.

"I know we don't have much time. And I really could use some new clothes." Jonathan kissed her nose and shed his coat. "Now, don't forget . . . your text said I would look good in anything."

That's right! That embarrassing text she'd sent him. "I still don't know what you replied." Conveniently, they seemed to get interrupted every time she asked him.

"I'm not sure I can remember now," he teased.

She held out her hand. "Then give me your phone. I'll bet I can find it."

"All right." He unlocked his cell and handed it to her. "I'll take off my clothes while you look."

Melody fumbled with the phone. "Wait, what?"

"In the *dressing room*." He shot her a naughty grin. "What were *you* thinking?"

"Wouldn't you like to know?" Melody shooed him away with a mysterious smirk. Her blush had likely made both her scandalous thoughts *and* desires obvious.

While Jonathan changed, she scrolled through their texts, and she had to go way back to that first exchange. There.

You'd look good in pretty much anything. She cringed one more time at those three eggplants in a row and then scanned his response.

You really think so? Maybe you're just being nice, but I'm going to take a risk and tell you something. Melody, I think you're beautiful. I have since the first time I met you. Beauty shines out of you and makes everything around you brighter. I know things never come out right when I'm talking to you but that's how I feel. Three fire emojis punctuated the declaration.

Tears blurred the screen in front of her. That was the sweetest text she'd never gotten, and the correct punctuation was adorable.

"You found it?" Jonathan stood a few feet away, hesitating.

Why was he hesitating? She lunged for him, hugging her arms around him, peering up into his vivid eyes. "Thank you. That would've been the best text I've ever gotten."

"Then I'll send it again." He pulled away and took his phone from her hand, tapping around on the screen.

A chime rang out from her back pocket.

"You have no idea how terrified I was after I thought the text sent." Jonathan clasped her hands in his and towed her back to him. "That's why I misplaced my phone. I was so afraid to see your response that I shoved it into my baking crate. Didn't find it until I unpacked everything the next day."

"That's kind of how I felt when I accidentally sent the eggplants," Melody admitted. "I didn't want you to get the wrong idea about me."

"I mean, I took that as a compliment." His laughter lured out hers.

"The truth is, Jonathan." She rested her hands on his chest. "I have feelings for you. They took me off guard and I wasn't sure what to do with them. But I think I'm starting to figure it out." She wanted this. She wanted him. For the first time, he had her reimagining her life—dreaming about what could be. Cupping her hand around his jaw, she drew his face to hers, watching his eyes the whole time.

Holding nothing back, she kissed him until she had to stop to breathe. "By the way, I really like this sweater on you," she murmured when her lungs had calmed. She smoothed her hands over his shoulders. "But I'm thinking blue might be even better."

"I agree. The gray is kind of blah." Jonathan pulled off the sweater. He pulled it off! Right there in the middle of her shop.

"Wow." The word came out in a squeak. *Woooowww.* She'd known he was broad and strong but the sight left her completely transfixed.

"You want me to dance or something?" Jonathan swiveled his hips, so cheeky!

"You're teasing me and it's not fair," Melody whined. Not when they were standing in her store and anyone could walk in—including their children.

"Is it working?" His steamy little grin told her he already knew it was.

"What do you think—"

Loud chatter outside tore her focus away from his abs. The kids were coming! "Go get dressed!" She threw the blue sweater at him, and Jonathan darted away, laughing. She couldn't seem to keep a straight face either. When she'd sat across from Mr. Braxton in his office, she'd never dreamed he was so playful and funny and . . . sexy.

"Hi, Mom!" Finn led the others through the door.

"Hey." Her face still radiated heat. "How was the shopping trip?"

"Awesome." Tate held up a bag. "We found some great stuff for the snowman part of the race."

"How're things going here?"

Melody took in the knowing smile Jonathan's daughter wore. She'd totally left them alone together on purpose.

"Everything's going great." She stooped to pick up the gray sweater that lay where Jonathan had dropped it during his striptease.

"What do we think?" Jonathan paraded out of the dressing room in his next outfit—the blue sweater, blazer, and dark jeans like he was walking the runway—stopping, turning, chin up, chin down.

He had all of them laughing, even the boys.

"I love it!" Ainsley hurried to straighten the blazer's collar. "You actually look cool, Dad."

"Very hip," Melody agreed, sending him another message with her eyes. *Hot.*

"That looks so uncomfortable." Tate shook his head. "Sorry you have to wear that, dude."

The sound of Jonathan's laughter brought Melody so much happiness.

"It's not that bad." He patted the sweater. "Actually, it's pretty soft."

"Cashmere," Ainsley told him. "We're getting it all," his daughter declared while Jonathan disappeared to change back into his old clothes. "The whole outfit."

"Good thing I brought my credit card." He emerged from the dressing room with the new garments on hangers.

"I forgot to tell you we're having a buy-one get-one sale this month." What good was owning a boutique if she couldn't make up spur-of-the-moment sales?

As Melody was ringing up his purchases, she did her best not to make eyes at Jonathan. But he openly stared like he didn't care who saw.

"Hey, Ainsley," Finn asked as Melody bagged up the clothes. "You want to come over to our house and help us keep planning tonight?" She'd never seen her younger twin speak so shyly.

That was sweet, but . . . "We won't be home tonight," she reminded him. "It's our family ice skating outing with Aunt Kelsey and Uncle Doug and Genevieve and Papa and Nonna."

"Oh man." Finn's shoulders slumped.

"Why do we have to go ice skating again?" Tate asked.

"It's a tradition. We go ice skating every year." The town park had the best rink on the frozen pond. When they were little, she and Thomas used to bundle them up in their snowsuits so they could hardly move and they'd hold her hands while they toddled around the ice. Someday, all of these traditions they'd shared would mean something to them. She had to believe that.

"Can we bring our hockey stuff instead of skating around in circles?" At least Finn hadn't asked in a whiny tone.

"Yeah, ice skating is boring unless you have a stick in your hands," Tate grumbled.

"I guess you can bring your hockey stuff if everyone wants to play."

Finn turned to Jonathan. "Mr. Braxton, can you skate?"

"Sure. I used to play hockey." He pocketed his wallet and took the bag of new threads from Melody. "A long time ago."

"Really?" Tate looked at him with a new appreciation. "That's so cool! Our dad was a hockey player too."

"So you and Ainsley will come to the skating rink with us tonight?" Finn had officially started to beg. "Please? Then we can have enough for teams."

"That'd be so much fun!" Ainsley rounded her eyes in a puppy-dog formation. "Please, Dad? I haven't been ice skating in years."

Jonathan hesitated, glancing at Melody as though trying to gauge how she felt about the invitation. "We don't want to impose on your family outing."

"The more the merrier," she told him with a raise of her eyebrows. Things were changing. She would always have the memories of Finn and Tate all bundled up at the ice skating rink, their chubby cheeks rosy. But they were entering a new era.

For the first time, that didn't seem like such a bad thing.

Sixteen

"I DON'T WANT TO WEAR THESE." TATE TOSSED HIS SNOW pants over a kitchen chair. "I'm *ten*, Mom."

"I'm thirty-seven and I'm wearing mine, but I guess it's your choice." The struggle for independence was starting, and now she had to figure out when to push and when to let natural consequences do their thing. "Remember, it's only twenty degrees outside. You can get frostbite in minutes." They should know that based on all those survival shows they loved to watch so much.

"I'll wear two layers of pants." Tate had always been the master of negotiation. One of his brows lifted. "And one of them will be my really heavy sweatpants."

How was wearing two pairs of pants any different than simply putting on his snow pants? She kept the argument to herself. He'd be the one who had to literally freeze his butt off. Not her. Besides, the park was only four blocks away. If Tate got too cold, he could always run home and change.

"Fine." She started to load the sandwiches she'd made and bagged earlier into the cooler. "But the gloves and hats are non-negotiable, mister. You don't want frostbite on your ears. And at least add a pair of long underwear as your base layer."

"Don't talk to me about my underwear." Her son tromped back up the stairs. He'd gotten smart enough to know when the negotiations were over.

Finn walked in from the garage. Surprise, surprise, he wasn't wearing snow pants either. But he did appear to be layered up. "I got our hockey sticks and pucks and the collapsible nets in the wagon."

"And what about our camping chairs?" Ice skating night was as much about sitting around the firepit Doug and Kels always brought along as it was about skating. At least for her.

"Whoops." He grinned sheepishly. "I'll go put those in too."

"Add this." She closed up the cooler and handed it to him.

"You've got it!" Finn rushed out the door. Ever since he'd invited Ainsley to meet them there, his enthusiasm for ice skating night had increased exponentially.

"Let's go, Tate!" she called up the stairs while she put on her puffer jacket, beanie, and gloves. When it came to doing anything outside during the winter months, she always chose warmth over her dignity.

Tate half ran, half skied down the stairs, already wearing his coat, beanie, and gloves! She'd take that as a win.

They met Finn in the garage and then skated their way down the icy driveway with Tate pulling the wagon.

Melody paused on the sidewalk, caught up in the razor-edge sharpness of a memory. "Aw . . . do you remember when you two were toddlers and Dad and I would put *you* in the wagon to walk to ice skating night?" They used to get excited to go anywhere in the wagon. Back then they'd worn whatever she'd dressed them in. "You had the sweetest little snowsuits with teddy bear ears on the hoods." Those were the days.

"Glad I don't remember the snowsuit." Finn stomped onward in his boots. "But I do remember skating with Dad. He was so much fun."

"Yeah, he was awesome." Tate grinned and Melody wondered if he knew how much he looked like his father.

"He was the best," she agreed, trying to keep up with them. Finn and Tate only had two paces—pause and Mach speed.

"No one could ever be like Dad." Tate led the way around the corner.

Melody's stomach immediately tightened. Was this an opening to start discussing the possibility of her dating again? She couldn't keep putting the conversation off.

"That's true. No one will ever take his place in our lives," she said carefully. "But, um, you know . . . *someday*, maybe there'll be someone special who comes into our lives again. Uh, not really *again*, per se, but . . ."

"You mean like a boyfriend?" Finn interrupted.

Whoa. This was escalating quicker than she'd wanted it to. "No. Not necessarily *boyfriend* . . . er . . . I don't know." She stared at the ground, mortified at her verbal stumbling. Why was this so hard? How did single moms bring up dating with their ten-year-old sons? There was no blueprint for this conversation! But they had to talk about this. She couldn't hide her and Jonathan's feelings for each other forever. Not when those feelings seemed to multiply every time they saw each other. "I mean, if I did want to maybe date someone someday, how would you feel about that, do you think?"

"I think it's pretty gross." Tate pushed the crosswalk button and they waited on the sidewalk.

"I don't." Finn shrugged. "You can have a boyfriend if you want, Mom. Heck, I'll probably have a girlfriend soon."

"Ainsley's too old for you, genius." Tate started walking right when the light changed. "And she's Mr. Braxton's daughter." He made a gagging noise.

That didn't bode well. "What's wrong with being Mr. Braxton's daughter?"

"Mr. Braxton is so boring and strict sometimes. He probably won't even *let* her have a boyfriend."

At one time she might've thought the same thing but she hadn't truly *known* Jonathan then. He was funny and playful and kind. She couldn't exactly tell them how she'd come to learn those things about him. "I don't know if he's *that* strict. He seems pretty great to me," she said, at the risk of giving herself away.

Finn frowned at her. "You're the one who's always telling us not to be late so we don't get in trouble."

Melody stared straight ahead so she wouldn't come across as too desperate. But where would she and Jonathan end up if the boys didn't like him or want him to be a part of their lives? She could never be with someone they didn't accept. "Being on time is an important life skill." The skating rink came into view down at the bottom of the hill, and her entire family was already all set up right next to it—her mom and dad sitting in their lawn chairs by a crackling fire in the portable firepit. Kels, Doug, and Genevieve already had on their skates and were gliding around the small oval pond.

"You're late," her niece announced when they'd made it down the hill with the wagon.

Finn cracked up. "That's because we haven't developed our life skills yet. Right, Mom?"

She ignored the comment and set up their chairs near her parents. "I brought the sandwiches and hot chocolate."

The boys got right to work swapping out their boots for skates while she sat next to the fire.

"You look nice." Her mom leaned in closer, studying her face.

"Nice?" A laugh sniffed out. "I'm wearing snow pants."

"But your hair is curled under your hat," her mother pointed out. "And you're wearing makeup again."

"So I'm putting a little more effort into my appearance. What's the big deal?"

"I'm simply wondering what the occas—"

"Hey. You made it." Kels came stumbling off the ice, and it was all Melody could do to not hug her and cheer. Her sister couldn't have timed that interruption any better.

"Yep." She heaved the cooler out of the wagon. "Brought the refreshments too." Her father was already digging into the sandwiches. She might suck at baking but she could make a mean club sandwich.

"Delicious, Melly," he declared.

"Whew." Her sister collapsed into the open chair next to her. "I swear ice skating gets harder every winter."

"That's why we only do it once a year." Melody found her skates in the wagon but wasn't quite ready to put them on yet. As usual, the boys were about ten steps ahead of her, already lacing up. "We'll set out the hockey goals a little later," she called. "After we all skate together for a while." She'd get her three laps in and then she could enjoy the fire the rest of the evening.

"Oh-kay." Tate shoved out onto the ice and skated backward past Genevieve.

"No fair," her niece squealed. "Teach me how to do that."

"I'll teach you!" Finn raced past his brother.

And they said they didn't want to go skating!

"Looks like the fire needs another log." Doug expertly glided to them and made it look easy to walk on the blades of his skates while he added the wood.

"I'll pour the hot chocolate." Her mother had given up on skating a long time ago, so she always concerned herself with the refreshments, but at some point during the evening their father usually still took a few turns around the rink.

With their mother out of earshot, Kels leaned in. "I logged into the computer before we came. Did Jonathan really spend that much money at the boutique today?"

Melody winced. "That was with a sudden buy-one get-one sale." She hoped he knew he didn't have to buy all those clothes just to impress her. Though he'd seemed happy about the new wardrobe.

"I hate to tell you this but someone's got it bad, honey."

Actually, two someones had it bad, but Melody couldn't admit that to her sister yet.

"Got what bad?" Doug pulled a sandwich out of the cooler.

"Oh, nothing." Melody let out a strained laugh. "Kels is just being her funny self." More like loudmouth self. She glanced to where their mother was pouring travel mugs of hot cocoa from the thermos. She wasn't quite ready to tell mama bear about her connection with Jonathan yet.

Their mother tended to make a big deal out of things like that. When she'd first started dating Thomas, her whole family had shown up on her doorstep all the way out in California for the weekend so they could meet him.

"Hey, Mom!" Finn skated past. "What time is Ainsley getting here again?"

Uh-oh. Melody shrank into her chair. "Soon," she called weakly. She'd have to figure out how to explain Jonathan and Ainsley's presence to her parents.

"Ainsley?" Her mother handed her a travel mug. "Ainsley Braxton?"

"Yep." Finn made another lap around. "She's gonna help me and Tate with the Great Cookie Race."

Her mom turned to her, confusion denting her brow. "I didn't realize you guys had been spending time with Mr. Braxton and his daughter."

"We haven't." She shot her sister a silent SOS plea. "But they came into the store earlier and she said she wanted to help. So *the boys* invited them to come ice skating with us." This hadn't been her idea. Ideally, she and Jonathan would spend more time alone together before she exposed him to her whole family.

"What was Jonathan doing at your boutique?" her mother demanded. "And don't tell me he was *shopping.*"

"Mom and Ainsley made Mr. Braxton try on all kinds of clothes," Tate yelled, skating away with his brother not far behind. "It was awful."

"Is that so?" Her lovely mother crossed her arms and leaned back in her chair, head cocked to the side. The woman had always excelled at silent interrogations. Melody nervously darted her gaze around while her mother's eyes narrowed.

"I *knew* something was going on with you and Jonathan." At least she lowered her voice. "Why haven't you said anything? You were actually *dressing* him? From the sound of things, you two are ready to pick out china patterns."

"First of all, no one gets china for their wedding anymore, so that doesn't even make sense."

Kels backed her up with an emphatic nod. "Truth."

"Second . . ." She dropped her voice. "Jonathan and I have gone on *one* date." In between sneaking moments alone here and there. "We don't even know what we're doing yet." Though with the bantering texts and the flirty FaceTimes, she had a pretty good idea where things were headed.

"You don't have to know right now." Dad raised his travel mug in her direction. "Have fun, that's what I say. God knows you deserve it, Melly."

"But what about Finn and Tate?" Her mother clutched her arm. "He's the boys' *principal*. At their *school*. I mean, can you imagine what they'll have to deal with if anyone finds out?"

Oh, she'd imagined, all right. But her feelings for him had only grown stronger. "That's why we're keeping things quiet right now."

"Quiet?" Her mother scoffed. "Honey, you can't keep anything quiet in this town. All it takes is one person who sees you two talking and the next thing you know, you're the hussy who used Mr. Braxton to make sure her kids got good grades."

Kels slapped her own forehead, but Melody only laughed. "Wow. Straight from widow to hussy. That's quite the leap."

In the dusky light, she caught sight of Jonathan and Ainsley making their way to the rink from their car. "They're here. So no more talk about china patterns and hussies. Please."

Her sister snorted.

"Amen." Her father helped himself to another sandwich.

Melody stood, anticipation already buckling her knees, and she hadn't even said hello to the man yet.

"Ainsley!" Finn careened toward the pair too fast, shooting off the ice and hot-footing his way right into the girl's arms.

She caught him, laughing hysterically, and Jonathan had to steady them both.

"Sorry." Finn extricated himself from the surprise embrace, his head hanging.

"Don't be sorry. That was awesome," Ainsley assured him. "You looked like a stuntman."

Finn laughed a little. "Thanks. Do you wanna get your skates on?"

"Yep. They're right in here." She patted her bag. Melody noticed that Ainsley happened to be wearing snow pants too. She'd have to point that out to the boys later.

Finn went back to the rink while Ainsley sat down and started to lace up her skates and Melody finally got to greet Jonathan. "Hi there." Even standing a foot away, the air between them seemed to crackle.

"Hi." His eyes said the rest—that he was happy to see her, that he felt this magic too. "I brought my grandma's red velvet cookies." He reached into the reusable grocery bag slung over his shoulder and handed her a plastic container.

"Well, I oughta try them out, then." Her father stole the container from her and sat back down.

Jonathan's laugh sent a ripple through her.

"Nice to see you, Arthur. And Patsy." Jonathan really should audition for toothpaste commercials with that perfect white smile. "How've you been?"

"Real good." Thankfully, her father answered for both of them. She didn't need her mother sharing her concerns about Melody becoming the town hussy.

"What about you?" her dad asked, munching on a cookie. "Looking forward to a break from school?"

"I am." His gaze crossed Melody's but didn't linger too long. "Maybe more this year than ever before."

An internal swoon nearly knocked her back to the chair.

She was looking forward to his break too. Maybe they could sneak down to Denver for a day while the boys were with Kels or her parents . . .

"And what're you planning to do over your break?" her mother asked Jonathan nervously.

"All right." Kelsey braced her hands on the chair arms and pushed herself up. "We're here to skate, so let's all get out there. Mom, will you take some pictures of Doug and Genevieve and me?" Kels half dragged her to the edge of the ice in an obvious effort to give Melody and Jonathan space.

"I'd better help her." Taking the hint, her father followed along behind them.

By now, everyone else, including Ainsley, had made it out onto the rink.

Melody sat down and invited Jonathan to join her. "You brought your skates?"

"Sure did." He pulled a pair of worn hockey skates out of the bag. "It's been a while since I've had these on."

"I only wear these once a year." Melody removed her boots and crammed her feet into the uncomfortable ice skates she'd had since college.

"I love that your family has so many traditions." Jonathan worked on his laces. "I wish Ainsley and I had more. But her mom and I were always so busy with work that we never made the time. That's one of my biggest regrets now that she's getting ready to go off to college in a few years."

"It's never too late. You can borrow some of our traditions." Melody stood up and immediately wobbled. "Whoa."

Jonathan might have steadied her arm but his touch completely destabilized her heart. If only she lived in a world where she could grab his hand right here in front of everyone.

And maybe brush a kiss across his lips like her body was begging her to.

"Easy," he murmured while they slowly made their way to the ice. The first step was always the hardest. Melody inched her way on, her feet clumsy and slipping while Jonathan effortlessly glided.

"I didn't realize you were such a good skater." Meanwhile, they were five steps in and a cramp had already worked its way into her calf.

"He was a hockey player in college." Ainsley cruised past them and then turned herself around to skate backward.

"That's so cool!" Tate zoomed by next. "What college did you play for?"

"I went to DU." Jonathan waited for Melody, sweet man that he was. Was it just her or was the ice choppier than usual this year?

"They won a championship." It was adorable how Ainsley loved bragging about him.

"Wow." Finn came to a twirl-stop and peered up at his principal with new stars in his eyes. "That's amazing."

"It was a long time ago." Jonathan offered his arm to Melody, and she took it gratefully. She'd thought physical challenges weren't supposed to get harder until you turned forty, but ice skating proved her wrong. At least her clumsiness gave her a good excuse to stay close to Jonathan. The boys wouldn't question that.

After a few slow turns around the ice, the boys closed in on her.

"Can we play a hockey game now?" Tate begged.

"With Uncle Doug and Genevieve and Mr. Braxton and Ainsley, we can have three on a team," Finn added.

234 £ ELIZA EVANS

Jonathan looked to her to make the decision.

"Sure." She wouldn't mind sitting back down with her hot chocolate anyway. Her feet were already starting to hurt.

Jonathan helped her make her way off the ice.

"You sure you don't wanna play, Mom?" Finn skated behind her. "You could be goalie, if you want. Then you don't have to move very much."

But she might very well take a puck to the face. "I don't think so, hon. I want to watch and cheer from the sidelines with Nonna and Papa and Auntie Kels."

"Forget that." Her father wobbled onto the ice, teetering on his ancient skates. "I get to be goalie for one of the teams."

While the players got themselves organized, Melody sat in her chair between her mom and Kels and tucked in a blanket around her. This was more like it.

The game started with Tate dropping the puck.

"Mr. Braxton! Pass!" Finn waved his stick and Jonathan delivered.

Melody watched him skate, transfixed. He could *move* out there, graceful and effortless and—

"Oh my God," her mother murmured. "You're in love with him."

Melody managed to pry her gaze off Jonathan to give her mother a proper glare, her irritation boiling over. "Would that be so horrible? If I cared about someone again? If I wanted to date someone? Wouldn't you be happy for me?"

It took her a few seconds too long to answer.

"Of course we'd be happy for you. Right, Mom?" Kels jabbed an elbow into her ribs. "No one's saying you shouldn't move on, Mel."

"You're right." Her mom clutched Melody's hand. "I'm

sorry, sweetie. I think I'm in shock, that's all. You haven't wanted to date anyone. And Jonathan is the last person I saw you being interested in."

She had her there. "There's more to him than I thought." He'd slowly been revealing himself to her. In a few weeks, they'd come a long way from those lectures in his office.

"We want you to be happy." Her mom leaned her head on Melody's shoulder. "I don't want you to hurt again, that's all. I never want to watch you hurt like you did after Thomas passed away. You've only just come out of it all."

"And I'm a lot stronger now." There were times it had felt like the loss would crush her soul, but it hadn't. Somehow she'd emerged on the other side, happy and healthy and ready to take on life again. Yes, she was ready. More ready than she'd realized.

"I know how people talk at the school, that's all," her mother said. "I'm being protective."

"And I appreciate that." She slung an arm around her mom and around Kels because they were the very best. "I appreciate how you've all been there for the boys and me. I wouldn't have survived without you." Even when they were being nosy and overprotective. "I didn't realize I was ready for something new until Jonathan told me how he felt. And I felt the same. We're taking it slow and we're being careful."

"And having some fun along the way too, I hope?" Her sister shot her a devilish grin. "Don't forget about the fun."

She couldn't if she tried. Thoughts of the fun were keeping her up late into the night. "Yes. We're having fun."

"Good. You deserve that." Her mother kissed her cheek. "You know we'll be supportive no matter what. I mean, I love Jonathan."

Melody suspected she did too. And what a surprise to feel

something so powerful again, something she thought she'd lost forever. She went back to watching him out on the ice, giving high fives to the boys, chatting with Doug. Yes, those weren't fleeting emotions coursing through her. They were real, deep and raw and sustaining.

"Wow, Ainsley's pretty good out there," Kels said. "She seems to fit right in with your boys."

"Better than I could've imagined," she agreed. The whole group fit—laughing and trash talking and zooming around the ice in near chaos.

Melody cheered for both teams, as did Kels and their mom, until everyone seemed to slow down.

"All right, Nonna." Her father came hobbling off the ice first. "I think it's time for you to take me home before I crack an ankle."

Everyone clustered around to say good night to her parents, and this was why she loved traditions so much. Family. Closeness. This was what wove their lives together and made them part of something bigger. Even on a cold night at the skating rink.

Before walking away, her mother hugged Jonathan. "You're a good one," she told him.

Melody winked at him to let him know she agreed.

"Hey, let's take a few more laps together before we go home." Her brave sister waved the kids out onto the rink. Doug caught up to her and held her hand.

But Jonathan sank into the chair next to Melody, legs stretched out while he rotated his feet around. "There's a reason I don't play hockey anymore."

Melody scooted a tad closer to him, a fire warming her from the inside now. "You looked pretty good to me."

"Yeah?" He always appeared so surprised when she said something complimentary like that.

"You looked really good, actually," she murmured.

He let his gaze run over her, lazy and unhurried. "You look really good to me too."

She laughed and patted the billowy material covering her midsection. "Even in my Stay Puft Marshmallow Man pants?"

"They're better than mine." He lifted the hem of his coat. "I had to safety-pin these bad boys because I haven't worn snow pants for a good ten years."

She must have it bad because she found those safety pins hugely endearing. "I hope it was worth it. Digging out the snow pants."

"I have no regrets." He watched the kids out on the rink. "I like your family. My family has never been close. I think my parents wanted my sister and me to be adults the year we started first grade."

Everything he revealed to her felt like a gift. "Where's your sister now?"

"She's a professor at Oxford. I became the big disappointment of the family when I went into elementary education." He shrugged. "I knew that was where I belonged. I love my parents but I wasn't going to live my life for them."

"I'm not sure my parents had any real expectations for me." They'd always given her such freedom in choosing for herself. "I think they've only ever wanted me to be happy." Even when they didn't agree or worried about her choices.

"That's a gift." He was gazing into her eyes now, steadily and seductively, and she couldn't do a damn thing about it with the crowd around. But she embraced the way her body simmered with anticipation.

After a few minutes, everyone came off the ice, tired and cold.

"Can we go, Mom?" Tate asked. "My legs are freezing."

Hmm.

"Seems like you should have snow pants on then, kid." Doug started to put out the fire. Good old Doug.

Her son got to work taking off his skates. "Yeah, you were right about the snow pants, Mom."

Melody held her cheers inside.

Ainsley and Finn sat down too, still chatting earnestly about the Great Cookie Race. And Kels was busy managing the removal of both her and Genevieve's skates.

"Thank you for sharing your family with us tonight." Jonathan slipped his boots back on and then stood up, offering a hand to help Melody to her feet. "I know this is something you usually do with the boys. But we don't have a lot of our own traditions and it was fun to be part of someone else's." He held on to her hand for a beat longer.

Melody walked with him a few steps toward the parking lot before stopping. She and the boys had to walk the opposite direction to get home. "I think this is the most fun I've had at an ice skating night in years. You and Ainsley are welcome anytime."

"Maybe next year I'll bow out of the hockey game." He winced and stretched his back.

"Bye, Finn! Bye, Tate!" Ainsley waved to the boys from the parking lot. "Thanks, Ms. Monroe. I had the best time."

"So did we!" Finn called.

Kels, Doug, and Genevieve left next. "You call me later," her sister instructed as she gave her a hug.

Once the wagon was all packed up, Melody and the boys started for home.

"Hey, Mom. I'm really glad we went ice skating tonight," Tate said. "And I'm glad Mr. Braxton and Ainsley came too."

"Yeah," Finn said thoughtfully. "Maybe traditions are better when you invite other people to be part of them."

She hugged her boys to her sides. "I think you're right."

Seventeen

MELODY USED TO DREAD BEING SUMMONED TO THE PRIN-
cipal's office, but right now she had to refrain from skipping
through the doors.

When Jonathan had texted her to stop in and see him on
her way to fulfill her cafeteria duty—with a winking emoji—
she'd run back upstairs to change her outfit yet again and had
added more eyeliner.

But she had to play this part cool or Nancy would get suspicious.

"Hey there, Melody." Jonathan's assistant smiled at her
over the computer screen. "You look lovely today. I mean,
you're positively glowing. Did you change up your skincare
routine?"

"Nope. I'm not doing anything different, really." Forget
Botox. Harboring a secret romance could take ten years off
easy. "I have a meeting with Mr. Braxton."

Or a rendezvous, depending on how you looked at it.

"Yes, he mentioned that. You two probably have all sorts of
things to discuss regarding Cookie Daze, I'll bet."

"Mmm-hmm."

Nancy waved her past the desk. "Go ahead on back. He should be waiting for you."

"Thanks." She started to float again, but hopefully Nancy was oblivious to the extra bounce in her step.

Outside Jonathan's door, Melody paused to inhale and straighten her brand-new white sweater. Nothing ever prepared her for the rush that hit when she saw Jonathan, though. He was sitting behind his desk and happened to be wearing the suede jacket he'd purchased at the boutique with the denim shirt underneath. "Don't you look nice!"

He pushed away from the desk and met her at the center of the room, his arms automatically coming around her. "I have a very talented stylist."

Her body sighed with relief. It was like she had a constant desire to be here, in his arms, close to him, and the craving had finally been satisfied. "Your stylist is officially reporting for cafeteria duty penance."

Jonathan took her hands and led her to the small love seat in the corner. "Technically, you didn't lose the bet. The Cookie Contest was never a fair fight. So you didn't have to come today."

"You're right. I didn't have to come." But then she wouldn't have seen him. Melody put on a good pout. "The contest wasn't even close to a fair fight. Going up against everyone's favorite single principal meant I lost before it even started."

"Am I single?" Sheesh. There was nothing sexier than that smirking frown on his face.

"As far as everyone knows." She made sure her tone hit a mysterious note.

"I'd change that in a heartbeat, you know," he murmured.

"If you wanted to. I'm not pressuring you, Mel. I'm only telling you where I stand."

"I'm making my way there too." She wanted to be there. Impatience flared again. "I kind of started a conversation with the boys before we went ice skating. But I ended up babbling and made a mess of it."

Jonathan slipped his arm around her. "It's not an easy conversation to have. Especially at their age." His soft smile offered her freedom. "Take your time. Ease them into it. I'm not going anywhere."

Melody clutched the collar of his jacket. "Being with you makes me want to rush into all kinds of things." It was probably a good thing they were sitting in his office instead of his living room or she might be peeling off his jacket right now.

"I know the feeling." Jonathan kissed her, slow and savoring. "But you're right to take it easy." He massaged her shoulders and she leaned into his touch. "I trust your wisdom. You've gotten the boys through so much and they're resilient. Like you."

Speaking of resilience . . . "I'd better not be late for duty." She forced herself to separate from him and stand up. "Wish me luck?"

"I'll do better than that." He stood too and towed her to him, wrapping her up once more. His lips found hers, already familiar and yet such a shock to her body at the same time.

"You are making it very difficult for me to want to leave," she murmured.

"Sorry." He drowned the word in another kiss.

She wasn't sorry. She kissed him back until guilt gnawed at her conscience. "Okay. I really need go."

"Can I see you again soon?" He let her step away but his hand caught hers.

"We'll figure out something." It was time for her to have the conversation with the boys, honest and direct. She'd tell them everything tonight. Then she and Jonathan could make real plans. "I'll text you later. If I survive the cafeteria."

"Good luck." He opened the door for her, but Charlene stood there.

Melody instantly felt a spotlight go to her lips. Did the woman know they'd been kissing?

"Hey, Charlene," Jonathan said casually.

"Well, isn't this something?" Charlene looked her up and down. "Jonathan, I'm here to meet with you about some concerns I have. Privately."

"Sure. I have a few minutes." He gestured her into the office and then stepped into the hall with Melody. "Come and see me after the torture?" he whispered.

She nodded, but her stomach roiled. What was Charlene doing here? Why now? "I'll see you later, Mr. Braxton," she said formally. Then she turned and got out of there, bidding Nancy a hasty goodbye.

By the time she'd made it to the cafeteria, perspiration itched on her forehead. There was no way Charlene could know about them. They'd been too careful. Too quiet. Squelching the panic, she found Gail, the lunchroom aide, posted by the door. Kids were already streaming inside.

"Hi there. I'm Melody Monroe, Finn and Tate's mom? I'm your volunteer today."

"Thank God!" Gail's voice was overly loud—probably a hazard of her job. "They're already hopped up on sugar. The last full day before Christmas break is always a doozy."

Tell her about it. From the high of kissing Jonathan in his office to the low of coming face-to-face with Charlene, she felt like she'd already been on a roller-coaster ride this morning.

"Well, put me to work." At least that would distract her from thinking about Charlene's mysterious meeting with Jonathan.

"Actually, I think I'll have you supervise out here the whole time," Gail said. "We're down a person in the kitchen, so I'll be going back and forth."

"Sounds good." The noise levels were already starting to rise. About half the kids were seated and half were in line to get their lunches. She hadn't spotted Finn and Tate yet. Or maybe they were avoiding her. "So I'm like the patrol officer, then?"

"Exactly." The aide gestured for Melody to walk with her along the wall. "If it gets too loud in here, turn off the lights for a few seconds. The kids know what that means. And keep an eye out for students swapping food. They know they're not supposed to, but you would not believe how often it happens."

"Oh, I'd believe it." With this many kids in one room? There was no way she could watch them all.

"Good luck." Gail saluted her and then hightailed it into the kitchen.

Good luck indeed. Melody sidestepped a group of girls who were huddled together, laughing at something on one of their phones. From her post against the wall, she assessed the task. There had to be at least six long picnic tables that could each seat twelve kids. What was that, seventy-two? She had to watch seventy-two children all by her lonesome?

"Hey, Mom." Tate passed by, giving her a wide berth. Finn came along right behind him, but he only waved.

"Hi." She shuffled alongside them for a few steps. "How're your days going?"

"Pretty good." Tate stared straight ahead.

"You're just gonna stand over here, right? Not by our table?" Finn spoke to her like they were both undercover operatives about ready to make a drug bust.

"Oh yeah." She edged back toward the wall to give them space. "I'll hang out on this side of the room."

The boys got in line, pretending they didn't know her. Fine, then. She needed to get on with patrolling anyway. Couldn't have a food swap go down on her watch. Melody walked between the tables, eyeing the countless faces, but for the most part, the kids seemed to be following the rules. Maybe this wouldn't be as difficult as everyone said it was.

Finn and Tate got their food and sat at the farthest table from her. The line had dwindled and she only had about twenty more minutes to go.

What had she been so nervous about? This might be the easiest volunteer gig she'd ever had at this school.

Out of the corner of her eye, she saw a girl hand another girl a small baggie over the table. *Uh-oh.* Melody approached them with a friendly smile. "Excuse me. Hi. Yeah, you're not supposed to swap food, so you'll need to give that back."

The girl tossed her long red hair over her shoulder and glared up at her. "Who said?"

"That's the rule, from what I was told." She could display every bit as much attitude as that girl.

"Whatever." She went back to eating the illegal pretzels.

Gail had neglected to tell her what, exactly, she should do if someone blatantly disregarded the rules *and* the volunteer. She needed backup. Melody made a beeline toward the kitchen for a consult.

"You take that back!" The shout silenced the entire cafeteria.

That was Finn's voice. She stopped and whirled. Her eyes scanned the tables until she saw him, standing up with his bowl of macaroni and cheese aimed at the boy across from him. Was that Charlene's son?

"I said take it back!" Her son wound up even more. He was going to throw it!

Oh no. No, no, no. "Finn!" A low hum in the crowd was quickly gaining momentum. She hurried past the first two tables at the end. "Finn!" The other kids were growing louder, and some had abandoned their seats to cluster around her son. She couldn't even see him anymore with all of his class-mates crowding him. "Finn!"

"I warned you!" he yelled.

"Everyone take your seats!" Her shouts were futile. She elbowed her way through the cluster just in time to see her son send the bowl of macaroni and cheese flying.

It landed on Blake's head, the pasta and creamy sauce spilling down his face.

"Finn!" She tried to get to him, but chaos ensued.

"Food fight!" someone shouted, and Melody got pelted in the chest with a container of applesauce. "Hey! Stop!" She shook the mess off her shirt, but there was really no point because food was flying everywhere. She ducked a half-eaten brown banana, but a chocolate milk container flew over her head and the thick brown liquid rained down, completely soaking her hair and her white sweater. "Oh dear God." This was so bad.

Screams and yells rang out all around her. She stayed crouched, pushing through the masses of children to find her sons.

All of a sudden, the lights went out and a whistle shrilled.

Everything stopped.

"You'd all better sit down right now," Gail barked.

When the kids sat back on the benches, Melody was the only one left standing. The aide marched to her like a drill sergeant captain, arms swinging and everything. "What the heck happened out here?"

"I don't . . . I'm not . . ." Melody slicked her chocolate-milk-soaked hair out of her eyes. This couldn't be happening.

"It was Finn Monroe," the girl with the illegal pretzels called. "And his brother, Tate. They started the whole thing. They threw macaroni and cheese at Blake first."

The cafeteria aide posted her hands on her hips, her glare bearing down on Melody. "Finn and Tate, as in your kids?"

"I guess?" This didn't make any sense. "But I don't know—"

"Finn? Tate?" The woman turned in a slow circle, her eyes scanning the rows of tables.

"It was me." Finn stood up and marched directly to the cafeteria aide, his hands on his hips too. "Tate didn't do it. It's not his fault."

"Oh yes it is." His brother joined him in the middle of the mess.

And Melody still couldn't seem to speak. What had gotten into them?

"Finn threw his macaroni and cheese at the jerk, and I threw my pudding at him." Tate crossed his arms. "And I'm not even sorry."

"Tate!" His name seethed out of her. What was he thinking? They didn't do this. They didn't throw food at people and create mass chaos in the middle of the lunch hour.

Gail's broad jaw set in a hard line. "I assume you're fine taking them down to the principal's office so you can explain the situation?"

Melody nodded meekly.

Finn and Tate were staring at her with varying degrees of concern—likely because they'd never seen her face so molten—but she simply pointed them toward the cafeteria's exit.

They'd almost made it there when Ms. Sanderson appeared with a towel. "Here, honey. You may want to wrap up. That sweater is a little see-through now that it's wet."

"Oh. Oh no." She wrapped the towel around her shoulders but not before she heard kids snickering behind her.

Eighteen

IN THE HALLWAY, FINN AND TATE BOTH MOVED QUICKLY, AS if they'd really be able to get away from her.

"What were you thinking?" She caught up to them in two strides. "What would ever possess you to throw your macaroni and cheese at another kid?"

"Blake was being a jerk," Finn grumbled.

That was it? His entire defense? "Blake is always rude." In this case, the apple didn't fall too far from the tree. Charlene's son thought he ran the place. "Who cares? If he was bullying you, you tell an adult. You don't take matters into your own hands. That's what I taught you." Or maybe she hadn't. Maybe she hadn't taught them anything. "I was right there. You could've come and told me."

"No, I couldn't." Finn stalked ahead.

"Why not?" She pulled him to a stop. "Help me understand what just happened." Because she was at a total loss.

"Melody?" Jonathan called her name, and a whole new humiliation washed over her.

She tried to smooth her hair out, but it was too sticky. "There's been . . . there was an incident."

"I know. Gail called down here to say you were on your way." He met them outside the office. "Are you okay?"

No. She wasn't okay. Tears scorched her eyes, and the smell of warm chocolate milk was starting to make her nauseated.

"Let's get into my office and figure this out." He looked around the hall nervously and kept his distance from her all the way there.

Nancy grimaced when they walked past but didn't say anything.

Jonathan closed the door, and the boys immediately moved to the other corner of the room. At least their heads were hanging with an appropriate amount of remorse.

"You boys want to tell me what happened?" Jonathan stood between her and them, almost as though he was unsure what to do.

"Blake was being a jerk so I shut him up," Finn muttered.

Jonathan blinked at him. "Um. Okay. How was he being a jerk?"

"He was—" Tate started, but Finn shook his head at his brother.

Melody looked back and forth between them. They'd always had this way of silently communicating with their expressions. What weren't they saying out loud?

"I got mad at him and I threw my macaroni and cheese at him, but I shouldn't have. I know that." Finn turned to her. "I'm really sorry, Mom."

"There has to be more to the story—" she said at the same time Jonathan said, "Sorry's not good enough this time. It sounds like there's a huge mess in the cafeteria."

"We can clean it up," Tate offered. "We'll mop and everything. That can be our punishment."

Jonathan sat down at his desk, rubbing his temples. "I don't think you two realize how serious this is. Someone could've gotten hurt in there. Did you think about that?" He didn't give them a chance to answer. "Of course not. You weren't thinking."

Melody shook her head in disbelief. They still didn't know exactly what happened and Jonathan was already starting in with a lecture? "I want to know what Blake said to you, Finny." Her voice wobbled.

"Nothing." Her younger twin wouldn't even look at her, so she focused on Tate. But he only shrugged. "I didn't hear what he said."

Tate shifted because he hated being dishonest, and Finn couldn't even make eye contact. They were lying right through their teeth.

"Well, I have to suspend you both." Jonathan had hardly looked at her once since they'd come in here. "I mean, that's my only option."

"Suspend them? Clearly they were baited into this." She pointed at the boys lest they get any ideas about her defending their bad behavior. "I'm not making excuses for you. You both know better, and trust me, there are going to be all kinds of consequences. But I want to know what Blake said to you."

"He said I was dumb." Finn still couldn't look at her, which meant he was lying again.

Jonathan checked his watch. He checked his watch! "I have a meeting with the superintendent. You need to take them home." He walked past her and opened the door as though shooing them out. "This is grounds for a three-day suspension, so they'll have to wait to come back to school in January."

Finn and Tate made a hasty exit out of his office and

disappeared, but Melody hung back. "Are you serious?" He wasn't even going to try to get to the bottom of this? "Are you going to talk to Blake too?"

"I can talk to him, but everyone saw Finn start the fight, Melody." Where was his soft, open smile that he usually saved for her now? "I can't give them special treatment. You know that."

"Fine. That's fine." She tightened the towel she still held around her shoulders. "I guess I'll see you around." She hurried away from him before he could get a good look at the tears in her eyes.

"Wait." He followed her to Nancy's desk. "I'm sorry. I don't have a choice."

Melody whirled. "You do, actually. You know them. You know this is completely out of character, so the least you could do is try to get to the bottom of it." But he had a meeting. So she walked away from him and found her boys engaged in a heated discussion outside the school.

They immediately stopped talking when they saw her.

"Get in the car." Melody trudged behind them not saying one more word. Because if she even opened her mouth right now, an avalanche of anger would come barreling out. Instead of completely losing it with them, she did every technique in the parenting books on the drive home. Slowly count to ten. One full minute of deep breathing. Reminding herself of five things she loved about each of her boys. By the time she turned onto their street, she had at least reined in the anger and the shock and humiliation. Only utter sadness remained. "You know what hurts the most?"

Neither boy spoke up. They were both staring out their respective windows.

"You're lying to me." She pulled the car into the driveway but not into the garage. "We don't lie to each other in this family."

"Oh really?" Finn snapped. "Then how come you didn't tell us you're dating our principal?"

An icy panic slithered through her, bolting her hands to the steering wheel. "What?" It came out as a gasp.

"That's what Blake was saying." Tate undid his seat belt and leaned between the seats like he wanted to gauge her face. "That you and Mr. Braxton are dating and it's only because you want us to stop getting in trouble at school."

"No." The ice had spread to her throat, freezing it over. "That's not true at all." Her knuckles ached from gripping the steering wheel so hard, but she couldn't seem to let go.

"You're not dating him?" Finn demanded as though he already knew the answer. "Because you *have* been spending a lot of time with him. You got him that mixing bowl. And you wanted him to give us special treatment in his office just now."

Melody's head shook. She finally broke free of the dread gripping her muscles. "Yes, we have spent some time together." She turned to face them. "But I wasn't asking him to treat you differently. I just wanted him to get to the bottom—"

"You didn't tell us." Her younger twin's lips twitched. He was on the verge of tears. "We looked really stupid in front of all of our friends."

Melody closed her eyes. Tears leaked out when she opened them. "I'm sorry. That must've been a horrible feeling. But I was only trying to protect you. I didn't want to say anything until I knew if we *liked* spending time together."

"Whatever." Tate pushed open his door. "We'll send ourselves to our rooms."

Finn climbed out of the car too, and both doors slammed in unison.

Melody let them walk away, into the house, before easing the car into the garage. Then she trudged into the kitchen in time to hear both of their bedroom doors slam too. They likely wouldn't be talking to her for a while, so she headed to her room too. She should've known Charlene would find a way to ruin things for her and Jonathan. Melody shed her chocolate-milk-stained clothes and stepped into the shower, letting a few tears fall under the stream of water.

While she was blow-drying her hair, her mother busted into her room. "I heard what happened at school. Are you okay?"

Melody backed to the bed and slumped to the mattress. "No." What a disaster she'd created.

"So it's true?" Her mom sat next to her. "Finn and Tate started a food fight in the cafeteria?"

See? She couldn't believe it either. "Because Blake was teasing them about Jonathan and me." Ugh. How had she gotten so caught up in her feelings that she'd neglected to consider what would happen if someone found out? "Charlene knows. I have no idea how. But who tells their kid something like that?"

"She's a piece of work, that one." Her mom patted her cheek. "She's just put out because the cookie committee is functioning much better without her, thanks to you."

"It doesn't even matter *why* she's causing problems." Melody pushed off the bed, a heaviness weighting her body. "You were right. This is exactly what you were worried about and look what happened. I should've listened to you."

"You should know by now never to listen to me, darlin'." Her mom stood too, pulling her into a comforting hug. "If you'd listened to me, you never would've realized how far you've come—that you're ready to open your heart again." She lifted Melody's chin so she'd look into her eyes. "What you did wasn't a mistake. It was brave. You put yourself out there. Maybe it didn't go the way you wanted it to, but never feel bad about pursuing something that makes you happy simply because you're afraid of how your kids will handle it."

"They handled it exactly like they should've." She shrank out of her mom's embrace. "They were humiliated and upset. And hurt. And I can't be the cause of their hurt." She should've known this would happen. Melody headed for her closet, pulling on a sweater and stepping into her boots.

"Jonathan is a good man." Her mother stood by the door, watching her. "One of the best I've ever met, in fact."

"Our timing doesn't work." That was the only thing that mattered. "Look at how this affected Finn and Tate." And they were supposed to come first. "Can you stay with them for a while?"

A sigh deflated her mother against the wall. "I suppose I can. But you shouldn't do anything rash. Wait a few days and let your emotions cool off."

"I can't wait." Both she and the boys had been completely humiliated today. She couldn't sit here and do nothing about it. "I'll be back."

Before her mother could try to talk her out of it, she left and drove to Jonathan's house.

Ainsley answered the door, her smile bright. "Hi, Melody!"

"Hey." She didn't even try to smile back. "Is your dad home yet?"

"Yeah. He just got home." Concern brought a guarded hesitation to her tone. "I'll go get him. Do you want to come in?"

"No. Thank you." This would be a quick, one-sided discussion. "I'll wait out here."

The girl nodded, her forehead creasing before she disappeared.

A minute later, Jonathan appeared at the door. "Melody, come inside so we can talk."

"We can talk out here." She crossed her arms to hold herself together. "Do you know why they threw the mac and cheese? Because of me. Because of us."

His expression fell.

"Rumors are already going around. And Charlene told her ten-year-old son all about them. Blake was teasing Finn and Tate at lunch." She refused to let any more tears fall.

Jonathan slipped all the way outside and closed his front door. "Why didn't they say something in my office?"

"Because Blake accused them of getting special treatment from you." And there's only one place that kid would've gotten that idea. "What was Charlene there to meet with you about?"

She wasn't sure she'd ever seen Jonathan truly angry until now. His entire face turned to stone and his mouth pinched. "She asked me if we're together. And she said the same thing. That people are starting to talk, and they're concerned the rules aren't being applied fairly across the board."

A humorless laugh slipped out. "I'm sure she's very concerned."

"I told her it's none of her business or anyone else's who I date." He stepped closer but Melody raised her hands, holding him off. She couldn't do what she had to do if he touched her.

"There's no policy against me dating a parent." His eyes were imploring her. "I don't care what people think or what they say. I've always treated all of my students fairly—including Finn and Tate—and that won't change because we're dating."

"You weren't exactly fair with them today," she said quietly. That was the truth. "I know you had to discipline them as their principal, but you could've tried harder to understand what happened." Instead he'd sent them off.

"You're right. I should've." He uttered a frustrated sigh. "The truth is, Charlene got to me. So I called the superintendent and asked to meet. I explained the situation to him. That's why I was distracted when you three were in my office. He was going to be there any minute." Jonathan reached for her hand. "I'm really sorry. I messed this all up. But he confirmed that we haven't done anything wrong. Us dating might not be ideal but—"

"Things would've gotten messed up anyway." She withdrew from his grasp, unable to hold back the tears any longer. "They've already been through too much, Jonathan. And I don't want to put you in a bad position either." God, it wasn't worth losing his job over. "Things need to go back to the way they were. That's the only solution. I'm sorry."

She stumbled down the porch steps and got into her car, refusing to look back at him before she drove away.

Nineteen

MELODY PUT A SHOT OF EGGNOG INTO HER DECAF COFFEE and tried to muster some good old-fashioned holiday cheer. Any minute, her entire family would show up so they could all pile into her parents' Suburban for their annual Christmas lights spectacular, but she wasn't feeling it tonight.

Sure, she'd put on her best ugly Christmas sweater—a requirement for this tradition—but she'd much rather curl up on the couch and bury her face in a pint of ice cream while she continued to mope, as she had been ever since she'd left Jonathan's house yesterday.

It was silly to miss something she'd barely had. But she'd forgotten the power of passion—how it *moved* her, made her blossom. She'd forgotten how it felt to have someone to say good night to—even if it was only over FaceTime. This morning when she'd woken, she'd grabbed her phone, anticipation building for a few seconds before she'd remembered that things had ended.

Who was she kidding? Nothing had ended for her. She might have told Jonathan their relationship was over, but her thoughts had wandered to him while she'd gone about her work for the day—paying bills and doing laundry and wrapping the boys' Christmas presents.

No one had really noticed her mood. The boys were still largely avoiding her, hanging out in their rooms playing their music and video games, probably. She hadn't gone over the terms of their grounding yet, seeing as how this was uncharted territory. What kind of punishment could she give them when she could've prevented this whole fiasco?

Tate rounded the corner into the kitchen, and lo and behold he was dressed for the weather.

"You're wearing snow pants."

"Yeah. Nonna said to dress warm because we're going to get out of the car a lot this year." Those were the first words he'd spoken to her since he'd told her he was going upstairs to read after breakfast. "I didn't want to be cold like I was when we went ice skating."

"Good thinking." Though she suspected he'd put on the snow pants for other reasons too. He was trying to make up for the whole food fight thing because he'd seen how upset she'd gotten. They were all still walking on eggshells since yesterday—the boys and her too. They were tiptoeing around their feelings, being overly polite like complete strangers, all doing penance in their own ways. This morning, she'd put extra chocolate chips in their waffles.

"Is it time to go?" Finn wandered into the kitchen carrying a stack of bowls she was pretty sure had been in his room for the better part of a month. "It's already getting dark." He. Put. The. Bowls. In. The. Dishwasher!

"Papa and Nonna should be here any minute." She finished her coffee and stood up.

"Here, Mom." Tate offered to take her mug. "I'll put this in the dishwasher for you."

"Thanks." She got teary for about the tenth time that day. In so many ways, the boys had started to take care of her every bit as much as she took care of them. But she didn't want them doing things out of guilt. "Hey, we should talk—"

"Knock, knock!" Her mother came through the front door wearing a sweater with blinking lights. "Who's ready for the Christmas lights spectacular?"

"We are." Finn tried but his tone fell flat.

"Then let's get going." She clapped her hands, ever and always the family's cruise director. "No dawdling now. We have an exciting surprise planned."

Melody handed the boys their coats, and they paraded through the door more like they were on their way to a funeral than a fun night out with the family.

"Everyone pile in." Her father stood by the Suburban's back door. Genevieve was already strapped into the way back, and Doug and Kels were in the middle seat. "Boys in the back. Melly, you can squeeze in next to Kels. No bickering, you two."

"Yes, Dad." She took her seat.

"How're the boys?" her sister whispered. Thankfully, Finn and Tate were already so busy talking to Genevieve about their latest Minecraft world, they didn't hear.

"They're not saying much." But it had only been a day. "Last night I had them write apology letters to everyone involved and Mr. Braxton." And they hadn't put up a fight. "But they seem pretty sad about it all."

"They'll come around." She peeked behind them and then leaned even closer. "What about you and Jonathan?"

"There is no me and Jonathan." A sense of loss hollowed

her voice. If only she had told the boys about them sooner. If only she hadn't gotten so caught up in the sneaking around. The regrets pressed in, burdening her heart. "It's too hard."

"If love were easy, it wouldn't be worth it," Kels whispered. "Think of all you and Thomas went through. You fought for each other. You stuck it out, even with all the complications. And you two were so in love. Right until the end."

Melody nodded, choking back tears. She'd met Thomas right when he'd started his medical residency. It had made no sense to pursue a relationship. He was working crazy long hours at the hospital while she was trying to work her way up in L.A.'s fashion scene. But there'd been this irresistible pull between them, one she couldn't deny, no matter how much she tried. So they'd figured out their schedules, stealing moments together, getting creative with their communication. She'd shown up to the hospital for his breaks. And he'd surprised her with coffees at her desk after he'd worked all night. They'd had to work hard for what they built. It hadn't come easy, and maybe that was why their love had been so strong.

She'd never thought she'd be lucky enough to feel that magic for someone else. But now she also had two boys who had to come first in her life. No matter what she wanted.

Trying to distract herself, Melody directed her attention to the front of the SUV, where her father was fussing with the radio. "We need to get going so we're not late to the last Cookie Daze meeting. I have to be there at seven o'clock sharp."

"Yes, ma'am." Her dad finally settled on a radio station, and her mom started to hand back the travel mugs. "We made dark hot chocolate with a hint of cinnamon from scratch this year. Sip and savor, people!"

"The drive is gonna be a little longer than usual, so

262   ELIZA EVANS

everyone needs to be on their best behavior." Her dad shot her and her sister a pointed look over his shoulder.

"Why so long?" It was already half past four. Usually their holiday light viewing excursion took around an hour.

"We found this amazing outdoor display near Evergreen. I heard Charlene talking about it at school pickup yesterday," her mom said excitedly.

Of course she had. Melody slumped in her seat. That was where those rumors had started, then. Charlene must've seen her and Jonathan at the Enchanted Forest together. Here she was trying to forget about Jonathan, and now she'd have to walk the same path she'd walked with him.

"Melly, do you think you could scoot over a little?" her sister half whined. "You're crowding me."

"Are you serious right now?" She didn't know what it was about the Suburban, but her fight instinct always engaged. "I don't want to scoot over. I want to scoot *closer*." She put her arm around Kels, who immediately elbowed her in the ribs.

"Do I need to pull this car over?" their father barked.

"You two are busted." It was the first semi-joking tone she'd heard from Finn since yesterday.

"That's nothing." Kels giggled. "Do you all remember when Mom and Dad got the brilliant idea to drive to Disneyland?"

Both of her parents groaned.

"I had to pull the car over at least three times in every state," her father told the kids. "That was the end of road trips. After that, we decided to fly everywhere."

"Tell us more stories!" Genevieve loved to hear stories about other people's bad behavior.

The rest of the drive, her parents took turns telling the kids what hellions they'd been tasked with raising. At least

Finn and Tate were laughing. Melody tried, but she'd never been very good at pretending.

When they pulled into the parking lot of the Enchanted Forest, she had to drag herself out of the car.

The magical night she'd spent here with Jonathan seemed like a lifetime ago.

They all followed the path into the glowing trees, with the kids chatting and running up ahead. Murmurs of awe interrupted the silence.

"Look at the pink trees!" Genevieve gravitated to the grove on their left with Doug following while he took pictures on his phone.

"I like the green." Finn veered right with Tate and her parents, so Melody decided to hang with Kels.

"I wish there were something I could do to cheer you up." Her sister tugged her jacket and slowed her down. "You've hardly said a word since we got out of the car."

Melody looked around them to make sure no one else would hear. "Jonathan brought me here. This was our date."

"Ah." Her sister linked their arms together. "It must've been a pretty romantic evening."

She really didn't want to think about it right now. "I guess so."

Kels gave her a jab and frowned.

"Okay, fine. It was the best evening I've had in a long time. Is that what you want to hear?"

"Yes, actually." Her sister stopped walking and faced her. "You care about him and he cares about you. It's so obvious. You can't let Charlene get her way in all this. You've got to put up a fight. You can't let her win."

"This isn't about winning. It's not that simple."

"She's only making trouble for you so she can start a cookie committee coup." Kels nudged her to start walking again.

"She can have the committee back." Melody turned toward the boys' voices. "I give up."

"But you've worked so hard on Cookie Daze," her sister argued. "And the live bake-off was really fun to watch, even if it didn't turn out how you'd hoped. We got more cookies donated for the daze this year than ever before too. You're doing a great job."

But her reason for taking over had been misguided in the first place. She'd thought the cookie committee would bring her and the boys closer, but the whole thing had only added more stress to all their lives. Hopefully it wasn't too late for her to salvage their holidays. "I'm going to catch up to Finn and Tate." She walked away from her sister and followed the sound of her sons bickering.

"So, what'd you guys think?" She walked between them, gathering them both under one arm. Forget the polite penance. Forget wallowing. They had to get past the food fight and start to focus on Christmas. Maybe that would help her move on.

"It's pretty cool." Finn gazed up at her, relief on his face. All day he'd probably assumed she was mad at him instead of just sad.

"It must've taken these people a lot of work," Tate said. "That's so many lights."

"I can't imagine how much work it was." Thomas used to spend hours putting lights on the house, but she hadn't even known where to start with all those cords and wires. So they all still sat in a box in the garage.

"We could do Christmas lights again." Tate stopped to examine a strand of colorful bulbs. "I mean, I know we haven't since Dad died, but we could now. Because we're big enough to help you."

Emotion got all jumbled in her throat. "That's true. You two would be a big help now." Letting them grow up wasn't all bad. They were taking on more responsibility. Maybe putting up lights could become a *new* tradition for them. "I can't believe how fast you're growing up." She did her best not to sound sappy, but she wanted them to know. "Your dad would be so proud of the young men you're becoming." She might have wanted them to stay little for a while longer, but they were maturing into good humans who would make a mark on the world.

"Dad probably wouldn't be proud of the whole food fight thing." Guilt still tinged Finn's expression.

"Everyone makes mistakes," she assured him. "Even he did. He told me a story about how he and his friend took the toilet paper from the bathroom and TP'ed the entire art room when they were supposed to be at recess once. He got suspended too." Hopefully they wouldn't get any bright ideas.

"Whoa. Really?" Tate cracked up.

"Really." She prodded them to keep walking through the mystical trees. "I think he would've understood the food fight thing. And even if he got a little mad about it, he would've loved you anyway, just like I do." They were her heart and her soul, these boys. They were what she had left of the husband she'd loved.

"Did you tell Mr. Braxton about Blake?" Dread weighted Finn's tone.

"I did." She squeezed his shoulder. "Because he shouldn't get away with his part in the whole mess either. You two took responsibility and had consequences, and so should he."

Finn leaned in closer to her side. "I didn't get so mad because you were dating Mr. Braxton." He peered up at her. "It was because we didn't know. And Blake did."

"And he was telling everyone and then even our friends started to talk about it," Tate added.

"I'm sorry that happened." She'd made a lot of mistakes as a mom, and she'd likely make a lot more. The best she could do was own them and learn from them and be authentic so her boys knew they didn't have to be perfect either. "Honestly, this is uncharted territory for me." Navigating the dating world again wasn't something she'd chosen, and yet Jonathan had made her *want* to put herself out there again. "I didn't think I'd ever want to date anyone again because I loved your dad so much. But Mr. Braxton and I started out as friends. And then our feelings went a little deeper. That wasn't our intention, but that's what happened." What else could she say? It was impossible to explain that kind of romantic connection to a kid. "But I promise, in the future, I'll be more up front. It wasn't fair for you to be caught off guard like that."

"I understand, Mom." Finn patted her shoulder. "You don't always get to choose who you crush on."

No matter how sad she was, these boys always helped her find her real laugh again.

"Mr. Braxton wasn't as bad as I thought." A huge compliment, coming from Tate. "I mean, he's a really good hockey player. That was a fun night. He laughs more when he's not at school."

"He surprised me in a lot of ways too, honey. But it's okay. We're not going to date, so you don't have to worry about any more problems at school."

Tate tugged her to a stop again. "But—"

"Snowball fight!" Genevieve ambushed them from be-hind, hitting Finn in the shoulder.

"Oh, it's on." Her son scooped up a huge double handful of snow and fired one back while Tate aimed for Doug. Melody took cover behind a tree.

Finally, Nonna declared a cease-fire so they wouldn't be late to the committee meeting. They all snapped a few selfies and then tumbled themselves back into the Suburban.

While her father stayed with the boys at her house, she and her mother and Kels rushed to the school for the meeting, arriving three minutes prior to seven.

Jonathan stood in the hall as though waiting for her.

"Hey, um, hi." She tucked her hair behind her ear, heat crawling up her neck.

"We'll go get seats." Kels dragged their mother into the conference room, leaving her alone with the man she'd been trying to forget about all day.

"You look cold." His mouth was drawn. "Your cheeks are rosy."

"Oh. Right." Now he had her touching her cheeks. Because she didn't feel cold right now. Jonathan still made her glow from the inside out. "We had a family lights night at the En-chanted Forest."

He nodded, his sad eyes staying intent on hers. "What did the boys think?"

"They were actually really into it." Those were maybe some of the best moments she'd had with them all season. "We had a lot of fun." But she was still missing him. Even more so as she stood here with him, feeling the heat between them but unable to do anything about it except step back be-fore she gave in and reached for him.

"I'm glad." Jonathan's gaze hit the floor and then traveled back up to hers. "So they're doing okay, then? I feel awful about that whole confrontation in my office. I should've handled things a lot differently."

Clearly she and the boys weren't the only ones steeped in guilt. "I don't think any of us knew what to do in that situation." How could they have? The boys weren't prepared, but she and Jonathan weren't either. "We can all give each other some grace and move past it." The words were forced because she didn't want to move past it, past him.

He reached out and took her hand. "I'd like the chance to talk—"

"Oh good." Charlene came barreling down the hall. "The meeting hasn't started yet. It looks like I'm right on time."

Fire traveled up Melody's sternum, a flame on a fuse. She shouldn't be surprised Charlene had shown up here. She ducked toward the wall. She couldn't do this right now.

Jonathan stepped in front of the door as if he could really block Charlene from attending the meeting. "What're you doing?"

"I thought it was important that I come to voice my concerns in person." The woman's sickly sweet smile had Melody clenching her hands. "Pardon." She stepped around Jonathan and went in.

Melody followed immediately, stacking her spine for a fight. The other committee members were already seated, but chatting stopped the second Charlene entered. "It's becoming common knowledge that Melody has got Mr. Braxton wrapped around her finger." She'd already worked on a speech, apparently. "And I'm not the only one who thinks it's a conflict of interest."

"Then why are you here alone?" Kels asked smartly. Mom and Aunt Bernice and Joan all snickered. Melody would've too, but her jaw seemed to have locked. If she forced it open, she had no idea what would come out.

"I mean, look at what happened with the Cookie Contest." Charlene set her duffel bag of a purse on the table. "Finn and Tate Monroe sabotaged the whole thing, and Jonathan made up a story to protect them. They weren't even punished for cheating."

Melody eased out a slow, methodical breath.

"That's because Finn and Tate weren't responsible for switching out my ingredients." Jonathan deployed a razor-sharp tone she'd never heard him use before.

"You don't know that. You have no proof they weren't responsible." Charlene darted her gaze to the others. "They're trouble. I don't have to tell you all what they did to Blake in the cafeteria."

"What about what Blake did to them, huh?" Her mother stood up, posture steeled. "That kid has been a bully since kindergarten, and—"

"Now, now, ladies," Nancy said. "There's no need for accusations and anger."

But Melody would stand up for her kids. "If you'll recall, Charlene, Finn and Tate were both suspended. They've written letters of apology and—"

"Actually, I've decided to revoke their suspension." Jonathan calmly took his seat. "I had a discussion with Blake yesterday. It seems he was badgering them about the gossip you yourself started."

The woman huffed. "I haven't started anything. You two are the ones sneaking around." She pointed at Melody and

Jonathan. "Blake did nothing wrong. I'll be forced to file a complaint with the superintendent."

"Go ahead." Jonathan smiled pleasantly. "I've already discussed the situation with him so he'll be ready for your call."

"Ha!" Aunt Bernice cackled. "Take that."

The woman looked around the room, her jaw hinged open. "The rest of you are fine with someone like her leading such an important committee for this school?"

"You want to take over, Charlene? Then have at it." Melody was ready to walk out. She didn't need this. "Unlike you, I don't need this job to tell me that I'm a good person."

Kels pushed out of her chair. "If Melody quits, I'm walking out with her."

"Me too," her mother called.

"And me." Aunt Bernice harrumphed. "You won't catch me working as one of Charlene's minions."

"That goes for the rest of us too, I think," Nancy said, although somewhat apologetically. Joan and Deb and Tracey nodded along.

"No one is stepping down and no one is quitting. But you're more than welcome to stay, Charlene." Jonathan gestured to the open chair across from him. "If you'd like to be a part of the team and help. It's a great group. I've never seen such effort and teamwork from this committee before."

Charlene scoffed, seemingly at a loss for words, and then stalked out of the room, lugging her gigantic purse with her.

"Shall we get on with our meeting?" Smiling at Melody, Jonathan patted the open seat next to him, and she pretty much wanted him more now than ever.

Melody sank to the chair, but how was she supposed to run the meeting with her heart clenched so painfully? Jonathan was everything she didn't know she'd been looking for and she couldn't have him. She couldn't turn to smile and hug him right now. She couldn't hold his hand under the table or text him kissy emojis or even look at him without aching.

"Would you like me to go over the volunteer assignments for Cookie Daze once more?" Kels offered.

She nodded, tears stuck in her throat.

After her sister had stalled with a very detailed rundown of what they could expect, Melody found her voice again. "If any of you have any questions before the big day, call or text me any time." She looked around the table, letting her gratitude show. "Thank you all for your great work on this team. I know things haven't exactly gone smoothly, but I feel like we've come together to get through the challenges."

"Because of you." Deb reached across the table to squeeze her hand. "You've done a wonderful job, Melody, especially taking over last minute the way you did."

"Christmas would've fallen apart without you," her mom added. "You kept the magic in Cookeville alive. Speaking of magic . . ." She gathered up her purse. "Ladies . . ." She turned to address everyone at the table except for Melody and Jonathan. "What do you say we give these two a moment alone?"

"Mom!" Melody gaped at her.

"I think that's a fabulous idea," Nancy sang.

"Me too!" Kels scrambled out of her chair.

"A moment . . ." Deb murmured with a smile. "Or maybe a whole evening."

If only.

"Bye, now," Bernice called, herding the rest of the cookie committee out the door.

"They're so subtle," Jonathan commented with a laugh.

His joking tone gave her the courage to turn and look at him. "My mother has never been subtle." But she couldn't complain right now. She had some things to say to him. The biggest one being . . . "Thank you. For taking care of the Charlene issue earlier." Melody wasn't sure she would've had the strength to face those accusations without him standing up for her. "I'm sure she's going to try to create problems for you later."

"Totally worth it." He inched forward in his chair, drawing closer but not reaching for her. "Besides, I'm not worried. I've recently adopted a new philosophy."

"What's that?" she asked softly.

He shrugged, grinning at her. "I've always lived by a pretty strict plan. But recently someone has inspired me to take life one day at a time."

"Yeah?" She found herself smiling back at him.

"Yeah." He might as well have been touching her for how hard her heart pounded. "Because things might not exactly fall into place today, but you never know what can happen tomorrow."

"That's true." Oh God. She ached to put her arms around him. But she didn't. "I suppose living life one day at a time leaves more room for hope." That was what Jonathan had given her.

And maybe hoping for him—for them—was enough to hold on to for now.

Twenty

"THIS IS GOING TO BE THE BEST COOKIE DAZE IN THE HIS-tory of all the Cookie Dazes ever to take place in Cookeville!" Finn made the declaration from the front porch, both arms raised to the sky, head tipped back in the sheer glory of joyful anticipation.

Melody snuck a picture on her phone before the moment passed, pretending she was checking a text so she didn't embarrass him. "We'd better get to the park." The rest of the team wouldn't gather for setup for another half hour, but she wanted to be early and make sure they had everything organized.

The entire committee had spent the previous afternoon collecting the rest of the cookies from people in town, storing them all in containers in the concessions kitchen at the park. Once more, Melody had double- and triple-checked the equipment and décor in the shed, making sure they had everything they needed to transform the park into a cookie wonderland.

"I've got the sleds for the race." Tate had rigged up one of the sleds to carry the other four, all stacked up. He pulled them across the snow with a rope.

"Everything else should already be there." Melody locked the front door and then followed the boys down the block. It was absolutely the perfect day to hold an outdoor event. The sun had warmed the air, melting off the dusting of snow that had fallen overnight—just enough to give the lawns an extra sparkle.

"Can we set up the race first, Mom?" Finn looked so much taller in his boots.

"Sure." She let Tate press the crosswalk button. "While you do that, I'll start to set up the carnival games." They'd had the same ones at the event every year—the inflatable limbo, the Santa snowball toss, the penguin sledding disc drop game, and, her personal favorite, the Christmas tree bowling game.

Jonathan had texted her last night to tell her he would be there to meet them at the park first thing in the morning, and then she'd proceeded to fantasize throughout the night. She was still hoping. Hoping for another moment . . . another date . . .

"What happened?"

Melody ran into Tate's back.

"Whoa. Sorry, buddy." She lifted her head and the park came into view. "Oh no." It was a mess.

"Our candy canes!" Finn tore away from them and sprinted to the various items strewn through the snow—all the huge foam candy canes they'd made for their slalom obstacle, the tunnels they'd built, the signs they'd painted only yesterday— everything lay in pieces all over the snowy fields and sidewalks.

Melody walked toward the scene in a haze. The bagged cookies that had been safely locked in the concessions kitchen were crushed and broken—scattered among the debris from the carnival games and the dress-up photo booth.

"I don't understand." Finn glanced around, his expression stricken. "We just checked everything in the shed yesterday. And we locked it up when we were done."

"Someone broke in." Tate picked up the broken padlock from the snow a few feet away. "Someone did this on purpose."

"Who?" the younger twin demanded. "Who would do this?"

Only one person came to Melody's mind. Charlene must've been so angry after the meeting the other night . . .

The sound of a car engine drew her gaze away from the pieces and parts of their ruined festival.

Jonathan's SUV pulled up against the curb and he and Ainsley got out, running to meet them.

"What in the world?" He stepped over the broken reindeer antler toss game.

"Someone ruined Cookie Daze." Finn was crying now, and Melody wanted to join him. All that work, all those hours, all the people who'd helped . . .

"What an awful, awful thing to do." Ainsley put her arm around him. "It'll be okay, Finn."

Melody appreciated the effort, but things were not okay. "Tate, that's your hat. Right there on the ground." The custom beanie she'd given him for Christmas last year that said *Laugh it up, fuzzball—Han Solo*.

"I didn't do this, Mom." Tate backed away from the hat. "I swear. I lost my hat at school a while ago but I didn't want to tell you."

"I know it wasn't you." He would've had to sneak out in the middle of the night when she was asleep. And he wouldn't have. He might've gone after Blake in the cafeteria to back up his brother, but Tate wouldn't purposely ruin the event he loved the best.

"I'm going to keep this." Jonathan picked up the hat and stuffed it into his coat pocket. "If that's okay."

"You believe me, right?" Tate directed the question to his principal.

Jonathan took a knee in front of him. "I believe you. I know you wouldn't do something like this. And we'll get to the bottom of who did later. I promise." He stood back up. "But right now, we need to come up with a plan for how we're going to save Cookie Daze."

Save it? "Everything's ruined." Melody scanned the debris. "Nothing is usable. None of the food, none of the decorations, none of the activities. Someone sabotaged us." Charlene was involved. She had to be. And that woman had actually planted Tate's hat there so everyone would think her boys were responsible? It was unbelievable.

"Everyone will be here in two hours." Finn sniffled. "There's not enough time to fix everything."

Melody took in her two devastated children, the shock and sadness snowballing into anger. "Sure there is." She whipped out her phone. "I'm texting the other committee members to go door to door to start collecting decorations and goodies—cookies or candy or whatever people have at home." She fired off the text. "And I'll get my family here to help Finn and Tate start the cleanup. Jonathan and Ainsley, you start on the north side of town. I'll start on the south side." And she knew exactly whose house she'd stop at first.

"Sounds like a good plan." Jonathan was gazing at her the same way he had before he'd kissed her for the first time—openly and intently—but Ainsley pulled her dad in the opposite direction. "This is gonna be awesome! But we'd better hurry. We have a lot of work to do!"

Yes, they did, but that didn't mean Melody didn't want a few minutes wrapped up in his arms. She turned her back on the craving and jogged through the snow all the way home to get her car.

Ten minutes later, she pulled into Charlene's driveway. Like everything else in the woman's life, her house projected perfection. A newer-model expansive two-story with a gleaming stone exterior and a wide front porch. Even the Christmas lights were straight and taut—perfectly spaced to cover every eave and window.

Melody climbed out of the car, her conviction gaining steam. She couldn't let Charlene get away with ruining Cookie Daze because of some personal vendetta. This rivalry, or whatever it was, had to stop now. She stabbed a finger into the doorbell, and Charlene opened it right away.

Melody opened her mouth to give the woman a piece of her mind, but she could only stare.

Instead of one of her expensive pantsuits, Charlene wore a pair of tattered joggers and an oversized sweatshirt. Her dark hair had been pulled into a crooked ponytail and there wasn't a trace of makeup on her face.

"What're you doing here?" Her voice wobbled like she'd been crying.

"Are you *okay*?" Concern overrode her righteous indignation. She moved to step inside the house.

"It's none of your business." A few tears slipped down Charlene's cheeks but she angrily swiped them away. "You need to leave. Please." She started to cry, *really* cry, and Melody couldn't seem to move.

"Charlene, is there something I can do for you?" She'd never seen her like this. How could she walk out when the woman was sobbing and all alone? "Do you need anything? You don't have to tell me what's wrong, but—"

"Ward left me." She buried her face in the crook of her arm like she wanted to hide. "Three weeks ago. I thought he'd be back. I thought we'd work it out, but he just told me he wants a divorce." She gasped out a sob. "A divorce! After everything I've done for him. Can you believe that?"

"Oh no." Without thinking, Melody threw her arms around her. "That's so awful." How could her husband walk out on her right before the holidays? "I'm sorry, honey. What a horrible, horrible thing to deal with." She knew how it felt to lose a partner.

"Don't tell anyone." Sudden horror gripped Charlene's features. "I don't want anyone to know yet. I can't imagine how people will talk."

"I won't say anything." Melody glanced around the foyer. With everything Charlene was going through, she had a hard time picturing the woman breaking into the shed and ruining Cookie Daze. "Do you want me to make you some tea or something?" Melody snuck a glance at her watch. She had so much to do, but she could spend a few minutes.

"No. No, no. I'm fine." Charlene raised her head, looking around like she was embarrassed. "Why did you come here? Clearly it wasn't to hear me blubber."

Melody thought about making up a lie, but she'd hear soon anyway. "Someone sabotaged Cookie Daze. The shed got broken into last night, and now everything's ruined—all the games and decorations and supplies we've worked so hard to collect—"

"And you thought *I* had something to do with it?" Charlene looked like she might cry again.

THE CHRISTMAS COOKIE WARS 279

"Not necessarily." At least not anymore. "We're trying to save the event before everyone shows up. So we're going door-to-door looking for decorations and cookies and treats and whatever anyone can contribute to make this happen. But I'm really sorry I bothered you. If I had known—" She started to head for the door.

"I'll help." Charlene moved in front of her. "I mean, if you want me to. I know I haven't exactly been supportive lately, but I could really use a distraction this morning."

Ha! She definitely hadn't been supportive. But Melody contained her reaction. She could let the past go. Things had been much harder for Charlene than she'd thought lately. Ward had left three weeks ago, and she had to wonder if that was the real reason Charlene had disbanded the committee. "We'd love to have you help."

"All right, then. I'll get dressed and cover this neighborhood." She was already on the move up the curved staircase. "In fact, I bet my neighbor Lynne will go door-to-door too. We can cover more ground that way."

"That would be great," Melody called. "Then I can go back to the park and help with cleanup."

"We'll meet you there soon!" A door closed upstairs, and Melody took that as her cue to make a hasty exit.

BACK AT THE park, Melody had just joined Finn and Tate on garbage duty when her parents and Kels and Doug pulled up in rapid succession.

"I can't believe this!" Her mother wore her full puffer snowsuit and a pair of matching earmuffs. "Do we know who's responsible? Because I'll give them a piece of my mind."

"Not yet." They didn't have time to get distracted right now, so she didn't give them the chance to speculate. "Mom, you team up with Finn and Genevieve. Dad, you're with Tate. Doug, can you go find a rake and some huge garbage bags?"

"You got it." Her brother-in-law sprinted back to their car and drove away.

She and Kels headed in the opposite direction and worked on piling up the bags of crushed wasted cookies.

"You don't think Charlene would be this desperate, do you?" Kels asked. "I mean, I know she's intense, but this is legitimate vandalism. We could report her to the police."

"It wasn't Charlene." Melody kept her promise to keep the divorce quiet, but she did tell her sister about Tate's hat lying on the ground in the middle of the mess—a clear setup. "So as far as everyone else knows, the only evidence points to *my* kids."

"Unbelievable." Her sister tossed another cookie bag on the pile. "Do you think it's the same person who messed with Jonathan's ingredients at the contest too?"

"It has to be." But she had no one on her list of suspects. "Jonathan said he was going to get to the bottom of it, but right now we need to try to pull off a miracle. And all this waste breaks my heart." She scanned the snowy field they were walking through. At least most of the larger debris had already been cleared by the others.

Doug pulled the car up near where they were walking and brought garbage bags and a rake. "I'll get the cookies raked up if you bag 'em."

"Deal." Melody dumped an armload of cookies into the trash while Kels held the bag open. Soon the boys joined in, turning it into a game of basketball, throwing the cookies from a distance.

They'd finished clearing the ground when a whole line of cars pulled up to the curb, filling the entire block.

"What's happening?" Tate tossed the last bag into the dumpster.

"I have no idea." But doors were opening and people were unloading things—lawn ornaments and decorations—even several giant candy canes Melody recognized from one of the yards on the outskirts of town.

"Mr. Braxton!" Finn pointed down the street. Jonathan was jogging toward them along with Ainsley.

The butterflies fluttering in her chest carried her to meet him.

"That was amazing." Ainsley was out of breath. "When we started to tell people what happened, they started to offer us all kinds of stuff."

"Wow!" Finn had joined them. "This is awesome! We can even use those candy canes for the race!"

"Yes, and there's a lot more stuff I thought we could use too." She directed him to follow her. "Let's start setting up."

Tate joined the two of them and they walked away talking through plans.

It took every ounce of willpower Melody had not to throw her arms around Jonathan. "We did it. We saved Cookie Daze." There had to be thirty cars parked along the curb and in the lot. And people. So many people. There was Charlene, unloading boxes out of her car while she barked orders at the neighbors she'd recruited.

Doug and Kels and her parents and aunt and uncle hurried to help various friends and neighbors unload, carrying box after box to the pavilion.

"The market donated cookies and brownies and pies and cupcakes." Jonathan laughed. "So we might have to change the name to Dessert Daze this year. But it'll work. We'll make this work."

"We will." Longing whispered through the words, and she didn't even care if he heard it, if he could see her real feelings all over her face. Maybe she couldn't have him today, but that didn't mean she didn't want him; that didn't mean they couldn't share a moment.

"Melly!" Kels waved her to the pavilion. "You two better come and help us get organized. There's a lot to sort out here."

A lot to sort out was an understatement. When the rec center had gotten wind of what occurred, they'd lent them all of their carnival games. "These can be set up on the cleared sidewalk near the playground," she told Doug. She deputized him and his project management skills to get the games ready.

"And Mom and Dad, you can start bagging and distributing the cookies. They'll need quite a few for the race. And the carnival games will be giving them out as prizes too."

"Say no more." Her mom found a wagon and the three of them loaded up.

"Jonathan, can you show all of the food trucks where they'll be setting up?" A few had just arrived.

"I'm on it." He jogged away and she watched him until Tracey tapped her on the shoulder. "Here are props we collected for the photo booth. We even have this fun backdrop."

"Great. You and Deb and Nancy can be in charge of that." She checked the list on her phone. They almost had just as many events and activities as they'd lost.

"What about a karaoke station?" Aunt Bernice asked. "I called my DJ friend, Mr. Spinz, and he should be here any minute."

"I love that addition." Kels looked at the diagram she'd drawn up last night. "We can do that in the outdoor amphitheater, if you can find some volunteers to shovel it out." They hadn't been planning on using that space, but she wouldn't turn down another fun thing for people to do today.

"No problem," her aunt assured her.

"What can I do?" Charlene asked behind her.

Once again, Melody had to shake off the shock. She actually wanted to help, and Charlene knew how to get things done. "You and I will both circulate and supervise." Melody pointed her toward the carnival games. "We'll share the director role and make sure everyone has everything they need."

"You've got it." Charlene smiled at her. A real smile!

The next hour flew by while Melody cruised from station to station, offering her help and opinions, watching the entire community come together to pull off a holiday miracle. At noon, they were ready to welcome their friends and neighbors who hadn't made it yet and even some tourists who'd heard the buzz.

Before she got too busy, Melody hiked up the hill to watch the boys kick off the first-ever Great Cookie Race, which already had a line winding back to the trees.

"On your marks, get set, go!" Finn waved a red flag he'd found somewhere, and the racers took off down the hill on their sleds to the cheers of everyone standing around.

"Did you see that, Mom?" Finn held up his hand for a high five. "Everyone loves the race. Look at our line!"

"It's amazing," she agreed. "In fact, I want to see the rest." She moved carefully down the hill in her boots and watched the racers go through the candy canes and through the tunnels and then build the snowmen at the end, where Tate was running back and forth keeping an eye out for the first team to finish.

"This is a big hit, huh?" Jonathan stood near the finish line.

There he was.

Melody had had her eyes out for him the whole time but hadn't been able to locate him in all the chaos.

"They're having a ton of fun." Her chest cramped with suppressed gratitude. "Thank you for helping to save the day. They were so upset when we got here." If Jonathan hadn't lent her his optimism and enthusiasm, she would've canceled the whole thing.

"Look at what we all did." Jonathan always seemed to distribute the credit. "This might be the best Cookie Daze the town has ever—"

"I got your text." Charlene hurried to Jonathan, Blake lagging behind her. "You said you needed to talk to us right away?"

"I do." Jonathan gave her a cool look. "I wanted to talk to Blake while you were here." He crouched until he was eye level with the kid. "I saw you take Tate's hat out of the lost and found the other day."

"No, I didn't." Fear rattled Blake's voice.

"You did," Jonathan said calmly. "Remember? I asked you if you found what you were looking for? You said yes and stuffed this very hat in your backpack." He removed Tate's hat from his coat pocket and held it out to Blake.

Melody watched the kid squirm. Unbelievable. *Blake* had been sabotaging them the whole time?

Judging from the genuine surprise on his mom's face, Charlene had had no idea.

"I don't understand," Charlene said to Jonathan. "If the hat was in the lost and found, it was fair game. It's not like Blake stole it."

"We found it here in the middle of the mess this morning," Melody told her. She hated to give her more bad news, but that was the truth. "Right outside the shed, where Blake apparently wanted us to find it. You wanted everyone to think Finn and Tate ruined Cookie Daze. But it was you."

"And you're the one who switched out my sugar with salt at the contest too, right?" Jonathan added. "I remember seeing you in the gym before the contest started and then you weren't there the rest of the day."

"He wasn't even at the Cookie Contest!" Charlene was shaking her head now. "We didn't attend this year."

"He was there." Jonathan had the kid trapped in an unrelenting stare. 'You said hi to me. And I saw you talking to some other kids, who I could ask to verify you were there."

Charlene whipped her head to gawk at her son. "How did you get to the contest?"

"I rode my bike," he muttered.

"Listen, Blake." Jonathan waited until the kid looked at him. "You can either tell us the truth, or I can file a police report and let them investigate for vandalism."

"It was just some stupid decorations." Blake wouldn't look at any of them. "I'm so sick of Finn and Tate always being the best at everything. They kept talking about their dumb race and they wouldn't even let me help."

Ah. Now she understood. Finn and Tate had a tendency to be exclusive when it came to projects.

"So you were trying to make them look bad?" Jonathan prompted.

"It was all a joke." Blake was looking up at his mom now. "They made me look stupid in the cafeteria, so I wanted to embarrass them too."

Charlene gasped. "I can't believe you would do this to me."

To *her*? Melody shared a look of disbelief with Jonathan.

"You're the one who said you hoped Cookie Daze would fail because no one appreciated you in this town," Blake retorted.

Melody backed up a few steps to give them some space. Maybe Charlene had been projecting her feelings about Ward's abandonment on the rest of the committee.

His mother looked around. "I don't think I said that, exactly."

"You did. That's all you've been talking about for weeks." Blake threw up his hands in obvious frustration. "I thought you'd be glad."

"No! I'm not glad. Blake, you can't vandalize things. I'm so sorry," Charlene seemed to say to everyone gathered around them. "You're going to fix this, mister." She grabbed his wrist and started to drag him away, going on and on about how embarrassed she was.

"Mystery solved."

She hadn't realized how close Jonathan was standing to her. But she felt his presence now, all the way to the very center of her heart.

"Mom, Mr. Braxton," Finn called from up the hill. "We need one more team to compete!"

Jonathan held out his hand to her. "What d'you say?"

"I'm in." She was all in. "As long as you pull the sled."

He laughed and didn't let go of her hand all the way up to the starting point.

"You two get the red one." Finn pointed out their sled. "It's the fastest."

Melody climbed onto the sled and Jonathan sat behind her, his legs coming around her. She leaned into him for one short second, feeling his strong chest against her back, and her whole body sighed with happiness. Today she could get away with this. Maybe not tomorrow, but today she would enjoy being this close.

"On your marks, get set, go!" When Finn waved the flag, they pushed off, the wind whooshing over her face. She couldn't seem to stop laughing as the bumps jostled them together.

Jonathan laughed too, his arms holding her.

When they came to a stop, he crawled out of the sled and pulled her around the candy canes and then through the tunnels, while she tried to help push and collected all the cookies she could grab.

"Quick! The snowman!" She scrambled to get out of the sled. "Let's roll the base." Thankfully, she'd had a lot of practice building snowmen with the boys.

On the sidelines, Finn and Tate and Ainsley had come together to cheer them on as they completed the body.

Laughing, they clumsily sculpted and rolled the last snowball for the head, and then she rifled through the goodies she'd collected in the sled.

"Here, we'll use these donuts for the eyes." She handed them to Jonathan. "And we can make the mouth with these miniature cookies."

"Perfect." Jonathan jabbed the cookies into the snow. "We're done!" He raised his arms in a victory formation.

Tate came over and took his time inspecting the snowman. "Three-piece snowman with desserts for decorations."

"And look how many cookies they collected in their sled." Finn pointed.

"I think you two are the winners!" Ainsley announced, and the kids closed in on them, cheering and hugging.

In the middle of the group hug, Jonathan's eyes found hers, and that tender expression on his face made her heart swell.

He moved in closer, until their faces were inches apart. Her breaths suspended in anticipation, but he didn't kiss her. Instead, he smiled and said, "We make a really good team."

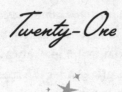

Twenty-One

THERE WAS NOTHING BETTER THAN SITTING AT THE KITCH-
en table on Christmas Eve morning, sipping coffee, inhaling
the aroma of cinnamon French toast baking in the oven while
you watched the snowflakes come down.

Except for having someone to share the moment with.

The rogue thought invaded Melody's peace, tightening her
throat and her chest.

She hadn't even had time to talk to Jonathan after the race
they'd won together yesterday. In the chaos of the Cookie
Daze cleanup, they'd each gotten pulled in a hundred different directions and then he and Ainsley had to rush off for a
play in Denver. When he'd gotten into his car, she'd waved at
him from a distance, a piece of her heart going with him.

A piece of her heart was still with him.

"Happy Christmas Eve!" her sister called, letting herself in
through the kitchen door, stomping snow off her boots onto
the rug.

Right on time.

This tradition had started the year after Thomas died—
Kels showing up on her doorstep with a surprise gift at exactly

nine o'clock on Christmas Eve morning. For a few years, Melody had tried to reciprocate, but her sister always refused. *Think of this as your gift from Thomas because I promised him I would still do his Christmas shopping every year, no matter how long he's been gone.* So now Melody always made extra coffee and she saved Kelsey's gifts under the tree for when they celebrated with the entire family.

"There's some kid shoveling your driveway." Kels poured herself a mug and plopped down across from her. "I didn't get a good look at him under the layers."

"What?" Melody stood and padded to the window above the sink, moving the curtain so she could see outside. Sure enough, a kid had carved wavy, uneven lines in the few inches of snow that had piled up overnight. *Oh, for the love.* "That's Blake. I'm sure his mother is forcing him to do something nice for us after everything he put the boys through. Poor kid. I'll be right back." She tied her fleece bathrobe and slipped outside, staying on the front porch so her slippers didn't get wet. "Hi, Blake."

He didn't look up from his mundane scraping. "Hey, Ms. Monroe."

"You don't have to shovel our driveway." She scrubbed her hands together. It was freezing out here!

"Yes, I do." He stopped to look at her, his cheeks every bit as red as his shiny shovel. "My mom said. She said I have to shovel your driveway for the rest of the winter or she'll take away my Xbox."

Ah yes, Melody had resorted to the Xbox threat a time or two herself. "Well, it looks like you're about done anyway. Why don't you come in for some breakfast and warm up?"

The boy's jaw hinged open. "What are you guys having?" he asked eventually.

Melody laughed. "I'm making some delicious French toast, and there's plenty of extra."

Blake looked around the neighborhood, most likely to make sure his mom wasn't hiding in the bushes spying on him. "I guess I could. For a few minutes, anyway. My hands are pretty cold."

She'd thought so. Melody held open the door for him and ushered him through the small foyer into the kitchen.

"Have a seat. I'm sure Finn and Tate will be up any time now." The heavy scent of cinnamon always lured them out of bed on Christmas Eve. "I'm just getting ready to take the French toast out of the oven."

Kels gave her a funny smile and followed her to the oven. "Look at you showing some grace," she murmured.

"It's Christmas Eve." Melody donned her reindeer oven mitts and slid the casserole out. The scent of cinnamon stung her nose in the best way. "Besides, it's barely above zero degrees out there," she whispered, noting that while Blake had removed his hat and gloves, he'd kept his coat on.

Kels harrumphed, nursing her coffee while she leaned against the counter watching Melody dissect the French toast.

"My mom said I should apologize again if I saw you," Blake said when she brought his plate to the table.

"There's no need to apologize again. Once is enough." She poured him a glass of orange juice from the pitcher and then handed him silverware and a napkin. "I bet Finn and Tate can move past everything that happened."

Footsteps creaked upstairs. "Speaking of . . ." She dished up their plates too and set them on the table just as the boys stumbled into the kitchen, all bleary eyed.

Finn stopped cold when he saw Blake. "What is *he* doing here?"

"Blake was shoveling our driveway," Melody said cheerfully. "So I invited him in to have breakfast with us." *And there'd better not be any food fights this time*, she told him with her eyes.

"Okay." Finn sat down next to him with a shrug.

Tate, however, sat across from Blake and gave him the evil eye. Her older twin had always had a harder time letting go of grudges.

"This is really good, Ms. Monroe," Blake said after a couple of bites. "Do you think you could share the recipe with my mom?"

Heck no. Who was she to call up Charlene—the catering queen—and tell her she needed to make one of *her* recipes? "Why don't you tell her about it, and then she can ask me if she wants it." She wouldn't be waiting for that phone call.

She shared an amused look with Kels and went to the sink to work on the dishes.

"I'm happy to call Charlene and tell her how much her son loved your French toast," her sister whispered.

"Now, now. It's Christmas." Melody rearranged a few plates and glasses in the dishwasher to fit in as many items as she could. "This isn't the time for vindictive phone calls."

"Fine." Kels huffed. "Maybe I'll save that for after New Year's." She leaned in even closer. "So, how's Jonathan?"

"I don't know." She'd obsessively checked her phone for texts until midnight, but nothing came. "Things got chaotic after the event, and I really didn't get to talk to him much."

"Maybe you'll talk to him today."

What was with the mystery in Kelsey's tone? "I doubt I'll hear from him on Christmas Eve." Melody closed up the dishwasher and glanced over her shoulder. The three boys were now laughing together. At least something good had come out of all this.

"The look on your face when the macaroni and cheese landed was priceless," Finn was saying.

"Yeah! You looked like this." Tate made a half-angry, half-shocked expression.

She was about to break up the teasing, but Blake cracked up too. "I can't believe you had the balls to throw your macaroni and cheese at me!"

Ugh. She hated that word at the table. But she didn't correct Blake.

"The food fight was kind of awesome," Tate said.

"But that's not something any of you will ever do again, am I right?"

"Right," all three boys said solemnly. In another minute, Blake stood up and carried his empty plate to the sink. "I'd better go before my mom comes looking for me. Thanks again for breakfast. It was delicious."

"You're very welcome. Anytime."

"Hey, Blake." Finn brought his plate to the sink too. "Maybe we could go sledding sometime over break."

"That'd be awesome." He pulled on his hat and gloves. "I'll probably be grounded from my phone for a while, but you could come and ring the doorbell when you're going."

"We will." Tate poured himself more orange juice.

With another seat open at the table, Melody and Kels sat back down with their own heaping helpings of French toast.

"What're you and the boys doing today?" Kels asked, drowning her breakfast in syrup.

"That's a silly question. It's Christmas Eve." Kels knew full well they maintained a very tight schedule of traditions on December 24. The day always started with Melody making their mother's cinnamon baked French toast for breakfast. She could check that off the list. After cleanup, the boys would open the new Christmas ornaments she'd bought them (they had to be wrapped, even though they always picked them out themselves) and put them on the tree. Then they always took the rest of the wrapped presents out of her closet and set them at the base of the tree before taking their annual Christmas pajamas picture in front of the display. Next, they moved on to playing their annual game of Risk—the boys' favorite. Typically they ate an early dinner—chicken noodle soup that her mother kept stocked in Melody's freezer along with a loaf of bread warmed in the oven. And, to cap off a busy but very relaxing day, they watched *The Polar Express*. "We have a lot to do today, don't we, boys?"

"Actually, we already told some friends we'd meet them at the park for sledding after lunch." Tate used his arm to swipe the orange juice off his upper lip.

"Oh." She set down her fork, her stomach suddenly cramping. Did she really have to give up on another tradition? She wasn't ready for this. "You don't want to play Risk today?"

"We play that every year." *Ouch.*

"We can miss one time, right?" Tate jumped up and put his glass in the dishwasher.

"Sure," she mumbled. "That's fine with me." She smiled so her lower lip would stop quivering. It looked like her plans had suddenly changed. She would sit here by herself, maybe pass the time by looking at pictures from when Finn and Tate were still totally devoted to their mom.

"Hey, Finn, let's go work on our Minecraft world before the tree stuff." Tate hooked his brother around the neck and they pounded up the stairs sounding more like a herd of water buffalo than two ten-year-old boys.

"Sorry, sis." Kels reached for her hand across the table, giving her a squeeze of solidarity.

"It's good, right?" She sniffled. "They're becoming their own wonderful selves. This is what's supposed to happen. And I have to start letting go a little bit." Ha! Letting go. It would be more like prying her fingers off one by one.

"I think this is a good time to give you your Thomas gift." Kels withdrew a small wrapped jewelry box from her pocket and handed it over.

"This helps a little." Kels always seemed to get her the sweetest things in Thomas's memory. She carefully picked at the tape to undo the paper and opened the box to find a necklace made of two interlocking hearts with Finn and Tate's birthstone in the middle. "Kels." She never tried to hide tears from her sister. "I love it. It's absolutely beautiful." She put it on, pressing the pendant to her chest.

Her sister held her hand again. "They're growing up, Melly, but that's only because you've done such a great job with them, all on your own."

"Now that's just not true." She used her napkin to mop up the tears. "You've been here the whole time. And Mom and Dad. And Aunt Bernice and Uncle Clive."

"But you're the reason they feel secure enough to embrace life." Now Kels had started to cry too. "You could've retreated after Thomas died. You could've lived in fear. But you didn't. You kept going and now they're thriving. They're strong and resilient and full of hope and joy. They know they always have a place to come home, no matter how big they get."

"Thanks, Kels." Okay, now she was just blubbering. They both were. "You're the best."

"I know." Her sister blew her nose into the napkin. "But I should get back home. Doug and Genevieve were still sleeping when I left, but they're probably ready to decorate the tree." That was one of her sister's family's Christmas Eve traditions. They always waited until the last possible minute to decorate the tree. "See you tomorrow?"

"See you tomorrow." Melody stood up and hugged her, holding on a little longer than usual.

After her sister left, she tidied up the kitchen and checked her phone again. Still nothing from Jonathan. Should she text *him*?

"Are we ready for the ornaments?" Finn wandered back into the kitchen, followed by Tate.

"'Cause we have to get going soon."

"I'm ready if you two are." She herded them upstairs and into her bedroom—the only room in the house that Thomas had had the chance to renovate before he got sick. They'd combined a small study and the largest bedroom into a suite, complete with a nice-sized walk-in closet that happened to be the perfect place to hide gifts. "Take these boxes out and we'll put all the presents under the tree."

"Are these mine?" Tate's eyes grew rounder.

"These have my name on them!" Finn took his box and she followed them down to the living room. The boys took out their presents one by one, shaking them as much as she'd let them get away with before setting them down.

"FYI, there are no Beatbox headphones in those packages." She'd better warn them now. After putting those in her online shopping cart, she simply hadn't been able to make the purchase. "They were a little too much this year."

"That's okay, Mom." Finn was inspecting one of the larger

presents with his name on it. "I don't *need* headphones. I can't wait to see what's in these!" He shook another package.

"Yeah." Tate continued to rummage through his stuff. "All that money for one pair of headphones is probably a waste when you could get like three Lego sets."

"Exactly." And each of them had a Lego set to open. Every once in a while she still got a glimpse of her little boys—that was her Christmas gift.

The last packages left in the boxes were their ornaments, so they both ripped them open—a feathered owl for Finn and a blown-glass snowman for Tate.

"We each made an ornament in honor of Dad too." Tate hopped up and disappeared.

"In art class," Finn explained. His brother brought back two small boxes.

"Wow." Melody carefully lifted out a stained-glass angel and a stained-glass star and held them up to the window, catching the sunlight. "Look at these colors. They're so cool. He'd love them." She handed them back and snapped a picture of the boys hanging them on the tree.

"Now it's real picture time!" Finn sure seemed to be moving things right along. He probably couldn't wait to go sledding.

"You two take your places while I set up the tripod." She fiddled with the thing for a good five minutes but finally found the right angle.

"Come on, come on." Tate waved her to join them impatiently. "We gotta hurry and meet our friends."

"Well, if we can all keep our eyes open and smile at the camera, this should be quick." But that wasn't possible. After six takes, they had a shot everyone agreed on. Before she could even disconnect her phone from the tripod, the boys were already suiting up in their winter clothes.

"Bye, Mom!" Finn raced back into the living room to give her a hug.

"We'll be back later!" Tate waved from the foyer.

"Have fun." She held her smile intact. "Be careful. But mostly have fun."

They stampeded outside, voices rising with excitement, and she collapsed on the couch and allowed herself five minutes of wallowing. But she couldn't sit around crying all day. So she got up and showered and dressed in a festive red sweater and jeans. She cleaned the bathrooms, since she was hosting her family for their big Christmas dinner tomorrow.

Even scrubbing the toilets didn't kill enough time for the boys to get back home.

Thankfully, the dishwasher buzzed. She'd just finished the silverware when there was a clamoring at the front door. "Boys?" She stepped into the foyer, and the door flew open. Finn and Tate walked in, along with Ainsley, who quickly closed the door behind her.

"Hey!" A hopeful breath sat suspended in her lungs. "What're you doing here?"

"We weren't sledding with our friends," Tate announced.

"We were working on your Christmas present," Finn finished.

"Really?" She couldn't stop glancing at Ainsley. The girl's smile hinted that a huge surprise was coming.

"Yep!" Tate looked at the other two and then back at her. "Here's the thing. We *want* you to date Mr. Braxton."

She didn't even know how to respond. "That's so nice, you guys, but—"

"He makes you happy," Tate interrupted.

"Your eyes get all bright every time you see him," Finn added.

She couldn't deny that. "I think very highly of Jona—I mean Mr. Braxton. But he's your principal and—"

"We're almost done with elementary school," Tate reminded her.

Yes, whether she wanted them to be or not.

"We only have five more months." Finn held up his fingers. "And then it won't even matter anymore. We'll be in middle school."

"True." But inviting someone into their lives would still introduce complications. It would change everything. For so long the three of them had functioned in their own little family unit. Were they ready for such a big change now? Was *she* ready?

"You do everything for us, Mom." Finn gestured for Tate to move closer to the door. "And we want you to be happy. So . . ."

"Merry Christmas," they said in unison. Tate threw open the door and there stood Jonathan on the porch with a huge red bow wrapped around him. "Surprise."

A laugh bellowed out, a huge guffaw straight from her belly. "They *wrapped* you?"

"It would appear so." He stepped inside the house somewhat tentatively. "This was all their idea."

"Mine too," Ainsley threw in. "I even found the bow."

Melody laughed again, and Jonathan joined in this time. "This probably isn't what you asked Santa to bring you."

"No." The laughter faded as she gazed into his eyes, but her smile only grew. "But this is the best Christmas surprise I've ever gotten."

"There's more surprises." Finn took the bow off Jonathan. "Mr. Braxton and you are going on a date to his house."

"We already made dinner for you, and Ainsley's gonna stay here and hang out with us while you eat," Tate added.

"And then we'll all watch *The Polar Express* all together." Ainsley squealed. "This is gonna be so great!"

Melody could only laugh again, joy bubbling up. "Thank goodness I showered."

"Go, go, go!" Tate all but pushed them out the door. "You don't want your dinner to get cold."

Before allowing herself to be swept away again, she turned to Ainsley. "You're sure you're okay staying with them?"

"I'm happy to." She slung an arm around each of them. "We're going to play Risk and then we'll heat up a frozen pizza."

"That was my idea," Finn told her.

"You three are full of good ideas." Melody took Jonathan's arm and stepped outside with him.

"So you're really okay with all this?" he asked on their way down the porch steps. "I didn't want to ambush you, but I didn't have the heart to derail their plans either. They were so excited."

"Are you kidding? *I'm* excited." She stopped him so she could finally put her arms around him. "I thought about texting you all night, but I didn't know if—"

"You didn't know if I was thinking about you too?" He checked the house behind them and then brushed a prelude of a kiss across her lips. "I was, Mel. I'm always thinking of you. I didn't want to push when you said things needed to go back to the way they were. But I'm not sure that's possible."

"It's not."

He smiled and held her hand the entire drive to his house. "So did the boys just show up at your house today and ask if they could wrap you up for me?" she asked when he helped her out of the car.

"They texted Ainsley yesterday and the three of them met in the park and hatched this plan." Her offered her his arm and led her to the front door. "It might not surprise you to learn that *National Lampoon's Christmas Vacation* is my daughter's favorite movie."

Melody let out a cackle. "Hence the red bow and delivering you to my doorstep."

"How could I say no?" He opened the door and steered her inside. "I didn't care how it happened, I only wanted to see you. All I want for Christmas is for you to give me a chance."

"You don't have to ask, Jonathan." She stepped into his space, circling her arms around his waist, drawing him as close as she'd wanted him all week. "I gave you my heart the night you saved our cookies." When he had so quickly and easily become part of the three of them. And now there was no going back.

She stretched onto her tiptoes so she could press her lips to his—and this would never get old, kissing him whenever she wanted. How had she lived without kissing for so long? Melody forced herself to pull back or they would never get on with the meal. "And then I tried to take my heart back, but I couldn't. I can't. It belongs with you." She knew because it had been the same with Thomas. They'd simply fit. She didn't need time to decide if the connection was there or not because she'd felt this before. This was real and powerful and lasting.

"I'll do my best to deserve your heart, then," he murmured, drawing her hands to his chest. "To hold it close to mine." He sealed the promise with a kiss, slow and savoring and freeing. Melody let herself sink into him, embracing the utter bliss.

"So, are you hungry?" Jonathan collected her to his side, walking her through his house into a great room. Now that they weren't lip-locked, she could get a look around. The space was neat without being overly clean. From the knotty floors to the dark kitchen cabinets along the left wall to the stone fireplace reaching up to the vaulted ceiling, the space had a rustic, homey feel. Mountain elegant. While the décor was clean and modern, it also had a lived-in feel. A few pairs of Ainsley's shoes sat near the couch, and she was glad to see she wasn't the only one fighting a constant shoe battle.

In the far corner, in front of large picture windows, the rectangular wooden dining room table had been all set, complete with dishes and a bottle of wine and two fondue pots with steam rising off the top. A platter of cut-up carrots and broccoli and cauliflower and cubed bread sat at one end. And another platter must've been the chocolate dippers—strawberries and pineapple and cookies and brownies. "Wow. Look at that spread."

Jonathan pulled out a chair for her. "Ainsley got a fondue set for her birthday a few years back and, after the divorce, that's become *our* Christmas Eve tradition." He picked up a lighter sitting nearby and held the flame to the wicks of two pillar Christmas candles sitting between the fondue pots. "I wouldn't let them leave the candles lit when we went to your house, but I promised I wouldn't forget to light them when we got back."

"Those kids are the sweetest." Melody felt herself tearing up again. "All three of them."

"They're pretty incredible." Jonathan sat across from her and filled their wineglasses. "Ainsley already thinks the world of you. Though I'm not surprised. I envy how open you are, how friendly, even with people you don't know well."

"You're friendly too." She took a few of the veggies and cubes of bread before handing the platter to him.

"But it's not as natural for me as it is for you." He used one of the fondue forks to dip an apple in the melted cheesy goodness. "I remember the first time I met you. When Finn and Tate were in second grade. It was my first week as assistant principal at the school, and you brought me a welcome package."

"That's right." She soaked a bread cube in the cheese. "I'd forgotten about that." She'd brought by some candy and local soaps and pumpkin bread from the bakery.

"You told me how happy you were that the school was in such good hands. It was the nicest thing anyone did to welcome me here." He was looking at her in that way he had, intently, focused, like she was the only thing he wanted to see. "It was the kindness I needed after getting through the divorce. I think that's when my crush started."

"That might be when mine started too." She chewed for a while, letting him sit in suspense for the rest of the story.

"You didn't have a crush on me." His head tilted. "Did you?"

"I thought you were way too handsome to be a principal," she admitted. But she hadn't been ready to do anything about it until now.

They talked about their respective losses, what they'd learned, how they'd grown, what they hoped for their kids. They could've sat and talked all night over that velvety smooth chocolate, but Melody knew the kids were waiting.

Jonathan seemed to be thinking the same thing. He cleared their plates before she could help and then assisted her with putting on her coat, stealing a few light kisses on her neck in the process.

When they arrived back at her house minutes later, Melody swore her cheeks were glowing.

Finn and Tate ambushed them the second they walked through the door.

"Did you have fun on your date?"

"Did you like the fondue?"

"Wasn't the chocolate amazing?" Ainsley asked hopefully.

"Yes to all of those questions," Jonathan said.

Melody turned to his daughter. "We ate the whole pot!"

"Yay!" Ainsley high-fived the boys.

"Now it's movie time!" Tate led the charge to the living room while Jonathan helped Melody make popcorn, and then they all nestled into the two couches—her and Jonathan snuggled up on one and Ainsley sitting between the boys on the other while the fire flickered below the television.

The movie started, but Melody wasn't watching the screen. She was taking in the moment. A moment she'd pictured deep in her heart. A moment she'd longed for without even realizing it.

The first of many more happy Christmases to come.

ACKNOWLEDGMENTS

This book would have never come to be without the hard work and dedication of countless other people. I am so grateful for my team at Putnam—Kate Dresser, my brilliant editor whose wise insight and attention to detail really made Melody's story sing, and Tarini Sipahimalani, whose positivity and organization continually offer me such strong support. A special shout-out also goes to the art department for designing this adorable cover and to the marketing and publicity team for working so hard to get the word out. I truly appreciate you all!

Thank you to my agent Suzie Townsend, as well as Sophia Ramos and Olivia Coleman at New Leaf for always steering me in the right direction and for handling the things I would not be able to handle on my own. I get overwhelmed just thinking about everything you all do. What a blessing to have such a great team working for me behind the scenes.

To my beloved reader friends—without you I wouldn't get to share the stories that flow out of my heart. Thank you for reading and reviewing and sharing my books with the world. You have no idea what an encouragement you are to me. While writing this book, I was walking through an incredibly difficult season with my family and I'm not sure I would've made it without the kind words and encouragement so many of you take the time to send me. What a beautiful community you are.

To my dad and mom, Phil and Emy, I could not be more grateful for this family that you have built and faithfully tended over the years. Even when things were falling apart, your strength and enduring devotion held us all together and somehow we made it through. I am also so thankful for my sister, Erin, and brother, Kyle, and their families for all the laughter and fun and adventures we get to share. Thank goodness we have each other.

Last but never least, thank you to Will, AJ, and Kaleb for your patience with all my creative shenanigans and for providing me with real-life inspiration on a daily basis. In so many ways, this story is a love letter to my mischievous little boys who grew up to be two of the most compassionate, adventurous, and dedicated people I know.

CRÈME BRÛLÉE EGGNOG "SPARKLEDOODLE" COOKIES

RECIPE BY AMANDA CUPCAKE
WWW.AMANDA-CUPCAKE.COM

This thick cinnamon-sugar cookie wears a crème brûlée "crown." After mixing, rolling, dipping, and baking into a snickerdoodle, the cookie is ready for accessorizing. The snickerdoodle is swirled with cinnamon eggnog buttercream frosting then torched with sugar for a crackly and soft caramelized cinnamonalicious sensation. Bedazzled with edible glitter, this cookie is transformed from an ordinary snickerdoodle into a "sparkledoodle."

Makes 12 large cookies (24 if made into a smaller version)

THE COOKIES

INGREDIENTS:

2¾ cups all-purpose flour

1 teaspoon baking soda

1 teaspoon cream of tartar

½ teaspoon salt

½ cup butter-flavor shortening

½ cup softened butter

2 eggs (room temperature)

1½ cups sugar

FOR DIPPING AND ROLLING:

3 tablespoons ground cinnamon

⅓ cup granulated sugar

TO PREPARE AND BAKE COOKIES:

Preheat oven to 325°. Line two baking sheets with parchment paper and set aside. In a shallow bowl, whisk the cinnamon and sugar together and set aside. In a medium bowl, combine flour, baking soda, cream of tartar, and salt. In a stand mixer using the paddle attachment, cream shortening, butter, eggs, and sugar together. Scrape down the mixer bowl with a spatula to incorporate all ingredients and cream together again. Slowly add the flour mixture to this creamed mixture. Using a two-inch cookie scoop, scoop out evenly sized cookie dough balls, hand roll until smooth, and dip or roll in the cinnamon-sugar mixture. Place on the baking sheets and flatten slightly until about one inch thick. Bake the cookies in the oven for approximately 10 to 12 minutes (being careful not to overbake) and let the cookies sit out until cool.

Tip: For a puffier cookie, refrigerate the cookie dough balls for approximately 20 minutes before baking in the oven.

THE CINNAMON EGGNOG BUTTERCREAM FROSTING "CROWN"

INGREDIENTS:

1 cup butter, softened

3 oz marshmallow cream

2 teaspoons vanilla extract

2 tablespoons eggnog

4–6 cups powdered sugar

1–2 teaspoons ground cinnamon

½ cup granulated sugar

Edible gold glitter

For a boozy sensation (optional): add 1 tablespoon of bourbon or replace regular eggnog with eggnog whiskey.

TO MAKE THE FROSTING:

In a stand mixer using the paddle attachment, mix butter, marshmallow cream, vanilla extract, and eggnog together on medium speed for 5 minutes until fluffy to combine their flavors. Gradually add powdered sugar until frosting has flexible peaks (for piping the crown onto the cookie). Add more powdered sugar for a stiffer piping texture. Fold cinnamon into frosting with a spatula until evenly distributed.

TO SWIRL FROSTING ONTO THE COOKIE AND CARAMELIZE FOR THE CRÈME BRÛLÉE "CROWN":

Line a large baking sheet with parchment paper and pour or spread the granulated sugar evenly onto it. Fill a piping bag with frosting, cut a medium-sized hole at the end of the piping bag, and pipe a mound of frosting on top of each cookie. Flip the cookies upside down and press the frosting mound flat onto the sugar-sprinkled parchment-paper-lined baking sheet. Let cookies set upside down on the baking sheet in the refrigerator or freezer for approximately 15 minutes. Set the cookies right side up and use a culinary butane torch to caramelize the sugar on top. Sprinkle with edible gold glitter while the sugar is still warm. The result: the cookies will have a satisfying crackly and soft texture.